The Haunting of Hayden Place

Book 5 in the Dreamist series

Kim Poovey

To God, my rock and my redeemer, with whom all things are possible.

The Haunting of Hayden Place

Prologue

Sarah's Diary
It's been a long few months since discovering I was a dreamist. After a lifetime of being told by my adoptive parents that I had an overactive imagination, I learned my ghostly proclivities are actually an innate gift passed down through the biological females of my family line. Spirits with unsettled circumstances surrounding the manner of their death seek out dreamists to help resolve their issues.

Part of me was relieved to know I wasn't crazy with all the apparitions I'd encountered during my life while the other part dreaded what it meant to be responsible for helping spirits move on. My best friend, Danni Cook, has stood by my side ever since learning about my otherworldly experiences even though she's not thrilled about the ghoulish activity.

One of the best things to come from all this was meeting Garrett Duncan and his ghost hunting team from Edgefield, South Carolina. If you'd told me in high school that I'd meet a man who investigates ghosts and isn't freaked out by my hauntedness, I'd have laughed. Yet, here I am dating this incredible guy whose dog, Dallas, has stolen my heart with his silly antics and ghost sensing capabilities. We're a formidable team. Harry and Ralph are part of Garrett's ghost hunting group and they've been just as supportive of my special skillset. Thus far, I've helped a Victorian lady, a murdered genealogical researcher, Lizzie Borden, and a college student from my mother's alma mater move on.

Every time I feel as if I'm getting a handle on all this, something else arises that requires further research and learning. Like discovering last Christmas that my paternal great-grandmother was also a dreamist. Somehow, I ended up with a double shot of the ability from both sides of my biological family. It's fulfilling and exhausting at the same time. Nevertheless, I don't have much choice in the matter. I'm a dreamist and there's nothing I can do about that except to embrace all it entails and do my best to help those who need my assistance.

There's a guidebook for dreamists that addresses the basic skills as well as the specific abilities affiliated with each family line. Unfortunately for me, these books were written as riddles, something I'm not very proficient at solving or understanding. Danni has been a huge help. As an attorney, she's pretty good at figuring out brainteasers and hard to understand situations.

One of the main reasons for this journal is to keep track of what I've learned so far. Each dreamist has her own special skillset. Mine is the ability to touch something that belonged to the deceased and get glimpses into their past lives. Recently, I discovered that buildings can also leave an imprint on me. Just when I feel like I'm getting a better understanding of my abilities another one pops up. I'm hoping this journal will help me keep track of my ongoing skills and possibly assist my children someday should I have any daughters.

Chapter One

"It's time you take the next step," a familiar voice whispered in her ear.

Sarah looked around at the deep green walls with matching floor to ceiling shelves filled with assorted books. Silk curtains puddled on the floor and comfortable chairs flanked the fireplace mantel. An evergreen and crimson hued rug sheathed the heart pine floors. She knew this space well. The library at Garrett's house.

Was she sleepwalking or dreaming? Last thing she recalled was curling up in Garrett's arms with Dallas snuggled at her feet. She'd stayed at Garrett's place after they'd arrived in Edgefield at 11:00 the night before. Exhaustion from almost two weeks of ghost hunting at the Borden House in Fall River, Massachusetts and then stopping at her mother's alma mater, Virginia Intermont College in Bristol, Virginia left Sarah too tired to drive back to her home in Beaufort, South Carolina. Of course, she loved staying at Garrett's house which had belonged to his late grandmother, Ola, a fellow dreamist. Now Sarah wondered how she ended up in the library.

"My grandson spent a great deal of time with me in this room," the voice said.

Turning, Sarah saw Ola standing behind her. A warm smile creased her twinkling blue eyes as she shimmered in the light pouring in from the window.

"Ola," Sarah muttered. "Why are you here?"

"I'm proud of all you've accomplished. Your work at Virginia Intermont was impressive. You're getting stronger and more confident."

Sarah felt her cheeks flush at the compliment and realized Ola's approval meant more than she'd realized. "I'm doing my best," she replied.

"It will get easier as you develop your skills. However, there are things that can make your experiences less complicated."

"Like what?"

Ola pointed to the top shelf but before she could explain, something grabbed Sarah's shoulder jolting her awake.

"What are you doing?" she groused.

Garrett leaned in and kissed her cheek. "Breakfast is ready. You said to make sure you were up by 9:00 a.m."

Sarah rubbed her eyes and sat up. "Sorry, I didn't mean to snap at you."

Garrett straightened. "Did you have a dream?"

"It was Ola. She was getting ready to show me something she claimed would make things easier for me."

Garrett's eyes darted around the bedroom. "She was here?"

"Actually, she was in the library."

"Then the answer is probably there. Come on," he said, heading for the doorway.

Sarah slid from bed and followed him down the hall to the library at the front of the house. Glancing around the space, she tried to remember exactly where Ola had been pointing in the dream. Her gaze settled on the top shelf of the bookcase where a set of leather-bound Waverly novels by Sir Walter Scott rested.

"Those are nice," Sarah said, pointing at the set.

"And valuable too," Garrett snorted. "Grams never let me touch those. Said they were old and worth a lot of money."

Drawn to the pristine spines on each tome like a child in a toy shop, Sarah glanced at the top shelf once more. "I wonder if this is what she was trying to show me in the dream?"

Garrett shrugged. "You're welcome to check them out. Keep in mind, you're the one she'll haunt if you damage them."

"Since she's already haunting me, I'll take my chances," she chuckled, climbing the wooden library ladder.

Sarah pulled one of the books from the shelf and cradled it in her left hand. The marbled end pages gleamed in the shadowy light illuminating the rich colors. They aren't even faded, she thought, admiring the condition. She paged through the *Castle Dangerous* before carefully sliding it back to its spot. She reached for another one, *The Talisman*.

"That's odd," she mumbled, holding the book in her hand.

"What is?"

"Something is rattling inside of this volume," she replied, furrowing her brow.

"Hand it to me," Garrett said.

Sarah gave the book to Garrett and climbed down the ladder. Standing beside him, she watched as he opened the cover. Instead of pages, it was empty, a box made to look like a book.

Garrett's eyes watered as the color drained from his face.

"What's the matter?" she asked, resting her hand on his forearm.

He held the box for her to see. Inside was a striking necklace with three charms. One had a thistle etched on it, one was

5

a rectangular cut peridot, and the other was a gold watch key set with an opal on one side and malachite on the other.

"It's lovely," Sarah mumbled, mesmerized by the piece.

Garrett continued staring at the object.

"What's wrong?" she asked.

"This was Gram's necklace. She wore it every day."

"I'm sorry. It must be hard finding something so personal of hers."

Shaking his head, Garrett spoke. "That's not it. We buried her in this."

An icy chill ran down Sarah's spine and crept across her skin.

"Maybe there were two of them," Sarah said, trying to lighten the thickness blanketing the atmosphere.

"No. This was one of a kind, she said so."

"Did she tell you anything else about it?"

"Nothing. But she wore it all the time. I don't remember ever seeing her without it."

Sarah took in a deep breath. She knew what she had to do. Reaching into the box, she gently lifted the necklace from within. As soon as her fingers made contact with the chain, a jolt of electricity raced through her body, nearly knocking her to the floor.

Garrett dropped the book shaped box and grabbed Sarah's arm to steady her.

"Are you alright?" he asked, his gaze fixed on her.

Sarah nodded. "This necklace is powerful," she muttered.

"How so?"

"Not sure but something tells me Ola will be in my dreams again tonight."

Chapter Two

Wind whipped a few strands of hair against Sarah's cheek while she drove home in the Beast, as she affectionately referred to her beat-up, yet reliable Chevy truck. Although cold natured, she'd left the driver side window halfway down so the chilly air would keep her alert.

Garrett had insisted she wear Ola's necklace in the hopes his grandmother's ghost might explain how the treasured piece ended up in a book shaped box on the top library shelf instead of buried with her. Sarah remembered how the nape of her neck tingled when the gold chain touched her skin. What did it mean and how did a family heirloom get from Ola's grave to her former abode? These were things only Ola could explain.

Three hours later, oyster shells crackled beneath the truck tires as Sarah pulled through the gates of Monroe Manse. A crow, its ebony feathers shimmering in iridescent shades of blue and green, stood in the center of the driveway staring at her. She inched the truck forward but the bird didn't budge. How bizarre, she thought.

She moved the truck forward a few inches. Still, the bird stared her down, its head cocked to the side as if pondering why she was trying to drive where he was standing.

Sarah tooted the horn. The bird didn't flinch.

Aggravated, Sarah swerved around the crow, parked the truck, and jumped out.

"Caw!" the crow sounded before taking flight.

"Unbelievable," she muttered to herself. Two weeks of ghost hunting, a necklace from the grave, and a bird with an attitude. How had her life gotten so complicated?

Granted, not everything had been stressful. While in Fall River, Garrett told her he loved her cementing their relationship. Even though she enjoyed being with Garrett, it was good to be home. At least she was familiar with the spectral activity in the house even though her great-grandmother's ghost hadn't visited for a couple of years ever since Sarah solved the mystery behind her demise.

After unloading her luggage, Sarah fixed a cup of tea and plunked onto the overstuffed leather chair in the front parlor. She startled when her phone rang.

"Hello darling," her mother's voice chirped. "Are you home yet?"

"Just got back. What's up?"

"Sorry to ask again, but I need Garrett's number."

"I gave it to you when Danni and I were driving home from Bristol."

"You did, but I've misplaced the note I wrote it on."

"What exactly do you want to talk to him about?"

"Nothing to be concerned over," her mother replied. "It's for a friend of mine."

Sarah could tell by her mother's tone that she was on a mission and wasn't going to spend a lot of time chitchatting or explaining the reason for her request. She gave her the number again and hung up. No doubt, Garrett would let her know the details of why her mother wanted to speak with him.

Sarah sipped her tea and fiddled with Ola's necklace. The last two weeks of travel combined with a restless night of sleep and a monotonous three-hour drive home was the perfect recipe for a nap. Placing the tea cup on the side table, Sarah leaned her head against the tufted leather of the wing chair, closed her eyes, and promptly drifted off.

The ground thumped beneath Sarah's feet as ladies and gents twirled about on the dance floor to a four-piece jazz band in the far corner. Her heart leapt. Based on the flapper dresses and fancy headbands, it appeared she was in the 1920s. This was her favorite era. For once she was having a pleasant dream and not a haunted nightmare.

One by one the dancers vanished as darkness crept along the walls and across the floor. A mustiness hung in the air, stinging her nose and making it difficult to breathe. It was a familiar scent, the dank, salty aroma of the Lowcountry.

Confused, Sarah took a step forward, careful not to stumble in the darkened room. That's when she heard a gurgling sound. Looking down, she noticed liquid pooling at her feet, its watery fingers wrapping around her sneakers. What was happening?

Panic gripped Sarah's chest stealing the air from her lungs as the rush of water grew louder. If she didn't calm herself, she'd succumb to whatever was coming for her. It was the most important lesson she'd learned as a dreamist. In order to face the entity seeking her assistance she must keep calm. Sarah had a deep fear of drowning despite growing up in the Lowcountry surrounded by tide pools and estuaries. If she couldn't assuage her fear, she'd call on Ola. That always worked.

He did this, echoed in her ear. The wall behind her crumbled, releasing a deluge of water. Sarah thrashed as the under-current surged forward carrying her along with the force of a tidal wave.

"Ola!" she screamed, trying to gain control of her body against the pull of the tide.

Something grabbed at Sarah's ankle and yanked her under. She struggled against it but her mind was swimming in panic from the lack of air. She coughed bringing in more water further compressing her lungs. Confusion blurred her senses when a hand reached out and took hold of Sarah's wrist pulling her upward. When her face crested the water, she sucked in air coughing and sputtering as her ability to breathe was restored.

Relief washed over her when she saw her mentor in front of her. Ola smiled, her reassuring gaze calming Sarah's pounding heart. Without warning, a face rose behind Ola, its skin swollen and blotchy. The apparition's eyes were hollow as its purple, bloated lips formed the words, *he did this.*

Ola's presence kept Sarah steady as she faced the gruesome creature.

"Who did what?" she asked.

The current crested like a watery hand crashing over Ola leaving Sarah alone with the entity.

"Ola!" Sarah screamed as the creature's rotting fingers reached for her. She slapped the hand away only to have more hands reach up from the water, bits of skin and flesh shedding from bones where sea creatures had nibbled at the bodies. Razor sharp nails clawed at her skin pulling her back under.

Screaming, Sarah bolted upright, still gasping for air. After a few deep breaths to steady her racing heart, she contemplated what she'd just dreamed. She was home so why was she having one of the most terrifying visions she'd ever experienced? Sarah could believe it was a typical nightmare except Ola had been there.

This wasn't a run of the mill dreamscape; this was a ghost in need of help. The spirit wasn't from her house so where was it from and why was it seeking her assistance? Obviously, something loomed in Sarah's future prompting the spirit to reach out. Even more frustrating, was the fact she didn't get the chance to ask Ola about the necklace.

Standing in a stretch, Sarah rubbed her eyes before padding up the stairs to the bathroom. She contemplated soaking in the tub but thought better of it. She'd just dreamed about drowning and didn't want to chance the entity trying to suck her down the drain. A shower would have to do.

Ten minutes later she was donning her comfiest pajamas and towel drying her hair when her cell phone clamored. Sarah tossed the towel in the sink and hurried into the bedroom. Her heart fluttered at the name on the screen.

"Hey, Garrett."

"How are you?" Goosebumps skittered across her skin at the sound of his baritone voice.

"A little rattled but okay."

"Haunted dreams?" he asked.

"Yeah, which doesn't make sense since I'm at home. I've already helped the ghosts here. Ola showed up when I called on her but I never got the chance to ask about the necklace."

Silence.

"Garrett? You still there?"

"I am. I was calling about a job in Savannah."

"Is this what my mom wanted to discuss with you?" Sarah asked. She'd wondered what it was about but hadn't been concerned until now. Why would her mother want to talk to Garrett about hunting ghosts? Perhaps this was what Veronica's spirit at Virginia Intermont was trying to tell her.

"Your mom has a friend who purchased a house on Hayden

Street near one of the squares in Savannah. She's asked the team to investigate the possibility of spirit activity."

"My non-believing mother asked you to do this?" Sarah queried, incredulous at her mother's request.

Garrett chuckled. "She reached out on behalf of her friend, Cheryl. Said she was worried she'd be taken advantage of by people who use ghosts as a front to take money."

That made more sense, Sarah thought, but it was still a stretch considering how adamant her mother was about ghosts being a figment of the imagination. Her mother didn't believe, but obviously her friend Cheryl did.

"Are you up for it?" he asked. "No one would blame you if you needed a break."

"I'll go," Sarah said with a sigh. "The ghosts will find me no matter where I am. No sense trying to avoid it. When do we leave?"

"Tomorrow. We'll pick you up around lunchtime."

"See you then," she said. "I love you."

"Love you."

Sarah hung up and slipped between the cottony sheets when it struck her. The water, the pungent smell of the Lowcountry, a ghost in need of help. Everything was beginning to make sense. Apparently, this spirit recognized her as a dreamist and decided to contact her before Sarah even knew where she'd be going.

Resting her head on the pillow, she contemplated all that had happened in the past twenty-four hours. The chain around her neck tickled her skin as the charms shifted. She hadn't removed the necklace hoping Ola would show up in one of her dreams to explain its purpose.

Regardless, it seemed Sarah had another ghostly endeavor waiting and the sooner she helped the spirit move on the sooner she could return to her own life. But first, she wanted to speak with her mother about this temporary shift in her otherworldly beliefs, or lack thereof.

As her breathing steadied, Sarah's lids fluttered a few times and within minutes, she drifted to dreamland.

Chapter Three

I t took Sarah a moment to realize she was in a dream. She saw a young woman hiding behind a door peeking through a crack. Oddly, Sarah could sense what the woman was hearing.

"We're making headway," one man said. "These simpletons are dishing out money like they're making it themselves."

"You amaze me, sir," the other responded. "Your ability to get people with barely enough to feed their families to hand over their wages is impressive."

"It's simple really," he chuckled. "Tell them what they want to hear and they'll believe anything else you say."

"What about the alcohol problem?"

"We're appealing to the family-oriented citizens. They're sick of public drunkenness and having to help people impacted by the inability of the alcoholic bread winner to provide for his dependents. If these families need money let the wife and kids get jobs. No excuse for taking hard earned cash from the rest of us."

The young woman standing at the door cringed at the

man's words. He was a heartless hypocrite. He married into money, not to mention her mother spent most of the day passed out. She always had a brandy nearby. Of course, her father would never let his voters know such a thing. Those close to the family were told her mother's drinking was medicinal. If being married to a tyrant was a disease, her mother was plagued.

"About the business of..."

"Miss Amelia," a voice whispered, making her jump. "Come away from there before you get caught. Your father and Mr. Warren won't take kindly to your snooping."

She turned to see Lanie the housemaid standing behind her, worry knitting her brow.

Lanie was right. She'd already taken a huge risk listening in on her father's conversation. If he'd caught her, she'd have been in a heap of trouble.

The scene shifted. Silverware clinked against china plates as dinner guests enjoyed roasted duck and some sort of fruity drink. In grand fashion, a tall gent stood silencing all those gathered at the table.

"I have an announcement," he boomed. "After quite a bit of deliberation, our family has decided to unite forces with the Warrens."

Clapping rounded the table like a ring of fire. Except for the young woman with dark brown hair. Her hazel eyes misted as she glanced at the other people in the room, her hands resting in her lap. This can't be good, she thought. The Warrens were as underhanded as her father when it came to business which is why they were two of the wealthiest families in the state. Granted, the Warrens were an old Savannah family, same as hers, except they hadn't made their way to Atlanta like her father to pursue politics. Savannah was her family's second home now that they had a permanent residence in Atlanta.

Sarah froze. Was she actually hearing what the young woman was thinking? She'd felt the emotions of previous ghosts but had never been in their heads like this. The clarity was astounding.

"By this time next year, our daughter, Amelia, will be the proud wife of Theodore Warren."

Cheers floated through the air as Amelia's head began to spin. Surely, she hadn't heard correctly. Was she being traded like a prize horse? Why hadn't she been informed of the proposal, if you could call it that. Her mother sat stoically at the end of the table, sipping her drink which Amelia knew to be sherry despite the non-alcoholic offering to guests. Congratulations buzzed. Theodore stood next to her father, a stupid grin forming as he glared at her with hungry eyes. This wasn't happening, she told herself. It couldn't be.

The rumors about an alliance between her and Theodore had been circulating since she was a little girl. But Amelia had other ideas. She was a romantic at heart and wanted to marry a man of her choosing, not the most affluent and powerful one her father could obtain for her. Being the youngest with four brothers was hard enough but being the only female made independence nearly impossible in their household.

"Bless her heart," Amelia heard Mrs. Simpson, the woman next to her, declare. "Her joy has rendered her speechless."

"Are you mad?" Amelia hollered. "I wasn't even informed of the arrangement!"

As soon as the words left her lips, she knew she'd crossed a line.

The room wavered and reformed. Sarah was in a man's office. Bookcases filled with legal tomes lined the wall behind a large desk. Amelia sat in a chair, her shoulders rounded and her face downcast.

"You're impossible!" her father roared.

Amelia's muscles were strained as she twisted her quivering palms. She hated being berated but expected this tirade after her outburst during dinner the night before.

"You've always been a difficult child," he continued. "But this is unconscionable! You humiliated me in front of the most important names in Atlanta! What have you to say for yourself?" he boomed, leaning over, his hot breath stinging her right ear.

"I'm sorry to have disappointed you, Father."

It happened so swiftly, she hadn't time to brace herself for the blow. She found herself, lying on the carpet her head spinning. Her father was a strong man and the force of his foot kicking the chair from under her sent her sprawling to the floor. Her left arm ached where she'd landed and no doubt, there'd be a bruise. Her father never did anything halfway, including doling out punishments for disobedience. Sadly, most everything she did was disobedient in his eyes. She'd spent much of her life sitting in a corner or banished to her room without supper. While he'd always been a harsh man, he rarely employed physical attacks.

"Get up!" he bellowed.

The room whirled as she pushed herself up from the Persian rug. Apparently, she wasn't moving quickly enough. Her father's hand gripped her right arm, sending sparks of pain radiating through her shoulder as he yanked her up.

His face was only inches from hers as his eyes narrowed. "Since you've managed to ruin everything I worked so hard to arrange for you, I'm going to do what I should have done years ago, you spoiled, ungrateful child."

Too terrified to speak, she stood there her stomach churning as his hate spittled across her chin.

"I'm sending you away, my dear," he said, straightening. A wicked smile creased his eyes sending unease gliding across

Amelia's skin. "You're about to learn what it's like to work for a living."

Amelia's heartrate kicked up, stealing the air from her lungs.

The scene shifted. Late afternoon shadows crept through the lace curtains across Amelia's bedroom floor. A knock on the door stirred her from her nap.

"Come in," she croaked, sitting up in bed.

Mrs. Carmicle, the head housemaid, entered the room. Her stormy eyes glinted from beneath her upswept gray hair.

"Has Father sent for me?" Amelia asked, hoping to find a way to reconcile the situation.

"No," Mrs. Carmicle replied, moving to the wardrobe where she removed a few of Amelia's dresses. "He said you're going to be staying with his sister in Savannah."

"For how long?"

Mrs. Carmicle straightened, her stern expression radiating displeasure. She'd always been a no-nonsense sort of woman who commanded respect from everyone in the household. It's probably why their house ran so efficiently.

"I'm doing as I was told," she said. "You'll have to speak with Mr. Danbury about the details." She resumed her work as if this were nothing more than dusting.

Amelia slipped from bed and hurried down the stairs to her father's study. She found him sitting behind the massive mahogany desk, his spectacles perched on his nose as he read through some papers.

"Mrs. Carmicle is packing my things. Why are you doing this?"

Her father looked up, his lips a thin line as he removed his glasses and set them on the desk top.

"You're a willful child and have never known want. Obviously, it has made you selfish. It's time you experienced what it's like to work for a living. You'll be staying with your Aunt Bessie and working at her husband's mercantile." He paused for a moment, steepling his fingers. "It's long hours and not suitable for a lady of your stature. Once you know the strain of being on your feet all day, having to bend to the will of unreasonable customers, and holding your tongue perhaps you'll reconsider the comfortable life you've been offered."

"I can't marry Theodore Warren," Amelia said more confidently than she felt. "I'm sure the Warrens' will understand. Just tell them I'm immature and need more time."

"You will stay with your aunt and uncle until you come to your senses and see reason. Until then, the Warrens' will consider the engagement official."

"But I don't even know my aunt and uncle. You never let me visit with them."

"Because they're beneath us," he retorted. "Since you want to lower yourself to their standards, it's only fitting that you stay with them. When you've learned your lesson, you can come home."

"Then I shan't ever come home!" Amelia declared, running from the room.

She made it as far as the entry hall where Mrs. Carmicle stood, her ruthless stare boring through Amelia's fortitude. Amelia's trunk rested by the front door. This was really happening. She started for the stairs when Mrs. Carmicle spoke.

"There's no reason to return to your chambers. I've packed everything you'll need for your stay."

"But I want to get..."

"You'll need nothing that's not already packed," Mrs. Carmicle said, raising her chin.

"This is my home and I'll do as I please," Amelia exclaimed as she grasped the newel post.

Mrs. Carmicle moved toward her. "This is not your home now," she said. "Per Mr. Danbury's orders. The car is waiting out front."

Amelia stared in disbelief.

Mrs. Carmicle opened the door and stood like a soldier fulfilling her duties. As Amelia walked through the door Mrs. Carmicle spoke.

"Are you not going to take your things?"

Amelia stared at the trunk, shock wavering through her limbs. "Mr. Hinson will load it," she replied.

"Mr. Hinson has been instructed to drive you to your destination, nothing more."

"You can't expect me to move that by myself."

"I don't make the decisions in this house. I only carry them out. Mr. Danbury was adamant you be treated as a regular individual without the privileges afforded to family."

Amelia's heart ached. Was she being disowned? She hesitated for a moment considering what to do next. It would be easier to acquiesce to her father's demands and continue with the privileged life she'd always known. Maybe Theodore wasn't the stiff, tiresome man she believed him to be. Lots of women married for practical purposes. Some even learned to love the men they wed.

Looking at the smug expression creasing Mrs. Carmicle's wrinkled lips, Amelia snapped out of her stupor. She couldn't marry Theodore Warren. She would not be traded like a prized brood mare.

"Very well," she said, grabbing the leather strap on the side of her trunk. Her shoulder strained as she pulled it along the floor. She smiled at the deep gouges digging into the heart pine boards and the galled expression on Mrs. Carmicle's face.

"Sorry about the floors," Amelia chortled, hauling the trunk down the front steps.

The door shut behind her followed by the clicking of the lock. The finality of it plucked at Amelia's heart releasing the tears that had been dammed up behind her hazel eyes.

Mr. Hinson stood at the side of the car; his stare diverted from her struggles. How was she going to get the trunk loaded? She caught Mr. Hinson glancing her direction, sorrow emanating from his gaze. He looked around and then hurried to her side.

"Let's get this affixed to the car quickly miss," he said, grabbing the other side of the trunk. Gratitude filled Amelia's chest as they hoisted it onto the back bumper of the car where he strapped it in place. He gave her a quick smile before getting behind the wheel and starting the engine. Amelia slumped against the leather seat in the back of the car watching her home fade into the distance. No one said goodbye, not even her mother. Of course, her mother would never go against her father's wishes. She'd always been a good and loyal wife. She was probably passed out and wouldn't notice her daughter's absence even when she did sober up. Those occasions were rare.

Amelia pondered everything that had happened since the argument with her father that morning. Was her mother upset with her? Had her brothers been informed? It hadn't taken her father long to make the arrangements to send her away.

Amelia hardly knew her aunt and uncle. Since her family had moved to Atlanta, they'd only gone to Savannah on short visits. Her father rarely spoke of his sister and her husband except to indicate they weren't as wealthy or respectable as he was. Yet he felt they were responsible enough to care for his daughter and put her to work. Maybe that was her father's plan, to leave her with irresponsible people and make her appreciate what she had and could have, if she agreed to the arranged marriage.

Tears trickled down her cheeks puddling on the floorboards of the vehicle. The water accumulated filling the inside of the car until Amelia was completely submerged. Sarah could feel the tightness in Amelia's lungs as her skin turned a splotchy, grayish hue.

Not right, she murmured, bubbles drifting from her blackened lips.

Sarah sucked in a huge breath and opened her eyes. She was in her own room. Sun peeked through the lacey curtains, tiptoeing across the floor in snippets of light.

As she leaned up, something tickled her neck. The necklace. Fingering the charms, Sarah contemplated the dream and the personal insight she'd experienced. Was this a new aspect of her dreamist abilities or was there something to the necklace she was wearing? And why hadn't Ola come back to explain more about it?

Trudging to the bathroom, Sarah stared in the mirror. She fumbled with the three charms, her fingertips prickling. She tried to take the necklace off but the clasp was gone. Her heartrate ticked up a notch. She'd affixed it around her neck the day before so what had happened?

"Ola," Sarah said. "I need to know about this necklace."

Nothing.

Sarah's head slumped forward. The last thing she needed was for Ola to be silent. Normally, something like this would have sent her into a panic; however, nothing in her life the past couple of years had been logical. Apparently, this was just another notch in her bizarre existence.

The grandfather clock in the hallway chimed six. Garrett and the guys would be here to pick her up at noon. If she wanted to pack and visit her mother, she needed to get moving. The mystery of the necklace would have to wait a bit longer.

. . .

An hour later, Sarah was at her parent's home sitting across from her mother with tea cup in hand. Morning sun drenched the room in a warm glow. "After all these years of claiming ghosts don't exist, now you suddenly believe?" Sarah asked, furrowing her brow.

"Not at all." Her mother sighed, placing the rose bedecked teacup on the coffee table between them. "Cheryl is one of those silly types who believes in ghosts. She's my friend and I'm trying to help her. She wanted to hire a medium but as you know many of them are scam artists. I trust Garrett."

"And you asked him and the team to go to her house and search for ghosts you don't believe in."

Looking away, Sarah's mother licked her lips. "Cheryl has invested her life savings in this place. She's always wanted an historic home in downtown Savannah and she finally has it. But she's ridiculous when it comes to this haunted stuff. Honestly, I think she's been listening to the neighbors and has it in her head that the house is swarming with spirits."

Sarah blew out a long breath. She knew her mother wasn't a believer yet the whispers of Veronica's ghost from the Virginia Intermont trip echoed in Sarah's mind. *She believes.* Why the ghost thought Sarah's mother believed in the otherworldly was still a mystery to her. One thing her mother had always been adamant about was that spirits and hauntings were nothing more than an overactive imagination. And yet, her mother was asking for ghost hunting help, even if she claimed it was only to save her friend from unscrupulous hacks.

Sarah's muscles were still tight after the restless night of haunted visions. She was tired and a bit cranky not to mention flabbergasted by her mother's actions.

"You know I'll be accompanying the guys on this endeavor," Sarah said, chewing her thumbnail.

"I don't know why you have to be involved. There's no

need to spend every moment with your boyfriend. You have a business to run," her mother said, pursing her lips. "Not that you need to after inheriting a fortune from your biological mother."

"I'm well aware of my responsibilities," Sarah huffed. Of course, she was concerned about leaving again after being away for so long. But Sarah had only continued her antique and estate business because she loved it. "Tiffany has done a wonderful job in my absence. Her knowledge of antiques is extensive. I doubt my customers even miss me. And I thought you liked Garrett?"

Her mother's expression softened. "I do like him," she replied. "I'm sorry for snapping at you like that. It's just...you know how I feel about all this ghost stuff and I don't want you having any *issues* again."

Sarah exhaled. Her mother still hadn't let go of Sarah's middle school encounter at Nancy's slumber party. She'd inadvertently described a ghost that happened to be Nancy's deceased grandmother which resulted in her being sent home in the middle of the night. Her parents wasted no time getting her an appointment with a psychologist. It was the main reason Sarah would never tell her parents about her dreamist abilities.

The more Sarah thought about it, the more she was convinced this is what Veronica's spirit had been trying to reveal. Her mother had plans to refer her friend to Garrett for some ghostly problems, not because she believed.

"I provide a great deal of support for the team and they like having me there."

"As long as you're only there for support." Sarah's mother gave a weak smile. "I'm grateful Garrett and his friends have agreed to help out. I know Cheryl will appreciate it."

Sarah shifted in her seat. This might be her trickiest venture yet. No doubt, her mother would be in touch with Cheryl throughout the ghost hunt which meant Sarah would have to remain as inconspicuous as possible. Maybe Garrett could ask Cheryl to stay away until they were finished. Tell her it would hinder their ability to capture the ghosts on film if she were around. She'd make sure to mention it to him when he picked her up.

"I'd better get back. The guys will be here soon." She sipped the last of her tea, hugged her mother, and headed to her house.

Sarah walked in the door of Monroe Manse, relishing the comfort of home. Her muscles were tight and her mind spun with everything her mother had said, especially since it revolved around ghosts.

"I need a long soak in the tub," Sarah mumbled to herself. There was still some time before the guys arrived so she decided to indulge. Images from her dream about drowning had drained from her mind at this point, making a bath a welcome respite.

Sarah trudged up the staircase to the master bathroom. Twisting the chrome knobs, she poured a generous helping of lavender scented bubble bath into the swirling water, lit a candle, and pulled her hair into a clip. She slipped off her clothes and lowered her body into the deep embrace of the antique claw foot tub. Aside from the fully stocked library, this was her second favorite thing about the house. The tub at her cottage had been the typical five-foot length but the one at Monroe Manse was a double-ended, 72-inch soaking tub. Sheer bliss.

Once the bubbles crested the edge, Sarah turned off the water and reclined, her shoulders and neck conforming to the gentle curve of the tub. Closing her eyes, she let the subtle hints of lavender wash over her as the steaming water melted the tension from her muscles. The popping divertimento of bubbles soothed her mind lending to the spa-like atmosphere.

Sarah's thoughts drifted to Savannah, a favorite place to visit. She'd attended numerous auctions there as well as clearing several estates over the years. It was a mystical place with the same enigmatic ambience that Beaufort held. Its residents were fiercely loyal to their city and the characters abounding in the town had been well represented in the books and movies set there. With a few deep breaths, Sarah felt the tension drain from her muscles. Relaxation took hold, escorting her to dreamland where salty breezes carried the secrets of scandal and deception.

A motor car rumbled along a rutted road past grand old homes nestled behind towering live oaks and lush gardens. Queen Anne, Italianate, Georgian, all the architectural styles that studded the squares of Savannah paraded through Sarah's thoughts like Rose Bowl floats. As the car rounded the corner, it came to a stop in front of a stunning Second Empire mansion.

Interestingly, the home had two front entrances on either side with covered porticos. A porch sprawled across the second floor with three sets of jib doors that opened onto it. Sarah loved how jibs altered from house to house. A common element of old homes, jib doors, sometimes referred to as windows, were usually of paned glass and offered entry onto outside porches. When opened they allowed breezes to cool the rooms. Legend suggested home owners used to be taxed on the number of doors in their houses and thus jibs counted as windows but functioned like doors. Sarah had never been able to find documentation to verify the stories but it seemed logical.

When she looked up, she caught a glimpse of a man with blood trickling across his face staring back from the upstairs porch. Sarah pressed her face against the car window craning her head in an effort to see him better. But he was gone. Funny how such a grisly sight would have disturbed her in the past. Now it was part of her daily existence.

Leaning back against the leather seat, Sarah jumped when a woman appeared next to her, her bloated face discolored to a purplish hue.

"He did this," she muttered, water dripping from her dress and fingertips.

Gasping, Sarah bolted upright, water sloshing over the edge of the tub leaving sudsy puddles on the octagonal tile floor. What on earth was happening? she thought with a shiver. The tepid water sent a chill through her body. She glanced around the space trying to get her bearings when reality struck her. She'd fallen asleep and had a dream. A dream set in Savannah.

"Great," she muttered. "The ghosts have definitely found me."

After drying off and dressing, Sarah called Garrett, her hands still trembling.

"How are you?" he asked. Dallas yipped in the background making Sarah smile.

"Alright, I guess."

"Something wrong? You sound strange."

"Just got out of the tub where I accidentally fell asleep," she replied.

"Uh-oh, what happened?"

Sarah proceeded to share the dream and the disturbing nature of the young woman who appeared next to her in the car.

"Have you seen a picture of the house?" Garrett asked.

"No."

"Then this could be a random dream not related to Cheryl's place."

"Doubtful," Sarah replied. "The ghost was definitely trying to communicate something; I could feel it. And it was in Savannah. I don't think that's a coincidence."

"We'll be at your place in about thirty minutes. Once we get to Savannah, see the house, and get more information from Cheryl, we can figure out how your dream ties in with all of this."

"Sounds good," Sarah said, relief washing over her. "Love you."

"Love you too."

Sarah hung up and went downstairs to fix a cup of tea. Now more than ever, she wanted to know more about Cheryl's home and what was so horrible that the ghosts were haunting her before she'd even been there.

Chapter Four

Clouds skulked across the sky shrouding the day in gloom. Sarah, Garrett, Dallas, Harry, and Ralph pulled up in front of 210 Hayden Street and parked. The guys emerged from the truck and stood before the mansion. Harry pulled out his phone and started snapping photos.

Sarah's heartrate ratcheted up as she gazed upon the Second Empire home with the two front entries, the same one from her dreams. Taking a deep breath, she held for a count of five, and released before exiting the truck. Sarah had been doing this since she was a child. Her parents had sent her to a shrink because they thought she was seeking attention by reportedly seeing ghosts. The breathing technique was the only legitimate thing she'd garnered from therapy aside from pretending she didn't believe in ghosts in order to stop the sessions and pacify her parents.

"Wow, this place is spectacular," Harry declared.

"Looks like a haunted house," Ralph replied with a broad smile.

Garrett looked over at Sarah who stood quietly staring at the structure with its peeling paint and rotting trim. "Sarah, are you okay?"

Swallowing the angst lodged in her throat, she nodded. "It's the same one," she mumbled.

"From your dreams?" Garrett asked.

"You've already dreamed about this place?" Harry said.

"Yup."

"Why didn't you say something?" Ralph queried.

"Didn't know until we pulled up."

Ralph grinned as he shook his head. "Incredible. The ghosts can find you before you even show up to a place. It's almost like you're psychic."

"Please don't add anything else to my repertoire." Sarah sighed. "The haunted dreams and eerie visions are more than enough."

Garrett squeezed Sarah's hand. "Ready to meet Cheryl?"

"Let's do this," Sarah said, blowing out a long breath. "The sooner we figure out what's going on, the sooner I can get back to my strange definition of normal."

The front door on the right side opened and a petite woman with blond shoulder length hair emerged. She stood on the porch, her eyes twinkling as a smile lifted her cheeks.

"Is she real?" Ralph whispered.

"Yes, she's real," Sarah replied with a chuckle. Stepping ahead of the group, she offered her hand. "Hello, I'm Sarah Holden. You must be Cheryl."

"Nice to finally meet you, Sarah. I haven't seen you since you were a wee little thing," she said with a dimpled grin. "Welcome to Hayden Place."

Sarah introduced the men and Dallas. "I hope you don't mind that we brought the dog but he's part of the team."

Cheryl knelt down and scratched behind Dallas's ears. "I

love dogs," she said. "I might be able to find a treat for him in the kitchen, if that's okay."

"He'd like that," Garrett replied.

They entered the house and stopped in the entryway. A grand staircase with painted spindles and a curved banister anchored the narrow hall. Blue tape held large swaths of brown paper in place to protect the floors while the work was being done. A corner piece was turned up revealing what appeared to be heart pine planks, typical for the time period.

Sarah scanned the space, looking for otherworldly activity. Nothing so far, although she didn't believe it would stay that way. If the ghosts had found her before she'd been to the house, chances were they'd make an appearance now that she was here.

"Cheryl, what do you know about the history of this place?" Garrett asked.

"Not much. It was built in the 1880s by a local couple. I purchased it from Mr. Jarvis who used it as a short-term rental."

"And you don't know anything more about the family who built it?" Harry asked.

"Nope. That's the only history I've been given so far. When I get a chance, I'll go to the local historical society and see what I can find."

Garrett, Ralph, and Sarah exchanged glances. They knew what this would lead to. A competition between Sarah's best friend, Danni and Ralph's brother, Walter, to see who could discover the details first. Walter and Danni had been wagering who was better at gathering information since the Edgefield Manor haunting. After Walter won that bet, an animosity had formed between him and Danni. The last wager ended in a draw. Now more than ever, Danni seemed determined to redeem herself as the better researcher.

"Is everything alright?" Cheryl asked.

"It's fine. We have a couple of people who may be able to help with unearthing more of the home's history," Garrett said.

"That would be wonderful. Not being able to find out more about this place has been frustrating. I fear something terrible happened here considering all the unexplainable occurrences."

"Are you living here?" Sarah queried, looking around.

"I stayed here for about a month before the renovations started. I removed the furniture from the first floor but the bedrooms are still furnished. As I said, the former owner used it as a short-term rental so it was in fairly good shape when I purchased it. But I wanted to bring it back to its former glory," Cheryl said with a broad smile. "I'm staying with my daughter across town until I can move back in."

Sarah's heart warmed. She and Cheryl seemed to share a similar outlook regarding the preservation of old buildings.

"What kind of things happened while you were living here?" Harry asked.

"It's quite strange," Cheryl said. "I'd walk into a room and hear water flowing nearby. When I searched for the source, I'd find one of the faucets running. I asked the plumbers about it but they couldn't explain it. One of the them actually suggested I'd left the faucet on and forgotten about it. Pfft. I may be getting older but I'm not senile, at least not yet."

Garrett shook his head. "They don't understand the paranormal. This isn't the first time we've heard about tubs and sinks mysteriously turning on."

"That's a relief, I think," Cheryl said, arching her brows. "As long as the ghosts don't flood the house, I can deal with turning off a few faucets."

"Anything else?" Harry queried.

"I keep seeing shadows even when there isn't any light in the room. It's quite unnerving. One night I heard footsteps in the hall. When I went to investigate, I saw a figure racing down the staircase. I thought someone had broken in so I locked myself in the bedroom and called the police."

"What did they find?" Harry asked.

"Nothing," Cheryl said. "They searched the entire house. All the doors and windows were secure. They said it wasn't the first time they'd been called out for something like this. That's when I realized the place was haunted."

"You're not spooked by the activity?" Ralph questioned.

"In the daylight, not so much but after the sun sets, it's pretty creepy. I'm going to be living here full time once the work is done. I can't have things scaring me. I've invested everything in this place. Not to mention, at my age, barreling down a flight of stairs in the middle of the night will likely lead to a broken hip."

Sarah's heart wrenched. She could see the conflict in Cheryl's eyes. It was difficult enough for Sarah to cope with her haunted visions and encounters. It must be terrifying to an ordinary person.

"Oddly, the occurrences seemed to ramp up once the renovations began," Cheryl added.

"That's not unusual," Harry said. "Ghosts don't like change and often become active when alterations are made to their former abodes."

"That would explain what happened a few nights ago with one of the contractors."

"What happened" Ralph and Harry asked at the same time, their expressions eager as if someone had offered them the winning lottery ticket.

"I was spending the night at my daughter's and the electrician was working late. He was installing something in the kitchen when he heard someone approach. He thought I'd come back to the house. When he turned around, nothing was there except a shadow against the wall. It scared him so badly, he left. He came back the next morning to finish what he'd started the night before but said he wouldn't return again. This may be a big city but it has a small-town mentality. It won't take long before contractors refuse to work on this place."

"That's interesting," Ralph muttered. "Sounds like a shadow figure."

Cheryl tilted her head.

"Some spirits can cast shadows without materializing." Harry explained.

"That's eerie," she replied, rubbing her upper arms.

"Don't worry, they're generally harmless," Ralph added.

"Would it be okay for us to stay at the house?" Garrett asked.

"By all means. The bedroom furniture from when the house was used as a short-term rental is still on the second and third floors. I've only tackled renovations on the main floor, so far."

"That'll work," Harry said.

"Okay if Dallas stays with us?" Garrett asked.

"Of course," Cheryl replied. "Let me get him that treat."

Dallas toddled behind her as she walked to the back of the house.

"Picking up on anything?" Garrett asked Sarah once Cheryl was out of earshot.

"Nothing so far but that could change at any moment."

Ralph's fingers flew across the screen of his phone.

"What are you doing?" Harry asked.

"Texting Walter so he can get started on the history search."

Sarah snatched the phone from his hands. "You can't do that yet. Danni will want to be part of this which means the two of them will likely be wagering again. Since the last bet ended in a draw, you know they'll be ready for another challenge.

Scrunching his lips, Ralph nodded. "Alright, I'll wait to tell him. But don't take too long, we need information as soon as possible."

Sarah handed the phone back and grinned. "We'll text them at the same time. First, we need to get things settled with Cheryl."

Cheryl returned with Dallas happily prancing at her side.

"Looks like you've made a new friend." Garrett chuckled.

"He's a sweet dog. I had some bacon left over from my breakfast biscuit; I hope you don't mind that I gave it to him."

"Not a problem. He runs enough to work it off."

Sarah sighed at the mention of running. She needed to start jogging again. With all the ghost hunting at Borden House and Virginia Intermont College she'd been derelict in her exercise routine.

"Do you need a tour of the place or would you rather explore on your own?" Cheryl asked.

The team looked at each other. "If you don't mind, we'd like to look around on our own," Harry said.

"Wonderful," she replied. "I have some errands to run and should be back in an hour or so."

"Thanks," Garrett said.

Cheryl gave a nod and disappeared down the hallway. Moments later the back door shut.

The team walked into the spacious front parlor. Heavy paper crunched beneath their feet protecting the wooden boards from further wear as light poured in from two large front windows. A slate mantel anchored the outside wall while ladders perched against interior walls where workers had been restoring the plaster. An ornate ceiling medallion encompassed a grand crystal chandelier that was sheathed in plastic. Despite the thick layer of plaster dust, the space exuded a regal air.

They went through the pocket doors separating the front parlor from the adjoining dining room. Plaster had been recently re-finished with original moldings and a sumptuous chandelier in the center of the ceiling. Another slate mantel, a match to the one in the front parlor, held court between two narrow French doors. Sarah peeked through one of the doors to a long room off the other front entrance. Large windows lined up with the interior French doors suggesting this had been an enclosed porch. The alignment of windows and doors was common practice at the time to create a cross breeze to help cool the house.

"Sensing anything?" Harry asked Sarah.

"Nothing except construction dust," she replied with a sneeze.

The group wandered to the kitchen at the back of the house. Newly installed cabinets and a center island topped in marble surrounded by bar stools welcomed guests to stay for a cup of coffee and a chat. Although modern, the room blended well with the Victorian style of the home.

"Shall we venture upstairs?" Ralph asked.

"Let's go," Harry replied.

Dallas led the way, his tail bobbing with each step. As they neared the second-floor landing, Sarah's lungs constricted. Was it mildew or something otherworldly?

"Is something here?" Garrett asked.

"Yes, although I can't quite distinguish what it is," Sarah replied with a shiver.

"Maybe there'll be something in the bedroom," Ralph said, hope glimmering in his eyes.

His enthusiasm warmed Sarah's heart. It almost made the frightening encounters worth it. Almost.

Multi-layered moldings lined the ceilings as they walked into a large bedroom at the front of the house with an ensuite bathroom, no doubt added later in the home's history. A four-poster bed with night tables on either side was situated between the front jib windows that lead onto a verandah. On the far wall was a massive armoire, its mirrored doors reflecting light from windows on either side of the hearth. The second-floor footprint mimicked the first-floor parlor and dining room with matching slate mantels, except there were windows on the exterior walls where the French doors were on the first floor.

"This bathroom needs a serious overhaul," Harry called from the next room.

"Most of them do in these old houses," Garrett replied, following him.

Sarah peered into the bathroom and gasped. It was glorious. Apparently, this had been another bedroom when the house was built but now was a spacious bathroom with a claw-foot tub, toilet, and what appeared to be a 1990's style vanity.

"What's wrong with it?" she asked. "Aside from the vanity, it looks perfect to me."

Harry shook his head as he stepped back into the bedroom. "I admire your passion for all things old, but a step-in shower with three shower heads would be much better."

Rolling her eyes, Sarah followed the guys from the room back into the hallway when something touched the back of her neck, sending a tingling sensation down her spine. Turning, Sarah gasped at the bloated figure standing behind her with its grayish skin and bulging eyes.

"He did this," the spirit muttered before vanishing from sight.

"Sarah?" Garrett whispered in her ear making her jump. "Everything okay?"

"She was here," Sarah mumbled.

"Who?" Harry whispered, looking around.

"Not sure but it was definitely the woman from my dreams."

"Did she say anything?" Ralph asked.

"Nothing that makes any sense," Sarah chewed her lower lip. This was the part she hated most. Not knowing where the haunting was going or how gruesome the scenes might be.

The team trudged up the stairs to the third floor where two more bedrooms were housed. These were more simplistic in nature and were obviously added later in the home's history as there weren't any fireplaces. Each hosted modest antique furnishings, threadbare rugs, and plaster in need of refinishing. Sarah loved when old houses retained their original features like plaster walls; however, the upkeep was cost prohibitive for most. Nevertheless, she was glad to see Cheryl putting forth the effort and expense to maintain the home's original state.

Glancing around, Sarah tensed, prepared for what might materialize. Nothing. She moved to the window at the rear of the room overlooking the back yard. The area had probably been used for gardens when the house was built. Now the space was a mound of dirt hedged by a six-foot privacy fence across the back and the side facing the road. Apparently, Cheryl was adding a parking area. What a shame, Sarah thought. A house without a garden was like a body without a soul. Then again, Cheryl was older and probably didn't want the time constraints or physical exertion of upkeeping a yard, especially during the oppressive heat of a Lowcountry summer.

Harry turned to Sarah. "Is anyone up here?"

Shaking her head, Sarah shrugged. "Nothing yet."

"Let's check out the yard," Garrett suggested, leading the group back to the main floor.

Sarah grinned as they descended the staircase. This reminded her of the Scooby-Doo cartoons she watched growing up. Except Dallas was smaller than Scooby-Doo and the ghosts Sarah encountered were real.

They stepped out the back door to the sandy expanse and glanced around. The space was unremarkable. The fencing was rickety with rotted boards bulging in places and the sound of cars racing past on the adjacent road echoing through. Sarah shielded her eyes from the sun as she gazed at the elaborately shingled mansard roofline. All manner of detail remained on the trim work of each of the three levels. The house was truly a Victorian gem.

Sarah walked around the side of the house when an image materialized. A young woman in a tattered flapper dress glared at her, the same woman from her dreams with the bloated face and decomposing body.

Dallas dashed to Sarah's side, barking. In that instant the woman's image dissipated and a quick glimpse of a man with a bloodied head flashed in Sarah's mind.

The men gathered around Sarah, staring at her.

"You saw something, didn't you?" Ralph asked.

Nodding, Sarah turned to face the guys.

"The woman from my dreams appeared. She was wearing a flapper style dress and a cloche hat. She vanished when Dallas started barking. Then a man appeared for a split second."

"A man? What'd he look like?" Harry queried.

"Hard to say," Sarah exhaled. "He was only there for a moment. But his head was covered in blood. I caught a glimpse of him in one of my dreams."

"Could you tell what kind of injury?" asked Garrett.

Sarah shook her head. "Like I said, it was so fast I couldn't make out details, only the blood."

"So, we have a woman in 1920s attire and a guy with some sort of head wound," Harry said. "It's a start."

"Sounds like something definitely happened here," Ralph

added. "Which explains the occurrences in the house. Cheryl said something about faucets running. Any idea how that ties in with what you've encountered so far?"

"Based on the state of the woman's body, she appears to have drowned. But I don't know how that connects to the faucets unless you consider the water aspect."

"Perhaps she drowned in the tub," Harry said.

"In a flapper dress? Doubtful. I'd say she lost her life in a boating accident or body of water." Sarah glanced around. This place was nowhere near the river, suggesting the woman's death didn't occur at the house. Unless someone held her head under the water in the tub until she drowned.

"What are you thinking?" Garrett asked.

Sometimes his intuition surprised Sarah. He always seemed to know exactly where her mind was drifting.

"I'm wondering how this woman could have been murdered in the house."

"I don't understand." Harry said.

"She's obviously connected to this place but drowning appears to be the cause of death. Since there's no body of water near here, the bathtub thing may not be as much of a stretch as I thought." Sarah paused for a moment, trying to find a way to explain what was swirling through her mind. "Being a flapper was a scandalous thing at the time. I know from one of my dreams that her father was strict. What if he caught her coming out of the bathroom wearing a flapper dress, lost his temper, and drowned her in the tub.

"Good theory but why would there be water in the tub if she was getting ready to go out? Not to mention, she'd probably be sneaking out," Ralph suggested.

"Maybe that's why she hadn't emptied the tub. It would make too much noise," Sarah replied. As she fiddled with the necklace, a memory from one of her previous dreams popped into her head. "Never mind. If she died in the tub, it couldn't have been her father. He was in Atlanta. He sent her to Savannah to live with her aunt and uncle."

"We're pretty early in this ghost hunt," Garrett said. "Based on our previous experiences, I'd say there's still a lot to uncover."

Chapter Five

Sunlight streamed through the kitchen windows illuminating the sparkles in the marble counter tops. Cheryl had returned bringing a box of dog treats with her. Dallas pranced at her feet in anticipation as she leaned over to give him one of the beefy bits. After patting the dog on the head, she straightened.

"So, what do you all think?" she asked.

"We'll take the job," Harry said.

"Wonderful," Cheryl replied, clapping her hands together. "What's your fee?"

Garrett glanced at Sarah. "None since you were referred by Mrs. Holden."

"Nonsense!" Cheryl declared, narrowing her eyes. "Sarah's mother told me this was something you guys are trying to do fulltime. You'll not get very far if you don't accept financial compensation for your work."

Harry shrugged a shoulder as the men exchanged knowing glances.

"How about no charge if nothing shows up. If we do capture something on tape then we'll need you to sign a waiver allowing us to post the video on YouTube and pay us what you feel is fair."

"Agreed," Cheryl replied, shaking Garrett's hand. "Do you need me to be here for all of this?"

"It's better if you leave," Ralph said. "We need to set up cameras throughout the house and the fewer people here the better our chances of capturing something on video."

"I've halted all renovations until I can get whatever this is under control. I'm running out of contractors and fear if word gets out that the house is haunted, I won't be able to find anyone within a hundred miles to work on this place."

"We packed all of our equipment in case you agreed which means we can start immediately," Garrett said.

"Perfect!" Cheryl declared. "I'll get my purse and be on my way."

Sarah followed Cheryl out the back door to her car.

"Excuse me, Cheryl," she said in a hushed tone. "May I ask you a question?"

"Of course, what is it?"

"Do you know why my mother referred you to Garrett when she doesn't believe in ghosts?"

Cheryl grinned. "She believes."

"How do you know?"

"That's her story to tell, not mine. You'll have to ask her."

Sarah nodded, disappointment weighting her shoulders. She'd hoped for answers sooner than later.

"Tell the men to text me if they find anything. I appreciate their willingness to help with this."

"I'll let them know," Sarah replied as Cheryl got into her car and pulled down the drive.

"Everything alright?" Garrett asked, causing Sarah to jump.

"Sorry, didn't mean to startle you." He rubbed her shoulders and kissed the top of her head.

"Cheryl said to text if we find anything."

"You mean *when* we find something," he responded. "Since you've already started dreaming about this place, I suspect we'll find a great deal."

"That's what I'm afraid of."

"Where should we start?" Harry asked when Garret and Sarah rejoined them.

"By getting Walter and Danni involved," Ralph said. "We need background information if we're going to understand who's haunting this place."

Ever since she learned about Sarah's ghostly proclivities, Danni had been stalwart in her support. She had helped Sarah untangle the brainteasers in the *Dreamist* book and taken time from her job as an attorney to join the team on the last two ghost hunts, despite being terrified of all things haunted. She was the best friend ever.

Sarah checked the time. It was 2:30 p.m. on a Saturday afternoon. Danni would probably be at home sitting in front of the television. "I'll text her."

Ralph smiled and sent a message to his brother Walter. Moments later, his phone dinged. "Walter said he's on it." Ralph's brows arched when another text pinged.

"Don't tell me he already has information," Harry chortled.

"No. He wants to know if Danni will also be researching."

Before Sarah could answer, her phone pinged. "She wants to know if Walter is involved."

"Looks like we have another wager in the making," Ralph grinned as he responded to Walter.

"So, it would seem," Sarah replied as her fingers flew across the phone screen. Seconds later her phone dinged again.

"What is it?" Garrett asked.

"Danni wants to meet us here."

"Seriously?" Ralph said. "That would give her an unfair advantage."

"Have she and Walter wagered yet?" Sarah asked.

Ralph shrugged.

"If she and Walter go at it again, they can work out the parameters of their bet. She was with us at Borden House and neither of them won so physical proximity doesn't seem to be a factor, especially with Walter's internet connections," Sarah replied, arching her brows.

"Whatever they decide, we need to learn more about the area," Harry said.

"Sounds like a good idea," Ralph replied.

The men started scrolling through their phones searching for museums and record offices.

"This sounds interesting," Harry said. "*Join Willow Knightly for a historically haunted tour through the oldest cemetery in Savannah.*"

"What time?" Ralph asked.

"According to her website she takes groups through the graveyard during the day or evening."

Sarah shuddered.

"Too much?" Harry asked.

"Graveyards are difficult for me. I can stay here with Dallas."

"But we'll need your insight," Ralph said with a pleading expression.

"Don't do anything that makes you uncomfortable," Garrett added.

"Being haunted is always uncomfortable." She snorted. "If I'm going to go, it would be easier during the day."

"That works," Harry said. "We need to be here after dark anyway."

"Looks like we're taking a cemetery tour," Sarah said, pursing her lips. "Danni will be thrilled."

Harry chuckled as he punched in Willow's number and made the reservation.

An hour later, Sarah met Danni at the front door and escorted her inside.

"Pretty creepy looking place," Danni grimaced, glancing around. "Kinda got an Addams Family vibe going."

"When Cheryl finishes the renos, it's going to be gorgeous," Sarah said.

"Still gonna be creepy." Danni replied, her upper lip crinkling.

Sarah took Danni to the kitchen where the guys were gathered.

"Hey Danni," Garrett said as she entered.

"You got here just in time," Harry announced. "We're heading over to Colonial Park Cemetery for a tour."

"A cemetery?" Danni whined. "Do I have to go?"

"Unless you want to stay here," Sarah replied.

"Are there ghosts in this place?"

"Wouldn't be here if there weren't," Sarah said with a mischievous grin. "Your choice. Stay here alone with the ghosts or come with us to the cemetery."

Danni rubbed her forehead. "How did I get caught up in all this?"

Sarah draped her arm around Danni's shoulders. "Because you drove all the way down here to help me which makes you the best friend in the world."

"Ugh," Danni said, rolling her eyes. "Alright, but if the undead grab me in the graveyard, this will be the last time I offer."

"If the undead grab you, you won't be here to offer," Ralph snorted, garnering a wicked look from Danni.

"Not funny," she grumbled, following the group out the back door.

Everyone piled into Garrett's truck. As they drove beneath a canopy of moss draped oaks, Sarah took in the mystical beauty of Savannah. It was just as picturesque as Beaufort with its historic architecture and sun dappled roads. The history of the city was as dense as its sandy soil making it a hotbed of ghostly activity. No wonder so many ghost hunting videos were filmed in the area.

"Have you spoken with Walter this morning?" Harry asked Danni.

"Yup," she replied smugly. "Whoever finds the most information about the house's history and any ghosts it may harbor, wins. Same prize as Borden House, dinner at the winner's favorite fine dining establishment."

"I assume the rules exclude my dreamist skills helping with your discoveries."

"Sadly, yes." Danni groused.

Sarah giggled at her friend's disappointment at not having an upper hand in the competition even though she knew Danni would never cheat to win. But having lost the Edgefield bet with Walter, she knew her friend was determined to win this one.

A short time later, they pulled up to Colonial Park Cemetery. People milled about chatting as they made their way to and from a stone archway with a sizable statue of an eagle towering above it. Iron fencing jutted from either side of the entrance encompassing the graves within. Even though it was daylight Sarah could feel the spirits pressing against her like metal to a magnet.

This was not going to be easy. Thank goodness Dallas was with her. Hopefully, he'd alert her to any approaching entities.

The last thing Sarah needed was for the tour guide to pick up on her ability to connect with the deceased.

Standing to the right of the archway, they watched for Willow's arrival. Meanwhile, Harry snapped photos of the cemetery entrance when Sarah noticed a woman with purple hair, a flowing black dress, and tattoos sprawling across her arms walking toward them.

This must be her, Sarah thought. "Willow?"

The woman gave her a derisive glance and continued down the sidewalk.

"Hello, are you my 11:00 tour group?" A lovely young woman with shoulder length brown hair and a bright expression approached them. She wore shorts with a pink t-shirt that said, *I dig graveyards.*

"You must be Willow," Harry said, offering his hand.

"I am. It's nice to meet you folks. Ready to learn about Savannah's oldest cemetery?"

Dallas barked as Danni groaned, sending a round of laughs through the group as Willow led them beneath the archway into a field of headstones. As soon as Sarah crossed the threshold onto hallowed ground, her skin began to crawl as if a thousand beetles scurried across her arms and down her back. There was more here than tombstones and the dearly departed. A host of unsettled spirits clamored for her attention. Swallowing hard, she squared her shoulders and took in a deep breath. She could do this.

Sunrays skulked beneath trees and between headstones. Sarah was thankful for the light; darkness would have been harrowing. The one thing she knew well was that apparitions preferred the dark; it seemed to strengthen them. Or maybe it just made for a more frightening situation. Either way, she was grateful the team was doing this during the day.

"Colonial Park has a rich history. Being the oldest cemetery in Savannah, it harbors a slew of ghostly tales," Willow said with a sweep of her arm as she led them along the path between gravesites.

Harry was filming with his phone. He'd use the footage as part of the final cut of whatever they captured at the Hayden Street house. Dallas toddled along, seemingly unfazed by the build-up of otherworldly pressure. With each step, Sarah's lungs tightened.

"Back in the day, priests required a nickel if you wanted to be buried here instead of the pauper's graveyard where criminals were hanged and entombed," Willow continued.

"Paying off priests," Danni mumbled. "This can't be good."

At that moment, Sarah glanced at the weathered headstone to her right where a nickel sat upon the crest of the grave marker. When she stepped closer to investigate, a shadowy hand popped from beneath the dirt, grabbed the nickel, and dissipated as a breeze shifted shadows across the headstone. Gasping, she stumbled backwards catching everyone's attention.

"Is everything okay?" Willow asked.

Sarah forced a smile. "Thought I saw something."

Willow grinned. "Mr. Grady's grave. He's a sly one. Likes to scare tour guests when we come through after dark. I'm surprised he'd show himself during the day."

Sarah's smile faded. Willow certainly seemed to know what had startled her. Could she see spirits too? Undaunted, Willow continued the tour as if ghostly appearances were a common thing.

Danni leaned into Sarah and whispered in her ear. "Maybe I should find a coffee house and wait for you guys there."

"Not a chance," Sarah replied. "You need to hear all of this so you'll know what to look for when you do your research. That is, if you want to beat Walter."

"You're mean," Danni said, her shoulders slumping as she trudged along.

Willow continued her dialogue. "At some point, the cemetery was running out of space so they started stacking coffins on top of each other. Many of the tombstones have been removed over the years so no one knows exactly where all the bodies are buried."

Danni halted and stared at the ground. "Are you saying we could be walking on top of dead people?"

Willow's smile broadened. "Exactly."

Sarah reached over and grasped Danni's wrist. "Remember your bet with Walter."

"I don't like walking over dead people," she grumbled through gritted teeth. "Don't want them haunting me."

"They won't haunt you," Sarah whispered to her friend. "That's what I'm here for. The worst thing you have to worry about is one of them reaching up from the grave and pulling you down with them." She snickered.

"Not funny," Danni replied, scooting nearer to Sarah. "But just in case, I'm sticking close to you. That way you can go with me."

They followed Willow as she shared tales of yellow fever and the fiasco across the street after Hurricane Isaac a few years earlier.

"Abercorn Street was the first to cut through the cemetery. Then a company purchased the piece of land on the other side. Construction began on the lot across the street shortly before the hurricane came through. The storm left standing water which must've weakened the foundation they'd poured, bringing skeletons to the surface."

"They didn't relocate the bodies before beginning construction?" Danni queried, furrowing her brows.

"As I said, there are dozens of bodies here without grave

markers. No one knows how many or where they're located. Exhumation would add to the bottom line and everyone knows developers hate that." Willow rolled her eyes and gave a disgruntled smirk.

Sarah's skin prickled as she glanced across the street at the building that was subsequently constructed on the site. Wavering images appeared near the building, their soulless eyes and sallow complexions boring through her fortitude. Shaking off the unease, Sarah diverted her gaze trying her best to focus on Willow's presentation.

They made their way to the far section of the graveyard where a towering brick wall spanned the length of the property with dozens of weathered gravestones decorating it.

"Why are the tombstones on the wall?" Harry asked, snapping pictures with his phone.

Willow gave a half grin. "These were placed here after the cemetery grounds were subdivided for development in the surrounding areas. Again, no one knows where the bodies are located."

Dallas growled, the fur on his back bristling. Willow looked around.

"Did he see a squirrel or something?" she asked.

"Probably," Garrett replied.

Dallas's growl deepened as he slunk toward the wall. He sniffed the dirt and then started digging.

"Dallas, no!" Garrett hollered, scooping up the dog. "Sorry, he must have smelled a critter or something."

Willow seemed to accept the excuse as Garrett and Sarah exchanged knowing glances. Obviously, there was something ethereal in that area and Dallas wanted to unearth it.

Danni, her lips a thin line, looked at her friend. Sarah could tell Danni was running out of patience for the spirit world and feared she would bolt at the next ghostly encounter.

"Another story follows a different storm when sanitation workers had to clean up this portion of the cemetery after the flooding receded. According to reports, workers were pulling finger bones from tree branches that were tangled in the Spanish moss."

Harry's smile broadened at the story and Ralph's eyes glinted. They were in their element. Danni; however, had had enough.

"I'm done," Danni announced. "Walking on dead people's unmarked graves, skeletons in foundations, and now bones hanging in tree limbs! I'm going to find the nearest coffee house, maybe a bar. Text me when you're done with the macabre march through the creepiest graveyard I've ever heard about."

Without another word, Danni headed for the back exit of the cemetery and disappeared down the next street.

"Did I say something wrong?" Willow asked.

"Don't mind her," Sarah replied. "She's not much into the spirit world."

"Then why did she come?"

"Fear of missing out," Ralph replied with a snort.

"She's with the research department and not one to face the entities head on," Sarah added.

"Research department?" Willow queried.

"We're here to do a ghost hunt and thought this would be a good way to get some background on the haunted side of the town's history," Harry said.

"Cool," Willow replied. "I'd love to see the final project when you're done."

"We can make that happen," Harry responded with a glimmer in his eye.

They meandered to the opposite corner passing several aboveground tombs.

"During the Civil War, Union soldiers camped here. They

showed no regard for the graves, destroying headstones as they rolled cannons and other equipment over them. When cold weather struck, some of the soldiers took the bodies from the crypts and huddled inside to keep warm."

Sarah hesitated as a foggy form in Union blue materialized next to the arched brick tomb to her left. The unwavering stare emanating from his empty eye sockets spoke of hate and discontent. Sarah feared he might come after her, rage seething from his spirit as his faceless skull followed her movements.

Dallas squirmed free of Garrett's grasp and bolted toward her. The dog's deep brown eyes met hers, alleviating some of her trepidation. Reaching down, she patted his head. He understood better than anyone how she felt. It was nice to have an ally.

"I wanted to share one of my favorite spots," Willow said, leading them to a tiny tombstone. "This is the grave of young Chester Barnes. He died of yellow fever but continues to haunt this area. Some have seen him jumping from the old oak beside his grave. He's described as having sandy blond hair, a mischievous grin, and a blue coat that's missing a button. He's harmless and wants only to find someone to play with him."

The group moved to the next section with Sarah trailing behind. She half expected to see the child sitting on a tree branch. The story was probably made up, she told herself. Many of the ghost sightings in cemeteries were usually people wanting to see something in a place likely to have spirits.

Sarah took a step forward when something crunched beneath her sneaker. Leaning down, she picked up a pitted brass button. A child's giggle tickled her ear as she studied the object. All of a sudden, the boy appeared, his legs swinging back and forth from the tree limb where he perched. A shiver rattled Sarah's body as Dallas ran to the base of the tree trunk barking and hopping on his back legs. The boy laughed as he peered down at the little dog. A moment later, the child leapt from the tree vanishing before his feet met the ground.

Not wanting the boy's spirit to follow her from the cemetery, Sarah dropped the button where she'd found it and hurried toward the group who was staring at her with Dallas at her heels.

"Sorry," Sarah said. "Thought I saw something in the tree."

"Apparently, the dog saw it too," Willow said.

Sarah lifted one shoulder as she took Garrett's hand and squeezed.

"What was it?" he whispered in her ear.

"I'll fill you in later," she replied in a hushed tone.

Willow concluded the tour with a few more haunted tidbits and a sincere thanks for the gracious tip. Reaching down, she scratched Dallas behind the ears.

"If I didn't know any better, I'd swear this little guy can see spirits," Willow said.

"Just squirrels," Garrett replied, with a sideways glance at Sarah.

Once Willow left, Sarah looked at the group and sighed. "For a while I thought Willow might have her own abilities regarding the spirit world. It's as if she knew what I was seeing. When she noticed Dallas's proclivities, I started to get nervous."

"Definitely a great storyteller," Ralph added.

"Maybe she does have some clairvoyant skills but doesn't reveal it to strangers," Harry said.

"I suppose we'll never know," Sarah replied. "I'll text Danni and find out where she ended up."

After a couple of back-and-forth messages, Sarah and the guys headed to a coffee house a few blocks away where Danni waited outside at a bistro table.

"How'd it go?" she asked as they approached.

"Pretty well," Harry said. "Got some great shots and the information was fascinating. We could do several episodes on that cemetery alone."

"Count me out if you do," Danni responded. "That place was seriously creepy. Don't know why y'all like stalking the dead. It freaks me out."

"Even though it was a great tour and will give us some good stuff for additional scenes, it didn't reveal any history related to Hayden Place," Garrett said.

"True," Harry replied. "But it sure was fun."

Sarah chuckled at the ongoing enthusiasm of this group and was thankful to have them all in her life. Even her ghost aversive best friend.

After a late lunch at a British pub downtown, the group returned to the house on Hayden Street.

"Are you going to stay with us or head back to Beaufort?" Sarah asked Danni.

"How haunted is this place?" Danni said, looking around.

"Won't know until after dark," Ralph replied.

"Think I'll pass on this one. Besides, I need to get online if I'm gonna beat Walter."

Ralph snickered, drawing an angry glare from Danni.

"What?" she asked in a firm tone.

Ralph's smile withered. "Nothing," he muttered.

"I *will* win this time," she announced, squaring her shoulders. Then turning to Sarah, she said, "Text me if you need anything."

"Thanks," Sarah replied, hugging her friend before she headed out the back door.

"Now what?" Ralph asked.

"We figure out where to place cameras," Garrett replied. "It would help if we knew more about the house and its ghost."

All eyes looked at Sarah.

"Let me guess, you want me to take a nap," she said.

"That would be great!" Ralph declared.

Garrett looked at her with a grin. "Only if you want to."

"I never want to sleep when the spirits are waiting but if it will help things along, I suppose I could try."

"Are you even tired?" Harry asked.

"Not really," she replied. "Maybe I could do some research on the house at a local museum instead."

"Thought I saw a sign on one of the homes across the street," Ralph said.

"A museum sign?" Sarah asked.

"I think so," he responded. Ralph took out his phone and punched in the street name. "Yup. It's the Hayden Street Neighborhood Museum." He turned the phone around to show her.

"Guess I'll take a stroll," Sarah said.

Chapter Six

Gravel crunched beneath Sarah's sneakers as she walked across the parking area next to the museum. Massive magnolias and live oak trees shrouded the tin roof of what could only be described as a gingerbread house. Ornate fretwork framed the porch and decorated the apex of the roof. Sarah half expected to see Hansel and Gretel emerge from within. A hand-painted sign read *Hayden Street Neighborhood Museum*.

Sarah turned the brass knob and shivered. The image of a dark-skinned woman flitted through her mind dissipating as quickly as it had appeared. Shaking off her trepidation, Sarah stepped into the modest cottage and inhaled. There was nothing more alluring than the smell of old wood and antique furnishings. A stout woman with gray hair in corn rows and glowing coffee colored skin entered the room.

"Good afternoon, welcome to the Hayden Street Museum. I'm Tilda."

"Hello, Tilda. I'm Sarah Holden," she replied, offering her hand.

"Are you visiting Savannah?"

"I'm with a ghost hunting group. We're filming at the mansion across the street and I was hoping to learn more about the neighborhood."

"This is a good place to start. Follow me and I'll tell you a little about this house."

Tilda shared the story about the Edwards family who built the house during the nineteenth century and then worked in the predominantly African-American neighborhood doing laundry.

"Back then, it was difficult for black people to make a decent living. The Edwards family provided a necessary service for the working class as well as some of the wealthier families nearby."

Sarah listened intently as Tilda continued the tour.

"As you can see this is a simple dwelling with four rooms on the ground floor and bedrooms on the upper level. The Edwards lived in this house until 1921."

"Where did they go?"

"No record of that but it was about the same time of Amelia Danbury's death."

"Who was Amelia Danbury?" Sarah asked, the name bouncing around her head. How did she know it?

Tilda smiled. "I seem to have gotten off track. It's a seedier aspect of the neighborhood history that's not part of the script for this house. Don't know why I ventured there."

"I enjoy the lesser-known facts, if you don't mind sharing."

"I suppose it wouldn't hurt..."

The bell on the front door jangled as a young couple with backpacks and camera's dangling from their necks entered.

"Welcome to the Hayden Street Museum. I'll be with you in a moment," Tilda said, turning to Sarah. "I need to get these people started on the tour. Feel free to look around the rest of the house. There's a twenty-minute video about the family and their business endeavors you can watch in the middle parlor."

"Thanks," Sarah replied, disappointment saturating her heart. She'd have to come back and find out more about the unscripted part of the tour.

Yawning, Sarah sat down on a long wooden bench to watch the video. She pressed the play button and leaned against the unforgiving back of the wooden church pew that served as seating. Images of days gone by flashed across the flat screen as the narrator's voice described life for the Edwards family during a transitional time in Savannah. Sarah's eyelids began to droop. She caught herself as her upper body rocked forward. Apparently, lack of sleep from the night before mixed with a cemetery tour and a full stomach was slowing her down. This was not the time or the place to doze off.

Sarah stood in a stretch and started for the door. As she reached for the knob, a cold breeze grazed her shoulders sending goosebumps across her skin. The words, *didn't deserve this*, brushed against her ear. Glancing over her shoulder, she saw Tilda pointing to a photo on the wall as she explained something to the young couple. Nothing else was there. She gripped the doorknob but before she could turn it, bloody fingers wrapped around hers. Sarah stifled a scream while trying to remove her hand from the knob. The more she struggled, the tighter the rotting fingers gripped. It was like the hand was a ghost itself.

She closed her eyes and tried to take in a deep breath but panic slinked up her throat preventing air from entering. All of a sudden, the grip released, allowing the knob to turn. Sarah scurried out the door without looking back in case something gruesome appeared. The crisp autumn air was a welcome respite from the suffocating terror she'd just escaped. Replaying the scene in her head, she realized the words *didn't deserve this* were more menacing than the other phrase she'd been hearing of *he did this*. It felt more aggressive almost as if a man was making the statement.

Her hands continued to tremble as she crossed the road. Now more than ever, she needed to pull herself together. If the team was going to help Cheryl, Sarah had to remain calm and focused. Her abilities would likely expediate helping the ghost move on so Cheryl could resume renovations and move into her dream home. That was the most important thing right now.

Since she hadn't garnered much at the Hayden Street Neighborhood Museum, Sarah decided a trip to one of the city museums might yield more information. She was tired but didn't feel like facing the ghosts that were bound to show up in her dreams if she napped. Stepping through the front door of Hayden Place, Sarah found the guys in the front parlor strate-gizing where the cameras would be placed for filming later that night.

"Did you find anything?" Garrett asked as Sarah entered.

"Nothing of significance," she replied. "However, the tour guide, Tilda, started to reveal something interesting when a couple walked in and interrupted. I'll have to go back another time and find out what she didn't say. The only thing I learned is that the Edwards family built the cottage across the street and ran a laundry. They left town unexpectedly in 1921 about the same time as a murder. Might try researching at a bigger museum."

"You can take the truck." Garrett offered. "Do you know where you're going?"

"The Georgia History Museum is a few miles from here. I'm hoping they'll have more information about this house."

"Text if you find anything," he said.

"I will."

Sarah drove several blocks and parked the truck beneath a

sprawling live oak and headed into the building. The displays and exhibits were remarkable, covering a range of topics from the Native Americans in the region to the Revolutionary War. Nothing about the specific residences in Savannah. Defeated at her lack of progress after visiting two museums, Sarah walked to the parking lot when her phone dinged. A text from Danni.

No luck on the research so far. Got anything I can use?

Other than a disembodied hand grabbing my wrist, I have nothing.

Sounds like you met Thing, she typed with a skeleton emoji. *Let me know if you need me to come back.*

Sarah's chest constricted. She really wanted her friend with her but understood Danni's trepidation and her desire to distance herself from the undead.

I'm good for now, Sarah replied.

Climbing into the truck, Sarah turned the key. The engine purred to life and the radio crackled as icy fingers scraped her back.

BAM!

Sarah jumped when a tree branch crashed onto the hood.

"Darn it!" she hollered, her heart pounding against her ribcage.

She got out and reached for the limb, hoping it hadn't done any serious damage. As her fingers made contact with the bark, the branch shifted into a skeletal arm, skin puckering from the bone in grayish hues. Sarah gasped as she recoiled, her fingertips still tacky from the sticky residue of the decomposing body part. Taking a step back, she closed her eyes. This isn't happening, she told herself. When she opened her eyes, the tree limb sat upon the hood just as it had appeared when it landed there moments earlier.

Gathering all her courage, she reached for the branch once more. This time it didn't alter as she flung it aside.

Sarah examined the hood, relieved there were no dents, only a tacky remnant where the limb made contact. There must have been sap on the branch, she thought, refusing to think about the rotting arm that appeared when she'd touched it. Climbing back into the truck, Sarah closed the door and screamed. A shadowy figure sat on the seat beside her. The woman's face was bloated and pocked and her eyes were nothing more than dark shadows.

"What do you want to tell me?" Sarah muttered, her pulse racing through her veins.

"Not fair," she moaned.

"What's not?"

"It's too late!" the spirit screamed in a high-pitched tone, her eye sockets glowing gold and her jaw dropping at an unnatural length as slime oozed across her swollen lips.

Sarah gripped her ears and squeezed her eyes shut. Her throat tightened, keeping air from entering her lungs. When she finally lowered her hands and opened her eyes, the entity was gone. It was definitely the same woman from her dreams. The question remained, who was she and what was her connection to the house on Hayden Street? Taking in a deep breath, Sarah held for a count of five and released. She did this several more times until the quavering in her limbs stopped.

Unnerved, Sarah headed to the house, parked the truck, and took the back stairs two at a time. She found the guys huddled around the kitchen island on a conference call with Walter.

"Sarah just walked in," Garrett said to the computer.

"That's all I have for now. I'll let you know when I get more," Walter said before the screen went dark. Classic Walter. He wasn't much of a conversationalist nor the type to engage in polite social interactions.

"Any luck finding information about this place?" Garrett asked Sarah.

Wow, no 'how are you' or 'good to see you're back,' she thought. "Didn't find anything," she replied, plunking onto one of the kitchen stools. "Although, there was the incident in the parking lot."

"What happened?" Harry asked.

Sarah told them about the tree limb falling on the truck and turning into a disembodied arm. "Thank goodness the truck isn't damaged, but the entire ordeal was unsettling."

"Glad you weren't hurt," Garrett said, rubbing her arm.

Sarah gave him a weak smile. "What did Walter have to share?"

"He found the names of the family members who built the house and lived here for several decades," Ralph said. "Joseph and Bessie Miller. Supposedly, Bessie was part of the Danbury family, a prominent name in the area at the time."

Sarah cocked her head. "That name sounds familiar." She hesitated for a moment trying to figure out where she'd heard it before. "Tilda mentioned Amelia Danbury. Wonder if there's a connection."

"Supposedly, Joseph and his wife Bessie owned a mercantile store on the Riverfront but didn't have any children. Bessie's brother, George, was a prominent citizen with five children, four sons and a daughter. He was a local politician who moved his family to Atlanta to make a run for congress. There was some sort of scandal that cost him the race."

"What kind of scandal?" Sarah asked, wondering if that's what Tilda was getting ready to share when the other couple walked in.

"Don't know. That's all Walter was able to find so far."

"Have you heard from Danni?" Harry queried.

"Not yet," Sarah replied with a yawn.

The men stared at her like she'd just scored the winning field goal.

"What?" she asked.

"If you're sleepy, maybe you need to lie down," Ralph said, excitedly.

Rubbing her forehead, Sarah sighed. "Alright, I'll rest for a bit and see if anyone shows up in my dreams."

"Thanks," Garrett said, kissing her.

"But I'm taking Dallas with me," she replied. "Come on buddy."

Dallas ambled up the stairs and waited at the top. Sarah went into the front bedroom on the second floor, crawled onto the bed, pulled a throw over her shoulders, and snuggled with Dallas. The heat from his body and his rhythmic breathing pulled Sarah into a state of relaxation. She hadn't done much that day yet her body felt as if she'd climbed a mountain. Closing her eyes, she took a few deep breaths and drifted off.

Sarah glanced around and realized she was at Cheryl's house. A young woman, the one Sarah recognized from previous dreams, stood in front of the grand mansion with its mansard roof, double porches, and sage green clapboard siding. Massive corbels supported the first and second story rooflines like decorative frosting on a cake. Amelia pondered the two front entrances. Was one for the family and the other for servants? It seemed strange since servant entrances were generally in the back where they were less conspicuous. At least that's how it was at her home in Atlanta.

Elaborately designed gardens surrounded the mansion with crepe myrtles, their fuchsia blooms glowing in the afternoon sun. Roses, lantana, and lilies exploded in a rainbow of color filling every corner of the yard.

The young woman's heart pounded within her chest. Why would her father send her to such a beautiful place as a punishment? Of course, their own house was grand with lush greenery around it. But there had never been flowers. Her father felt flowers were a waste of resources because they didn't last long and needed constant care. Money was his only pleasure and the thing he cared about most.

One of the front doors opened and a petite lady with a bobbed hair cut stepped from within. Her brown eyes sparkled as a smile lifted her cheeks.

"You must be Amelia," the woman called out.

"Yes ma'am," she replied, her throat dry.

"I'm your Aunt Bessie," she said, moving to the porch railing. Looking around, she tilted her head. "Where's your father?"

Amelia's gaze dropped to the ground. "He had his driver drop me here."

"Without helping you in with your bags?"

"Father instructed him to let me do for myself since I'm too selfish to accept help from others." Amelia braced for a cruel retort from her aunt. She'd never been allowed to spend time with her father's sister. She assumed it was a long festering disagreement. Whatever had separated the siblings years before hadn't stopped her father from dumping his only daughter on someone who was essentially a stranger.

"Ridiculous!" she hollered, making Amelia jump. "Wait right there, I'll get someone to help you."

Bessie scooted back into the house and moments later appeared with a lanky dark skinned young man.

"I'm sorry but my back has been acting up the past few days and Joe would have a fit if he knew I lifted anything heavy. This is Jackson," she said, motioning toward the young man. "He'll take your trunk."

Bessie's welcoming expression radiated kindness. Amelia held her breath, unsure how to react. Would she be staying with the servants? Not that it would bother her, after all, she'd spent most of her childhood sneaking to the servant's quarters in her father's house. She preferred their company to her own family. Her brothers were always engaged in what her father referred to as 'boys business' and her mother was generally passed out.

"Are you alright?" Bessie asked, gently touching Amelia's arm.

"Yes, ma'am," Amelia whispered. "I don't want to be any trouble. If you could please show me where I'll be staying, I can get everything inside on my own."

"Good gracious, it's worse than I suspected!" she declared, throwing her hands in the air. "I knew that scoundrel would be ruthless to his children."

"Ma'am?" Amelia muttered.

"Let's get some things straight. To begin, I'm not *ma'am*, I'm your Aunt Bessie. Apparently, your father has forgotten that I am not as stubborn and bullheaded as he is. I can assure you my husband is not either."

Amelia took a step back. She wasn't sure if she should be terrified or wrap her arms around this tiny spitfire of a woman. Her aunt seemed to take notice of her trepidation and softened her tone.

"My goodness, you're like a scared kitten. My apologies for being so brusque about your father. You've no need to fear me or your uncle. I was thrilled when your father contacted us about having you come for a visit." Turning to Jackson, she smiled. "Would you mind helping Amelia with her things? She'll be staying in the blue bed chamber on the third floor at the front of the house."

"Of course," he replied. A smile spread across his face as

warmth emanated from his dark eyes. Lifting the trunk, he started toward the front door. "You comin'?"

Amelia nodded unable to find the words. It was like stepping into an imaginary world where everyone was kind, something she'd only dreamed about as a child. She'd never known anyone to stand up to her father and a large part of her was enjoying her Aunt Bessie's gumption.

Turning toward Sarah, Amelia's visage began to alter, her skin taking on a sallow glow and her eyes bulging from their sockets.

Help them, she uttered.

A slimy substance coated Sarah's face as her chest tightened. She jolted from the dream to find Dallas standing on her rib cage licking her cheeks. Temporarily disoriented, it took Sarah a moment to figure out where she was. Hayden Place. She finally remembered the identity of the woman who'd been dominating her dreams and her name was Amelia Danbury.

Chapter Seven

Climbing from bed, Sarah took a moment to steady her wobbling legs. Dallas stared at her with deep brown eyes and his head cocked. She ruffled his ears and smiled.

"Looks like I have a name."

"Yip," he replied.

Dallas followed Sarah downstairs to the kitchen where the guys were setting up the monitors for filming later that night.

"Hey," Garrett said, walking over to Sarah and kissing her gently. "Any good dreams?"

Sarah bristled. She understood the team's desire to get information about the ghosts in the house but sometimes she just wanted to be seen as herself without the haunted proclivities. Not to mention, she needed some time to wake up before being bombarded with questions.

"Yeah, I guess," she mumbled.

"Sounds intense," Harry said, looking up from the camera he was fidgeting with.

"Not intense, more like mysterious."

Garrett reached for her but instead of accepting his embrace, Sarah sidestepped him and plunked onto the stool at the kitchen island. She leaned her elbows on the marble counter top, refusing to meet his befuddled gaze.

"I saw the ghost that's been visiting my dreams in her living state. She arrived at this house where her aunt and uncle lived. I was expecting the same kind of meanspirited people as her father. Except her aunt was kind. Before the dream progressed, the young woman morphed into the gruesome creature that's been haunting me."

"Wow, that's a lot," Harry said, crossing his arms over his chest. "Still no idea who this woman is?"

"Actually, yes. Amelia Danbury."

"The same Danbury who was running for congress?" Ralph asked.

"I assume so since Walter found that information and they're connected to the house," Sarah replied, her words clipped.

"I'll share Amelia's name with Walter and see if he can find anything about her," Ralph said softly, pulling out his phone.

"In that case, I need to let Danni know too," Sarah said sharply, her fingers tapping a message to her friend.

Ralph flushed at the boldness of her statement as his thumbs raced across the screen.

Garrett and Harry exchanged worried looks as they continued working on the equipment for the after dark ghost investigation. Cameras were placed in the front parlor, the hallway leading to the kitchen, and the third-floor bedroom at the front of the house. Ralph had monitors set up in the kitchen and would watch all of the camera feeds while Garrett manned the one in the parlor and Harry stayed with the one on the third floor. EVP recorders, to capture utterances from the entities, were placed with the cameras. It seemed the haunted visions, Sarah's mood, and the competition between Danni and Walter were intensifying.

Darkness shrouded the house in a blanket of gloom. Since there wasn't any furniture in the parlor or dining room, Garrett brought in a stool from the kitchen island for Sarah to sit on while he manned the camera. The air was electrified as if several spirits were lingering nearby. As he adjusted the camera settings, a chill slithered down Sarah's spine.

She wasn't sure what she was facing, only that the entity in need of her help was Amelia. Based on the bloated nature of her body, the pocked skin, and soggy state of her attire, Sarah surmised the woman must have drowned. The idea rattled her. Drowning was something she'd always feared as a child even though she was a fairly strong swimmer.

Closing her eyes, she could still see the dream as if it were projected on the big screen. Without warning, Sarah found herself underwater. Something held her under as she clawed at the unseen force. Her lungs were losing strength like a leaking balloon ready to deflate at any moment. Light drifted down through the water's surface teasing her with the promise of air if she made it to the top. If only she could break free but her arms and legs were too weak. Panic squeezed her chest as the air filtered out of her lungs and water came pouring in.

Sarah jolted as she opened her eyes. Had she fallen asleep or was the memory etched in her mind so deeply she'd conjured it back to life? Hopefully, this wasn't a foreshadowing of what was to come. Rubbing her eyes, she tried to steady her breathing but apprehension weighted her chest. She wanted to run from this house and its ghosts. They were playing on her greatest fears. How was she supposed to stay calm when the spirit brought to life the very thing that haunted her psychological fortitude?

"You ready?" Garrett asked, startling Sarah from her ruminations.

"Ready as ever," she replied, her shoulders slumped. Obviously, he hadn't noticed her distress.

"Are you okay? You've been distant today."

Shaking her head, Sarah exhaled. "I'm just a bit worn out. We've been going non-stop with the ghost thing for a couple of weeks now and I'm tired." How could he not realize the stress she was under?

Garrett leaned in and kissed her softly on the lips. "I promise we'll take a break after this. First, we have to help your mother's friend."

Sarah gave a slight smile. "And I appreciate it," she muttered, her lips brushing his once more. She felt like an empty husk; all her emotions strained to the point of feeling nothing. It wasn't as if she could take a break from the spirit world. Sure, she didn't have to help with ghost hunts every weekend, but the entities would always find her no matter where she was.

Dallas stood at her feet and let out a resounding bark.

"Do you want to sit here with me or hang out on your own with Dallas?"

Sarah contemplated staying but the pressure in the room was building. "I'll go to our room on the second floor. Maybe Amelia will be drawn to the quietude. Hopefully, she'll be more communicative there."

"Sounds good. Holler if you need me."

"No need, I've got Dallas," Sarah said. Having another being, even one of the canine species, who could sense the entities swarming through the house offered a slight bit of comfort.

Garrett rolled his eyes and shook his head.

As she climbed the stairs to the second floor, Sarah fingered the charms dangling from the chain around her neck. Her ability to feel Amelia's emotions was different than previous experiences. She could actually hear Amelia's thoughts. Was the necklace the reason or were her dreamist skills developing?

Dallas reached the top of the stairs first and waited for her to catch up. They entered the room at the front of the house. Shadows shimmied across the wood floors as Sarah made her way to the window. She stared at the yard where a street light glimmered across piles of lumber awaiting installation. From what she could recall from her dreams, there'd been flora and shrubbery edging the space in a rainbow of colorful hues. What a shame all of it was gone. Now the roadway occupied that part of the yard.

Sarah released a breath and turned back to the room. She plopped onto the four-poster bed and considered lying down. If she could dream something significant, she'd feel more productive. Was this her life now? Feeling useless unless she was dreaming about ghosts?

Dismissing her gloomy thoughts, she went back to the window and stared at the night shadows skulking across the street. She sucked in a breath when her reflection in the glass window panes altered to Amelia's water-logged visage.

He did this, she groaned, sending Sarah stumbling backwards.

Swallowing the bile inching up her throat, Sarah managed to speak. "Who did what?" she muttered.

He did this! the apparition screeched. Sarah covered her ears and squeezed her eyes shut as Dallas yowled.

Moments later, footfalls echoed from the hall as Garrett rushed into the room and grabbed Sarah by the shoulders.

"You okay? What happened? Was the ghost here?" he blurted out, his words jumbled.

"I'm fine," Sarah replied. "And yes, Amelia was here."

"What did she say?"

Even in the darkness, Sarah could see the anticipation glimmering in Garrett's eyes. All of a sudden, she felt used, like a spirit vessel, only valued for her ability to speak to the dead.

"Same thing as before, *he did this.*"

"And you don't know who she's talking about?"

"No," Sarah responded, shorter than she'd meant to.

"You sure you're alright?" Garrett asked, rubbing her upper arms.

Sarah shirked away from him and turned toward the window. "I told you, I'm just tired from the past few weeks. Being a conduit for the dearly departed is exhausting."

"Yeah, I get it," he replied, softly. "I'll be in the parlor if you need me."

Sarah continued staring out the window as Garrett left the room. Dallas whimpered, pawing at her jeans. Guilt weighted her chest as she reached down to pet the dog. "Sorry little fella. Didn't mean to upset you. I'm not angry with Garrett. I'm only frustrated with all this haunted stuff. I could really use a break," Sarah sighed. "Too bad I can't get one."

Dallas let out a groan as he plunked down with his chin resting on his paws. Sarah chuckled. It was like Dallas agreed with her. After all, he sensed spirits and probably got tired of it too. Except he couldn't express his frustration.

For the next half hour, Sarah paced back and forth, nervous energy coursing through her veins. Why was she so agitated? She'd never felt this way before and it bothered her. Sitting on the bed, she pulled out her phone and texted Danni.

Find anything yet?

Dots scurried across the screen.

Nothing substantial. Any word on what Walter found?

Not supposed to tell you. Sarah typed.

I know but thought I'd give it a try.

Aside from dreams of drowning and a speakeasy scene, I have nothing else to share.

Speakeasy? Danni responded.

It was from an earlier dream but haven't seen it since.

Okay. Need to get back at it.

Sarah hesitated for a moment. She really wanted to share her feelings with Danni. Then again, her friend needed to focus on finding information, not coddling Sarah through another bout of insecurity.

Good luck, Sarah typed with a sigh.

Sliding the phone into her pocket, Sarah leaned against the headboard. She closed her eyes and quieted her thoughts, hoping something would come through. Nothing. Relief washed over her when Garrett rapped on the doorframe.

"We're calling it a night," he said softly.

Sarah stood and walked over to him. She brushed her hand along his stubbled cheek. "Sorry about earlier. Don't know why I was so grumpy." She planted a quick kiss on his lips. "Did you guys capture anything on tape?"

"Nada," he breathed. "It's only the first night though. Chances are we'll have more luck tomorrow. Of course, once Ralph and Walter work with the videos something might show up that we didn't see. Maybe you'll get more from your dreams."

"Let's hope so," she said, kissing him once again. "Don't know about you, but I'm ready to get some shuteye."

"Me too. I'll be back after I take Dallas outside."

Sarah squeezed his hand before he left the room. The great thing about staying in the house was that the guys didn't have to pack up the equipment each night. Her chest tightened at the idea of what her dreams might reveal. The underwater scenes were disturbing and she didn't look forward to facing them.

After washing her face and changing into her pj's, Sarah slid beneath the quilt and rested her head on the pillow. The charms on the chain around her neck slinked to the side as she turned over.

Fingering the trinkets, she pondered what they meant. There had to be some meaning to them otherwise Ola wouldn't have led her to find the necklace. Just once, she wanted something affiliated with her dreamist abilities to be straightforward and simple. Deep down she knew that would never happen. At least things were getting a little easier as her skills developed.

Dallas leapt onto the bed and snuggled next to Sarah. Garrett joined them moments later.

"Goodnight," he said.

"G'night," she replied. Even though fatigue gripped her limbs, Sarah was wide awake. "Garrett?"

"Yeah."

"Do you think Ola enjoyed being a dreamist?"

He reached over and grasped her hand. "I'm not sure. Why do you ask?"

"It's all so complicated. I feel like I get good at one aspect only to have another more complicated one show up. Did Ola have that problem?"

"Don't know. She never said if she liked it or didn't. I know she took it seriously and felt responsible for helping the spirits move on."

Silence blanketed the room as Sarah pondered Garrett's statement.

"She never complained about it?" Sarah asked.

"Nope, but Grams rarely complained about anything except people who didn't return their library books on time."

Sarah giggled. "I suppose it would be annoying having to track down overdue books."

"I think tracking down the truth about ghosts would be more stressful but if it was, Grams never mentioned it."

Shame sat on Sarah's chest, compressing her ability to take in a deep breath. She felt horrible for being so negative about her dreamist abilities all the time. Then again, Garrett didn't learn about Ola's skills until he was a teenager. By then, Ola had probably perfected her abilities, not to mention, she had the guidance of generations of women before her. Sarah looked forward to the day when all of this would be second nature. Until that time, she was stuck with a serious learning curve and terrifying dreamscapes. Closing her eyes, she stroked Dallas's soft fur until she fell asleep.

"Aunt Bessie asked me to bring this to you," Amelia said, handing Jackson a glass of sweet tea.

"Thanks," he replied, wiping the sweat from his brow before downing the amber drink.

"What're you working on?"

"An old jalopy that oughta be scrapped for parts," he chuckled. "But old man Roberts loves this car. I keep patching it up so he can rumble around town in it."

"He must be rich if he can afford to keep that thing running."

"He ain't rich. Don't charge him for it either. Mr. Roberts been good to my family so I do this for him."

"That's nice of you," Amelia said, glancing over her shoulder. "Should I keep this a secret from my aunt and uncle?"

"They know all about it. Your aunt and uncle are some of the kindest people I know. They use their money to help others. Got my family set up with the laundry. My mother does your family's washing for free. Folks 'round here take care of each other. Goodness knows, anyone outside of the neighborhood don't much care what happens to us."

"Jackson!" a man hollered from the doorway. "Need you to take a quick look at something for me."

Amelia turned to see a man standing there, his crumpled hat sitting on top of unruly hair that poked out from underneath like straw from a haystack.

"What's the problem, Eddie?" Jackson asked, wiping his hands on his coveralls.

"Think something's misfiring in the engine. Can't get any power. Need it for a delivery this evening," he said with a wink.

"Let me take a look at it," Jackson replied.

Amelia watched as Jackson tinkered with some things in the engine.

"That oughta do it," he proclaimed, slamming the hood. "Be careful tonight."

"Careful is for sissies," Eddie said, slipping behind the wheel and revving the engine. The car disappeared in a cloud of dust as he sped down the drive and onto the road.

The scene shifted. A sleek Cadillac, its ebony finish shimmering in the sunlight stopped in front of a flat front building off one of the Savannah squares. A tall gent in a bowler hat and dark suit emerged from the vehicle. He took a handkerchief from his coat pocket and wiped his brow as he stared at the structure. *Miller's Mercantile* was printed in large letters across the top of the front wall at the roofline. Sarah's heartbeat ticked up a notch. This must be Amelia's aunt and uncle's store, she thought.

She followed the gentleman inside where the smell of lemon oil and lavender greeted them. Sarah scanned the neatly organized space. Shelves of canned goods along with barrels of flour and grits lined one side while the other hosted an array of items such as leather boots, bolts of cloth, and a few hats.

Amelia stepped from the back room and froze. Chewing her lower lip, she handed a loaf of bread wrapped in brown paper to a woman waiting by the front counter before making her way over to the man in the tailored suit who'd just entered. Why was Theodore Warren in Savannah instead of Atlanta helping her father with the campaign, Amelia thought.

Sarah sucked in a breath. Had she actually heard what Amelia was thinking? She'd had insight into a ghost's mind before but never to this degree. Was this a new skill developing or was there something about Amelia that allowed Sarah to connect with her on such a personal level?

"What are you doing here?" Amelia said quietly.

"I came to see you," Theo replied, looking around the place with a grimace. "Seriously, Amelia, is this a more attractive existence than being married to me?"

Squaring her shoulders, she took in a deep breath before answering. "This isn't about living a pampered life. It's about controlling my own destiny."

"Come on, Amelia. How long are you going to keep up this charade? You're angry with your father. There's no need to take it out on me. When have I ever treated you with disrespect?"

Her brows arched. "When you arranged to marry me without consulting me first," she replied through clinched teeth. "Please leave, Theo. I have customers to help."

"Do you hear yourself?" he grumbled, leaning toward her. "You sound like some sort of low-class tramp."

Amelia's eyes narrowed as she balled her fists. "It's a good thing I'm working or I'd have slapped you for that. I'll have you know this is honest work and I enjoy the people I meet."

"This isn't a garden party. It's below you, Amelia. Why can't you see that? You've proven your point. You're an independent woman. But this has gone far enough," he said, grabbing her arm. "Come home with me so we can announce our engagement and start making wedding plans."

"I'll do no such thing," she retorted, yanking her arm free. "Hear me now, I am not going to marry you. Not ever."

Sarah could feel the heat radiating from Theo as he straightened his suit coat.

"I see you still haven't learned your lesson," he spat. "Go ahead and work in this hovel like a shop girl. When you've had your fill of this nonsense, let me know and we can move forward with our lives."

He turned on his heel and marched out of the store leaving Amelia standing there, a slow grin creasing her eyes. She did it. She stood up for herself and it felt good. Deep in her heart, she was certain her father had sent him to bully her.

"Miss?" a woman called from the fabric section. "May I get a yard of this blue broadcloth?"

"Of course," Amelia replied, going over to the cutting table. As she measured the fabric her heart rate resumed a restful pace.

All of a sudden, Sarah found herself on Hayden Street after nightfall. The windows of the house were dark, save the one on the third floor. Amelia's room. Unease filtered through Sarah's veins when she caught movement from the corner of her eye. She looked around and saw someone move through the bushes of the small brick church across the street next to the Edwards' gingerbread cottage.

Although Sarah couldn't make out the details, she could see the figure was tall and slim. She moved across the street to get a better look but whatever had been there was gone.

Sarah blinked and found herself on the porch of the Edwards' cottage where Amelia stood with a bouquet of flowers. Knocking, Amelia listened as footsteps approached and the door swung open, light pouring across the porch floor from inside.

"Come in Amelia," the woman said, stepping aside.

Amelia looked around the front parlor which was much smaller and more modest than the one at her aunt's house. Despite its quaint size, it was beautifully furnished with bright blue walls and a brick fireplace in the opposite corner. A braided rug covered the pine floors and a large painting of a river scene anchored the wall across from where she stood.

"Your home is lovely, Mrs. Edwards," Amelia said, handing her the flowers. "I thought you might like these."

"That was sweet of you," Mrs. Edwards said, a broad smile crossing her face. "Come with me. Dinner will be ready in a moment."

Amelia followed her to the dining room. A rectangular table shrouded in a lace cloth was bedecked with stoneware plates and yellow cloth napkins. Ladder-back chairs were crowded around the table leaving little room between.

"Have a seat. I'll be back in a moment," Mrs. Edwards said. "Mr. Edwards and the others will be here soon."

"Can I help with anything?"

Mrs. Edwards stopped abruptly, her brows arching. "You're our guest."

"I'd still like to help if I can."

Mrs. Edwards' eyes narrowed as a slow smile crept across her face. "Jackson said you was special. If you want to help, come with me."

Sarah watched as the entire family squeezed around the table, hardly a hand's width between them. Apparently, the Edwards had three other children besides Jackson, two girls and another boy. The kids were energetic but well-mannered as they chattered throughout the meal.

Amelia's thoughts infiltrated Sarah's mind. She envied the

Edwards with their simple, contented lives. People always thought money brought joy but Amelia knew better. Love and kindness were the basis for happiness. And it was abundant in this house.

Sarah shuddered when Amelia turned towards her, her porcelain skin turning sallow as the life drained from her face. Water dripped from her dark hair as she mouthed the words, *help them.*

Before she could respond, Sarah found herself at the riverfront, her head forced in the icy river, water pushing the air from her lungs. She managed to get her face above the surface, momentarily catching a glimpse of her attacker. He was tall and slender. His grip on her hair tightened as he shoved her head under the water once again and everything went dark.

Gasping for air, Sarah sat up in bed. Garrett was sleeping soundly as the streetlamp peered through the window in a golden glow. She was safe. But Amelia hadn't been as fortunate. Someone had killed her. Someone tall and lean like Jackson. The question being, was Jackson the one who did it? The dream had gone from dinner at the Edwards to Amelia's drowning. And the repeated phrase of 'help them.' What was that about? It seemed as if she was asking Sarah to help the Edwards' family. But previous encounters with Amelia had also suggested her aunt and uncle were in need of assistance. Which one was it?

Sarah exhaled. Now that she thought about it, the man holding her under the water and the figure she'd seen across the street bore a striking resemblance to Jackson Edwards. Yet Jackson seemed so kind in previous dreams. Obviously, Amelia liked him too or she wouldn't have been dining at his family's home. If Sarah had learned anything from past endeavors it was not to make judgements based upon how agreeable the potential killer could be. She'd been fooled in the past and didn't want to make the same mistake again.

She glanced at Garrett's sleeping form. She desperately wanted to talk this through with someone but didn't want to wake him. Their relationship had to be founded on more than hauntings and dreamist discussions. And what was happening with her ability to hear Amelia's thoughts? Only one way to find out. Rolling over, Sarah squeezed her eyes shut and willed herself back to sleep.

Water dripped from a broken pipe splashing to the ground in a popcorn like rhythm. Cobblestones glimmered in the darkened alleyway where two figures stood a few feet from where Sarah watched.

"You know what to do?" one man asked.

"I got it," the other replied. "The little lady needs to learn a lesson. I'll make sure she gets a good scare."

"I'll deny any involvement if you screw this up. And I won't be responsible for what happens if you do."

"Don't threaten me," the taller one growled. "I'm not afraid of you or anyone else."

Sarah stifled a scream when something grabbed her by the shoulder and pulled her into the shadows. The scent of decay stung her nostrils. Squeezing her eyes shut, she froze, too terrified to move. That's when Sarah felt something icy tickle her ankles. With the hand still holding her in place, she glanced down and saw water flowing about her feet.

The words, *didn't deserve this*, brushed against her cheek, the rancid odor of the spirit's breath sticking to her skin. As the water crept up her calves, the grip on her shoulder tightened until she couldn't stand it any longer.

Wrenching free, she bolted into the flooding cobblestone

lane, water splashing as she ran. She didn't dare look back for fear of what she'd see. Breathless, Sarah stopped. The water was rising to the point she couldn't move forward.

Something grabbed her ankle.

Her scream was amplified by the buildings on either side of her. Whatever was wrapped around her leg, yanked her beneath the flow of water where everything was dark. The water's movement rushed through her ears as she flailed her arms in an effort to break free of whatever was pulling her under. Opening her eyes, a light from above glowed through the current, highlighting the hand that was holding her down.

Panic seized her chest and muddled her mind. Sarah clawed at the hand, trying to free herself. Bits of flesh and skin sloughed off leaving only bone behind. The sight startled another scream allowing the water to flow freely down her throat choking the remaining air from her lungs. As her sight began to fade, Sarah caught a glimpse of who was holding her down. The facial features were distorted by the water but it was clear to her it was a man. A man who resembled the one she'd seen earlier in the alleyway.

Death wrapped its sinewy fingers around her even though she knew ghosts couldn't kill her. Yet her consciousness seemed to be going out with the tide. Her right arm went limp as her left hand floated toward her neck brushing against the necklace. How odd that she was wearing it in the dream.

Ola flashed before her, concern shrouding her usually sanguine expression. Her lips moved as she mouthed something but Sarah couldn't make out the words. As Sarah's fingertips grazed the tiny thistle charm, the hand holding her under the water retracted, the tide flowed away, and Sarah found herself gasping for air on the edge of the Savannah waterfront.

Ola stood on the grass a few feet away, her countenance returning to one of warmth and compassion.

"What happened?" Sarah groaned, her throat still raw from nearly drowning.

"There's much to explain but at a later time."

"Wait!" Sarah called, jolting up.

"Sarah?" Garrett croaked, sitting up in bed next to her. "You okay?"

Closing her eyes, Sarah fought back tears. "No, I'm not."

Chapter Eight

"Tell me about the dream," Garrett said, running his hand through his bed tamped hair.

"It was strange. There were two men in what appeared to be an alleyway behind Hayden Place. One was threatening the other. That's when a hand grabbed me and pulled me into the shadows. I tried to break free but couldn't." Sarah paused trying to remember everything as accurately as she could. She knew this was important or the ghost wouldn't have shown it to her.

Garrett waited, his soft stare giving her the courage to continue.

"Then water began rising and someone was holding me under. When I started losing consciousness, Ola appeared."

Garrett's eyes lit up at the mention of his grandmother. "What did she say?"

"Something about more to learn but at a later time."

"Nothing else about Amelia?"

"No," Sarah huffed, plopping back against the pillow. She rubbed the heels of her hands against her eyes, frustration pulsing through her limbs. Couldn't he see she was upset? Instead of trying to help her understand what was happening he asked about Amelia. "I'm sick of all this. Why can't someone just tell me what I need to know without all of the cryptic messages?"

Garrett reached for Sarah's hand but she yanked it away.

"I know this is hard," he said tenderly. "Is there anything else that might help us understand what Grams was trying to say?"

Tears christened Sarah's eyes as she revisited the dream. "Yes!" Sitting up, she looked at Garrett. "Right before Ola arrived, I touched the necklace."

"Did it summon her?"

"Not sure but she did appear at the same time. Didn't you say she always wore this?"

"Yes."

"Even at night?"

"All the time. She never took it off."

"Maybe that's its purpose. The necklace can connect me with Ola when I'm facing something horrible in my dreams."

The idea of the necklace being some sort of talisman that could assist her as a dreamist washed away the irritation she'd felt towards Garrett only moments earlier. Seeds of hope sprouted in her heart.

The team gathered around the kitchen island watching footage from the night before. Grainy glimpses into the darkened spaces of Hayden Place filled the screen. Sadly, nothing significant materialized.

"That's disappointing," Sarah said.

"At least we don't have time constraints for this one," Ralph replied.

"Except we have to get back to our real jobs at some point," Harry added. "We really need to get this done in a few days."

Garrett rubbed his chin. "There may be something we can do to expedite the process."

"What's that?" Ralph queried.

"Let me do some reading and I'll let you know."

Ralph, Harry, and Sarah exchanged glances.

"Is it something we can help with?" Harry said.

"Not really. You guys keep looking for information about the house." He turned to Sarah. "Can I talk to you?"

"Alright," she responded with a nod. Sarah's stomach churned. It wasn't like Garrett to be secretive with the guys, making her wonder what he had in mind and what she'd have to endure to help.

Sarah followed Garrett up to their room and plunked onto the bed as he closed the door.

"What's going on?" she asked.

"I think there's something special about Gram's necklace."

"We kinda know that already."

"I'm going to search her *Dreamist* book," Garrett said. "There's got to be something about it in there, especially if it's an heirloom related to her abilities."

"What makes you think there's a connection?"

"When I was little, I remember asking Grams about the necklace. She said something about inheriting it from her mother after she'd passed."

"Did you know your great-grandmother?"

"No, she died when I was little. But I recall seeing a photo of her wearing it."

"How does that help us?"

"Obviously, the necklace is linked to their dreamist skills. We know women are the only ones who can possess the ability and it skipped my mother. Maybe that's why Grams led you to it."

"Except I'm not part of your family so whatever purpose it served them wouldn't be the same for me."

"Exactly. We have to figure out what powers it held for my family and how that applies to your skillset."

"I suppose it wouldn't hurt to look into it." Sarah cocked her head. "Do you still have the photo of your great-grandmother wearing the necklace?"

Garrett looked away.

"Garrett?"

Turning back to her, he blew out a long breath. "I do. It was taken at her funeral. She was wearing it in her casket. I assumed they removed it before her burial."

Sarah swallowed the bile rising in her throat. What sort of witchcraft was this thing? It vanished from the depths of the grave and showed up on the living? All of a sudden, the chain around her neck felt ice cold burning her skin. Gripping the chain, Sarah tugged but all it did was pull against her.

"Stop!" Garrett declared, grabbing her hand. "What are you doing?"

"I don't want any part of this wickedness!"

"There's nothing sinister about it. Grams would never have engaged in anything with the occult."

Tears crested in Sarah's eyes as she sucked in the sob threatening to escape. "Then explain how this got from a casket to a hidden box in your library. Now it's around my neck and I can't get it off!" Sarah screeched, hysteria strangling her words.

Garrett took both of Sarah's hands in his and squeezed. "I don't understand it either. Next time you're asleep..."

"That's not what I want to hear! I'm tired of haunted sleep and I'm sick of not knowing what to do!" She wrenched her hands from his, slid from the bed, and stormed to the bathroom, slamming the door behind her.

Sarah leaned over the sink and splashed cold water on her face. Reaching for the hand towel, she caught a glimpse of movement behind her. "Garrett, I'm not in the..."

When she looked in the mirror, it wasn't Garrett. It was Ola. Her presence released the sob stuck in the back of Sarah's throat as she turned to her deceased mentor.

"I'm sorry," Sarah cried. "Please tell me what to do. I'm exhausted and can't go on like this anymore. I'm not as strong as you were."

"My dear girl, don't be so hard on yourself. Being a dreamist is a difficult thing. Very few have handled it as well as you have, especially given your recent introduction to your abilities."

Ola's form wavered.

"Don't go! I need to know about the necklace!" Sarah cried out.

"Removed...my grand...heirloom." Ola's words came in between flashes of her calming face. "Not much energy left... stay calm..." And she disappeared.

Taking several deep breaths, Sarah felt the angst flow from her muscles as her mind returned to a rational state. Ola would find a way to help her. Guilt gripped her heart. Why had she been so hostile with Garrett? He was only trying to help. And he was correct; Ola would never put Sarah or anyone else in danger.

Maybe a hot shower would help. Sarah turned on the water and stepped beneath its heated spray. After letting the water pound the tension from her muscles, she dressed, and walked into the bedroom to apologize to Garret but he was already gone.

Great, she thought. What a way to start the day. Grabbing her phone, Sarah made her way to the kitchen.

Silence. Where was everyone?

"Garrett! Harry! Ralph!" she called.

Nothing.

Voices echoed from the back yard. They must be outside, she thought. Turning the old brass knob on the back door, Sarah jumped when a zap of electricity stung the palm of her hand at the same time an image flashed through her head. It was so fast she barely had time to register what it was but she was fairly certain it was a man. Maybe one of the guys from her dream the night before? Opening the back door, Sarah stepped outside. No one was there yet she heard voices.

Must be out front, she told herself and started down the side of the house. The voices carried from the front yard, making Sarah chuckle. Obviously, the guys were moving around the house and she was a few steps behind. Except when she reached the front yard, they weren't there either. That's when she heard laughter booming from inside.

Agitation niggled at her nerves as she climbed the front steps and followed the boisterous guffawing echoing from the house. With each step, the air grew colder, breath puffing from her lips.

"Garrett!" she called, her chest tightening. "Harry, Ralph!"

Silence.

Even the traffic on the side road had gone quiet.

Fidgeting with the necklace, Sarah stepped inside and climbed the staircase to the second floor, her eyes scanning the area as she went. Where was Dallas? she thought with a shiver. Apparently, something otherworldly was here so why wasn't he barking?

With each step the air warmed, giving her the confidence to keep going. When she reached the second floor, the voices grew louder. Irritated that the guys refused to answer her calls, she marched toward the sounds which now emanated from behind the closed door of her bedroom. What were they doing in there, she thought.

Sarah drew in a deep breath, threw open the bedroom door, and stepped inside, anger lacing her words as she yelled, "What is going...?"

Sunlight scrabbled across the multi-colored rug in snippets of gold like disembodied fingers crawling toward her. Clothes spilled from her suitcase at the foot of the unmade bed. No one was there. Not a sound, not a chuckle, nothing.

Sarah touched the necklace once again, her fingers trembling.

"Ola. Are you here? What's happening?"

A tear streaked down Sarah's cheek. The silence was deafening. Her fortitude was failing.

"Ola!" she screamed. "I can't do this without you!"

Sarah crumpled to the ground, sobbing. She jumped when something brushed her shoulder. Turning, she saw Ola's translucent image standing over her, worry etched in her furrowed brow.

"Stay resolute," she whispered. "And listen with your heart. The answers are never far..." Ola's voice faded along with her face.

Sarah sat on her knees and wiped her dampened cheeks. What was happening to her? And why was Ola so drained of energy? Pushing up from the floor, Sarah steadied herself and looked around. She needed to get a grip and find the guys. That's when it hit her. Garrett's truck hadn't been in the driveway when she was walking around outside. She pulled the phone from her pocket and texted him.

Where are you?

Dots paraded across the screen.

At the Georgia Museum doing research.

Why didn't you tell me you were going?

Didn't want to upset you more.

Sarah swallowed hard. She'd been rude, there was no doubt about it. There was no reason to take out her frustrations on Garrett. He'd been nothing but supportive and he loved her. Before she could text him back, her phone pinged. Danni.

Be there in fifteen. Sitting in the drive-through at Perks. Need anything? Chai tea, yogurt, or something naughty like a bear claw?

Nothing, thanks.

Sarah blew out a long breath. Danni was on her way. Their friendship bordered on psychic. Now more than ever, she wanted her best friend. Knowing Danni would be there soon was all Sarah needed to face the confusion needling her fortitude.

Half an hour later, Sarah and Danni sat at the kitchen island with the scent of freshly brewed coffee wafting from Danni's to-go cup.

"You don't look well," she said, taking a long sip.

"I feel strange," Sarah replied, bobbing a tea bag in her mug.

"How so?"

"Can't explain it. I can feel Amelia's presence and the dreams are clear enough but when I wake up, I'm agitated."

"I would be too if all my dreams were haunted. How is this any different than your other dreamscapes?"

Sarah shrugged. "I don't know. Ola keeps trying to tell me something but her energy levels seem low so she only gets a few phrases out before she disappears. And this blasted necklace is as much a mystery as the haunting," Sarah grumbled, running her fingers along the chain. How she wished she could rip it from her neck even though she knew that wouldn't solve anything. Better to wait it out and see what Ola revealed.

"Where'd you get that?" Danni asked.

"It's a bizarre story," Sarah replied. "We found it in the library at Garrett's house. It belonged to Ola."

"That was sweet of him to give it to you."

"Except that's not how it happened." Sarah paused. "Ola was buried in it."

Danni's eyes widened as her mouth dropped open. "What are you saying?"

"I'm not sure I understand it myself, but somehow this got from Ola's grave to my neck."

Swallowing hard, Danni grimaced. "That is seriously weird, and kinda gross. What does Garrett think?"

"He's confused too. Speaking of Garrett..."

Danni reached over and took Sarah's hand. "What happened?"

"Nothing, that's the point. He hasn't done anything wrong." She sighed. "And yet I feel like nothing more than a conduit for his ghost hunting."

Danni released Sarah's hand and straightened. "Garrett loves you. He's not using you if that's what you're implying. He wouldn't do that."

"I know but for some reason I get annoyed every time he asks about my dreams."

"Are you sure you're not projecting your inner struggles with all this haunted stuff onto him?"

Sarah furrowed her brow. "Why are you taking his side?"

"Taking his side?" Danni declared. "Do you hear yourself? I don't take anyone's side if they're doing something wrong, especially to my best friend! I know about men who use people to get what they want, or have you forgotten about Brady?"

Sarah froze. She hadn't meant to cross Danni or upset her. Brady would be a sore subject for years to come. Danni had loved the man. Discovering his deception not to mention standing at the other end of his revolver had left an emotional scar on Danni's heart. One Sarah wasn't sure would ever fade.

"I'm sorry, I didn't mean to be insensitive. But something is wrong and I can't figure it out."

"Wrong between you and Garrett?"

"No, it's me although it's impacting my relationship with him."

Danni took another sip of coffee before responding. "Listen, you've been through a lot in the last couple of years. You learned you're a dreamist and that ghosts will haunt you for the remainder of your life. You discovered you were adopted and that your biological father is one of the most odious creatures in town. You inherited a small fortune and a haunted mansion. And now, you have a boyfriend who not only adores you but also has experience with dreamists. It's a lot. Don't feel badly about struggling with it all."

Sarah hadn't thought about it that way. Maybe this was nothing more than stress from a series of unusual events that would have sent many rushing to a therapist or a bar. She was lucky. She had a strong support system. Although Sarah had never known her biological mother, her adoptive parents were incredible. Her best friend and boyfriend were loyal and supportive. There was no reason for her cranky mood. She had a responsibility to Amelia, and she intended to fulfill it regardless of her personal frustrations.

With a nod, Sarah looked at her friend. "Thanks, Danni. I needed to hear that." Wiping a stray tear from her cheek, Sarah stood. "Let's get going."

"Where?"

"Where ever you planned on taking me. I know you didn't drive all this way for a cup of coffee and a pep talk."

Danni's brows arched. "Should we add mind-reading to your list of abilities?"

"Please, nothing more," Sarah said, waving off her friend.

"Actually, I found some information about the buildings surrounding the property." Danni pulled out her phone, scrolled through her photos, and turned the screen toward Sarah. "Here's this house," she said, pointing to an old layout of Hayden and Prince Streets. "Right here are several cottages that I noticed are still standing. Behind that is a cinder block building."

"Did they belong to the Millers?"

"Yes. They rented the cinder block structure to the Edwards family who ran a laundry out of it."

"The neighborhood museum I went to the other day belonged to the Edwards family. The tour guide mentioned that they owned a laundry service," Sarah replied. "Garrett and the guys are at the Georgia Museum. I'll text the info to them so they can look into it."

"No!" Danni scolded, grabbing Sarah's phone. "I got this from a friend who works in the archives. For once, I've got a lead that Walter doesn't, and I want to follow through *without* him knowing about it."

"Alright, but I don't like keeping things from the team. They have a right to know."

"We aren't keeping it from them; we're going to investigate further before sharing what we find."

Sarah rolled her eyes. "Where do you want to start?"

"The Prohibition Museum."

"That's where you want to go?"

"After you told me about a speakeasy in your dreams and the flapper dress the ghost was wearing, I decided to look into it," Danni said, excitement glimmering in her eyes. "That's when I found the museum."

"How is a museum about prohibition going to help us?"

"Maybe we can find something about local speakeasies that might lead to information about Amelia Danbury. Since she was wearing a flapper dress there has to be a connection or you wouldn't have dreamed about it, right?"

Sarah nodded. "I suppose."

They got into Danni's car and drove toward the City Market in downtown Savannah.

"Did your friend at the archives find anything else?" Sarah asked as they sped beneath towering live oaks, Spanish moss swaying from the branches as if waving them along.

"Not yet," Danni replied.

They pulled into a parking space by a taco place with signs advertising the best Margaritas in town.

"Hmmm..." Danni said, the car door beeping as it locked. "Best Margaritas in town. Might have to stop there after the museum."

"Seriously?" Sarah chuckled. "We're going on a tour about prohibition and you're already thinking about drinking?"

"How long have you known me?" Danni replied with a roll of her eyes as she buttoned her coat.

Sarah drew her jacket around her body as she stepped from the car into a bracing wind. Even though the south rarely saw snow, it still endured cold temperatures and brisk breezes coming in from the water. Lowcountry winters were generally a damp kind of cold making it unbearable at times. At least the buildings lining the streets helped block the wind.

As they walked along the crowded street, Sarah watched merchants emptying trash containers and folding boxes into recycle bins. A tall man across the road was taking a photo of a ticket left on his windshield in the public parking lot while a grungy looking guy rode by on a bike loaded with plastic grocery bags filled to the brim. Varying scents of frying burgers to baking pizza wafted from several old buildings. Sarah's stomach rumbled. She hadn't eaten anything this morning and the delectable smells were wreaking havoc on her senses.

They rounded the corner, where a three-story brick building caught Sarah's attention as they passed. The door was open inviting guests inside for a meal. A scruffy looking gent in a plaid shirt with ragged trousers held up by old-fashioned braces leaned against the doorway. A sneer wrinkled his upper lip as his hollow eyes met hers. Above him at the top of the door frame was a sign that read, *Most haunted building in town.* Goosebumps paraded across her skin.

His jaw dropped to an unnatural level, the words *get outta here* tumbling over yellowed teeth as he rushed down the stairs toward her. Right before the apparition reached her, Sarah leapt into the road. A car horn blared at the same time Danni grabbed Sarah's arm yanking her back to the fractured sidewalk.

"What are you doing, trying to join the dead?" Danni hollered.

"Sorry," Sarah mumbled. "Wasn't paying attention."

Danni's expression wilted as her stare darted around the area. "You saw a ghost, didn't you?"

"Yes. He was standing in the doorway of that restaurant," Sarah replied, pointing to the building they'd just passed. "He told me to get out of here and charged toward me."

Danni turned to look at the building, her brow wrinkling. "Definitely won't be eating there. Maybe this wasn't such a great idea after all."

"Don't worry about it. It was one ghost and he's gone."

"There's bound to be more than one. Isn't Savannah considered one of the most haunted cities in the country?"

"Not a point to focus on at the moment," Sarah responded. "There's the museum."

Midway down the block was a two-story brick structure with a large sign that read, *Prohibition Museum*. A young man with dark hair curling down his neck wearing a heavy coat and a knit hat boasting the museum's logo stood behind a kiosk.

"Welcome to the Prohibition Museum. I'm Chris," he announced. "Did you purchase your tickets online or will you need to buy them here?"

"We need two tickets," Danni said, handing him her credit card.

"Do you want the tour ticket or the package with one of our signature drinks in the speakeasy at the end?"

"Definitely the one with drinks," Danni replied.

"It's only 10:30 in the morning," Sarah whispered in her friend's ear.

"Won't be by the time we finish touring the place." Danni gave a triumphant grin, her nose as red as Rudolf's. "Besides, it would be uncouth not to partake of a mixed drink after learning about the history of liquor bans. I'd think this would be right up your alley with all the time you and Garrett spend at Fitzgerald's."

"The 1920s themed place in Edgefield?" Chris said, his eyes glinting.

"You know it?" Sarah asked.

"Sure do. My cousin lives in Edgefield. We go to Fitzgerald's every time I visit," he said, his smile growing.

"Guess this is the perfect job for you," Sarah added.

"Keeps the lights on," he said, shrugging one shoulder. "Here are your tickets. Enjoy the museum."

They stepped inside the warm building, thankful for the respite from winter's grasp. Sarah smiled as she looked around. It was like traveling back in time. A gent dressed in 1920s style trousers with a plaid shirt and hat approached them. His broad smile added to the upbeat atmosphere.

"Welcome to the Prohibition Museum, I'm Nick," he declared, sweeping his arm through the air. Taking their tickets, he explained how the self-guided tour worked.

"Is the building old?" Sarah asked.

"Built in the 19th century."

A blast of cold air whooshed past as the heavy front door opened and several people entered. As Nick began the spiel about the museum to the group, Danni and Sarah took in their surroundings. The far wall was designed like the outside of a two-story building one hundred years prior with a couple in rag time attire standing next to a set of double doors. Just above was a woman on an upstairs balcony hanging clothes on a line. In front of them was an actual Model A car with a smiling fellow waving from the driver's seat. The wax figures were so realistic, Sarah almost expected them to speak.

"Wow," Danni said, staring at a group of wax women with prohibition signs. "These people look so real."

"It's like the automated mannequins you see at Disney except these don't move."

Danni shot a worried look at her friend. "Oh no," she moaned. "Please don't tell me any of these mannequins are actually spirits."

"Don't be silly," Sarah huffed. "If they were, they'd be invisible like ghosts."

Sarah started for the staircase at the back of the room with Danni close behind her. "Wait a minute," Danni said. "You're not inferring there are people here I can't see, are you?"

Sarah smiled as she ignored Danni's question and jaunted up the steps to the second floor. Nothing like keeping her friend on alert. After all, an old building like this was bound to have a few spirits outside of the fermented kind.

They entered a room beautifully decorated with an antique bar and liquor bottles lining the shelves. With a gasp, Danni stopped abruptly. "What is Lizzie Borden doing here with an ax?" she declared, her eyes wide.

"That's not Lizzie Borden," Sarah replied. "And it was a hatchet, not an ax."

Rolling her eyes, Danni stepped closer to the wax figure of a Victorian lady dressed in black grasping a hatchet.

Sarah read the placard near the figure. "It says Carrie Nation, otherwise known as Hatchet Granny, was a staunch supporter of the temperance movement long before prohibition. She was known to take a hatchet to bars."

"That's extreme," Danni replied, stepping away from the menacing figure. "What's with these turn-of-the-century women and their need to butcher stuff?"

"Must've been the corsets. Needless to say, I've had enough of these hatchet brandishing women for a lifetime. I say we keep going," Sarah said with a shudder.

The air thickened as they stepped into the next room, Danni grumbling under her breath. Sarah stopped and turned around.

"This museum was your idea," she said.

"Didn't realize it would have realistic wax figures in an old building that's probably haunted."

"Perhaps you should've researched it better," Sarah teased with a wink.

"You're mean," Danni whined as she followed Sarah into a grand space filled with memorabilia and another large Model A automobile. A corpse slumped against the steering wheel and a dead couple were slouched in the back seat.

Apparently, this was the gangster room. Black and white images of men sprawled in puddles of blood covered the walls with details of Capone and other rum runners.

"This is morbid," Danni said.

Sarah glimpsed at the wax figures in the back seat of the vehicle. The woman wore a flapper style dress and a glittering head band with fake blood trickling from the hole in her head. The gentleman beside her was in the same condition. Sarah shivered. Even though they weren't actual people, the life-like appearance was unnerving. Sarah had witnessed too many gruesome scenes in her nightly visions not to be moved by the wax depictions before her. Anxious to escape the morbid feel of the room, Sarah hurried to the next exhibit. From there they moved through several more rooms housing everything from period photos to prohibition banners to news articles.

"Look at this," Danni said, pointing at a plaque. "It says income tax was implemented to make up for the lost taxes from alcohol producers during prohibition." Her expression hardened. "If that's the case, why are we still paying income tax? Liquor sales are copious."

"Sounds like you're paying double," Sarah snorted. "Between your liquor purchases and income taxes, you're funding most of the governmental operations."

"Very funny," Danni retorted. "Keep in mind, you're contributing plenty too."

They made their way to the next room where Sarah stopped to snap a few photos of an authentic flapper dress along with shoes, a beaded purse, and a lady's hat. "Check it out," Danni said, excitement accenting her words. A mock door with a window in it showed the hologram of a woman with bobbed hair and a 20s style frock waving them closer. The image proceeded to hold her finger to her lips and then swoop her hand up as if she was taking a shot of something.

"She's so life-like," Danni said.

"She really is," Sarah replied. "Kinda gives me the creeps."

Danni planted her hands on her hips. "You communicate

with the dead every night in your dreams and a holographic woman signaling you to a speakeasy spooks you?"

"If you hadn't pointed her out, I might have believed she was a spirit."

"That's what they look like?" Danni gasped, looking back at the woman who continued motioning people closer for a drink on the sly.

"Pretty much, except they're usually in some stage of decay. Until I solve the mystery behind their death. Then they look like her."

Danni sneered. "Eww, realistic rotting bodies does not sound fun."

"Trust me, it's not," Sarah said as she moved to a large floor-to-ceiling mirror. On the floor in front of it were footprints guiding guests in the steps to the infamous Charleston dance.

"You and lover-boy dance the Charleston, don't you?"

"It's one of my favorites." Sarah stepped into the alcove and shimmied a few steps. When she glanced in the mirror another image was staring back at her. Amelia stood in front of Sarah, her flapper dress hugging her slim figure. Taking a step forward, Sarah reached out to touch the glass. "What do you want? Are you affiliated with this museum or the building?"

"Who are you talking to?" Danni whispered, her complexion paling.

Ignoring her friend, Sarah stepped closer. "I can help if you tell me why you're here."

Amelia's misty frame moved nearer causing tiny lines to crackle across the glass.

"Sarah?" Panic choked Danni's voice.

With a shake of her head, Sarah kept her eyes focused on the spirit in the mirror. Without warning, Amelia's appearance altered, her hollow eyes bulging as her puffy blue lips opened exhaling an ear shattering scream. She lunged at Sarah sending her stumbling into the display behind her.

He did this! Amelia thundered.

Unable to catch her breath, Sarah grasped her chest. As quickly as she'd appeared, Amelia was gone.

"Sarah?" Danni's cheeks were flushed as she shook her friend's shoulder. "What's going on?"

"Nothing," she murmured. "Let's get out of here."

They hurried down the corridor without viewing any more displays until they reached a huge wooden door with a password posted in the top right corner.

"It's the speakeasy!" Danni announced. "Thank goodness. I don't know what's happening, but something tells me a drink is in order."

Sarah followed the directions on the wall, gave the password, and the door screeched open.

"There better be a living creature on the other side of that door or I'm jumping out of the first window I find," Danni groaned, taking a step back.

Sarah held her breath, half expecting Amelia's rotting corpse to appear on the other side. She exhaled when the melodious sounds of glasses clinking and laughter floated from the other side. The two friends exchanged glances before stepping into an old-fashioned speakeasy replete with stained glass windows, tables and chairs, and a bar nestled in a brick archway that spanned the length of the room. People milled about with drinks in their hands laughing and chatting. The only thing distinguishing it from the 1920s was the fact the patrons were dressed in modern day clothing.

"This is amazing," Danni said a slow smile bringing the color back to her cheeks. "We should've started here."

Sarah nudged her friend's shoulder. "Let's get a drink."

They sidled up to the bar, placed their orders, and watched

as the bartender poured and mixed with the grace of a butterfly. They took their drinks to a nearby table and sat.

"Wanna tell me what happened back there?" Danni asked.

"Sure you want to know?"

"Not really but it's probably better if I do."

"Amelia was staring at me from the mirror."

Danni placed her drink on the table and leaned in. "Was she dead?"

"Of course she was dead. She looked normal at first. Then she came at me in a state of decomposition when I started asking questions."

Danni downed her drink. "I know I'm going to regret asking this, but did she say anything?"

"Nothing that makes any sense. She hollered, *he did this.*"

Staring at her empty glass, Danni hesitated before speaking. "Do you think she's connected to this building? Your ghost encounters usually only happen in places associated with the spirit, right?"

"Generally. What I need to figure out is whether Amelia is affiliated with the theme of the museum or the actual structure."

"You said Amelia is always wearing a flapper dress. Since that correlates with the start of prohibition it makes sense there may be a connection with the subject matter, not the building. Unless she was murdered here," Danni said.

"Not likely," Sarah replied. "It's obvious she drowned."

"Looks like we've got more digging to do." Danni sighed. "As informative as this has been, I didn't see anything specific about the Hayden Street house or any local speakeasies that might be linked with your ghost."

"I agree. This was enlightening but I don't think there's any connection to what's happening at Hayden Place."

Danni's shoulders slumped. "I guess I was hoping..."

"That you found something before Walter?" Sarah said, exasperation tinting her words. "Which means we just wasted the morning in a museum with no affiliation to the haunting."

"There must be a correlation or Amelia wouldn't have made an appearance." Danni said. "We need to figure out what that is."

A smile crept across Sarah's face. Danni was right. There had to be something related to Amelia's death for her to show up here. Initially, Sarah believed Danni suggested this place because there could have been a link between the way Amelia was dressed as a flapper and prohibition. Now, Sarah suspected the promise of alcohol may have been a bigger factor in Danni's choice of museums to explore.

Since Hayden Place wasn't mentioned at the museum, Sarah pondered why Amelia had appeared here. This was the hardest part, figuring out the why behind the hauntings. Regardless of her ethereal encounter, Sarah had enjoyed the excursion and was feeling a bit better. Her worries about her spat with Garrett that morning had dissipated.

"I wonder how the guys are doing," Sarah said.

"You haven't heard from them so I assume that means they're still looking for something. Which also means Walter hasn't had any leads from them either."

"I don't mean to upset you, but Walter doesn't need any leads. Not to mention, this little outing took some time. He may have found something of significance already."

"Not necessarily," Danni retorted, straightening in her chair. "He does have a job."

"Walter can multitask."

"That was really low," Danni replied, her eyes narrowing. She grabbed her purse and stood. "Might as well get back to the house so I can resume my researching."

Slipping out the back door, they stepped into the brisk

winter air. They strolled past a bronze monument of African soldiers during the Revolutionary War with plaques at the base describing their heroic efforts in the battle for this country. As Danni and Sarah crossed the street, they were met by the delectable scents of everything from pralines to pepperoni wafting from the market square where people bundled in coats and scarves milled about.

"Let's grab something to eat before we head back." Danni suggested.

"Thought you had research to do," Sarah replied.

"Right now, I want to research that pizza joint on the corner."

The two friends joined a line of people streaming from an outdoor pick-up window. They placed their orders for two slices of pizza and huddled near the building as they waited. Ten minutes later, a man with a ponytail and tattoos inching up his forearms, called their names. They took their order, strolled to the car, and huddled inside.

"Oh my gosh," Danni declared as she opened the pizza box.

Sarah's eyes widened at the sight. The pizza slice was as big as her head.

"Good thing we didn't order more than one slice," Sarah said, lifting the cheesy triangle to her lips. Drops of grease dripped to the box as she bit into the saucy crust. Closing her eyes, she savored the rich flavors as they slid over her tongue. "I think this is the best pizza I've ever had," Sarah said with a satisfied moan.

Danni nodded in agreement as the two of them devoured the head-sized slices and washed it down with a couple of sodas.

An hour later they were pulling up to the house on Hayden Street. Sarah's stomach twitched at the sight of Garrett's truck. Normally, she'd be excited to see him but right now she wanted to run away. She wasn't up to facing him after the way she'd treated him that morning.

Trudging up the back stairs into the kitchen, Sarah and Danni were met by the aroma of freshly brewed coffee. The guys were gathered around the island as Dallas bolted toward Sarah. She reached down and tousled his fur before removing her coat.

"Hey Danni!" Harry said with a smile. "When did you get here?"

"Few hours ago. Needed to take Sarah somewhere."

All eyes were trained on them like a pack of hungry wolves.

"Did you find something?" Ralph asked.

Sarah gave her friend a 'you better tell them' look.

Danni sighed. "I have an old friend in the records office who shared a layout of the structures in this area from the late 19th century."

"Anything else?" Harry asked.

"Since the ghost Sarah has been seeing in her dreams is dressed as a flapper, we went to the Prohibition Museum hoping to find some answers but there was little there about local stuff. Mostly the national fight for and against liquor sales," Danni said.

"There's a museum dedicated to prohibition?" Ralph declared.

"Yup," Danni replied. "Even has a speakeasy at the end with some pretty good drinks."

"And a few ghosts," Sarah added.

"When were you going to share that?" Harry asked, his eyes wide.

A smile crept across Sarah's face. "It wouldn't be unusual to see a few entities in an old building. The strange thing was seeing Amelia there."

Garrett looked at Sarah, his gaze seeping into her soul. She really did love him and needed to apologize for her rudeness earlier that morning. When they were able to break away, she'd tell him she was sorry.

"What happened?" Ralph asked.

"It was strange. Amelia reflected from a mirror at the museum. She started out in her flapper dress but then morphed into her corpse self and bolted toward me."

Ralph's mouth gaped open while Harry grinned like a kid in a toy store. Danni looked like she'd swallowed a lemon. Obviously, she wasn't happy reliving the incident.

"Did she say anything?" Garrett asked.

"Actually..." Sarah started when Garrett's phone rang.

Glancing at the screen, he furrowed his brow. "Gotta take this," he said, heading out the back door.

"That's odd," Ralph said. Then turning back to Sarah, he smiled. "So, what did the ghost say?"

She said, 'he did this.'

"Who did what?" Harry asked.

"That's the million-dollar question," Sarah replied. "Find the answer to that and we're closer to solving this mystery."

Garrett stepped back inside, his cheeks flushed. "I need to run an errand. I won't be gone long."

His statement was matter-of-fact and extremely uncharacteristic for him. Nothing diverted his attention when he was working on a ghost hunt with the team. Without another word, he slipped out the back door. His truck engine roared followed by the crackling of gravel beneath tires as he drove off.

"What was that all about?" Ralph asked.

"Who knows," Harry said, throwing his hands in the air. "Right now, we need to focus on figuring out who's haunting this house and why."

Sarah twisted her hands as she chewed her lower lip. Danni patted her shoulder with a reassuring grin letting her know everything would be okay. The beauty of their friendship was their ability to communicate without saying a word. Swallowing the lump lodged in her throat, Sarah exhaled. "What did you guys find?"

"Names of the people who lived or worked in the buildings behind the house." Harry shared. "There was also a small building in the back of this property used as a garage for auto repairs." Harry showed them a copy of the layout of buildings on Hayden and Prince streets from the 20s. "These cottages were built in the latter part of the 19th century about ten years after the house was built. And this cinder block building was the launderer."

"This is the same stuff my friend shared with me," Danni said, tapping her finger on the laundry building. "Who preserves a cinder block building used as a laundry mat?"

"Savannah," Harry chortled. "The structure was built in the 1890s making it historic even if it's non-descript."

"The Edwards family rented it from the Millers," Sarah added. "They lived in the gingerbread cottage across the street which is now a museum. It's where I went yesterday."

"Anything connecting them to your ghost?" Harry queried.

"Only the proximity of the buildings to this place and the fact they rented from Amelia's aunt and uncle," Sarah said. "Since the old laundry hasn't shown up in my dreams, I'd need to be in the building to know if something happened there."

"We need to get access to that place," Ralph said.

"Let's find out who owns it and see if they'd be willing to let us look around," Harry replied.

Danni's thumbs flew across her phone screen as a half-smile curled the right side of her mouth. "Dewey Jones owns the place. Here's his number," she said, turning her phone for the guys to see.

"Impressive," Ralph said. "Looks like Walter's rubbing off on you."

"Or maybe I've been the gifted one all along," she responded, pursing her lips.

"Except Walter won the first bet."

"And it was a tie on the second one." Danni retorted.

"First, we need to contact this Dewey person and find out if we can see the place," Harry said. "Hopefully, Sarah will be able to pick up on any spirits that might be hanging around."

Sarah bristled. Maybe she didn't want to seek out the undead in the old laundry. Why couldn't they see her instead of her abilities?

"Who wants to call?" Ralph asked.

"I'll do it," Harry said, walking to the other room.

"You okay?" Danni asked.

Sarah exhaled. "I'm fine."

She knew how much the guys wanted to redeem themselves after the Borden House fiasco. Guilt rolled through her gut. Deep down she hoped Dewey didn't answer, or even better, refused to let them see the place. It was hard enough trying to maneuver a relationship and figure out how to help a dead woman without adding another building to the repertoire.

A few minutes later, Harry returned, a broad grin on his face. "Great news! He can meet us in half an hour."

Ralph rubbed his hands together. "Think he'd be willing to let us video while we're there?"

"Probably. He seemed excited that we were looking for ghosts. Said he's had renters complaining about unexplainable occurrences for years and he'd like to know more about it. I texted Garrett. He's going to meet us there."

Dread pounded inside Sarah's chest. This could be intense. As a laundry, the building probably had several entities connected to it and right now she didn't feel like facing a ghostly jamboree. The last thing she needed was extraneous hauntings. Amelia's presence was strong enough.

Danni whispered in Sarah's ear. "Do you need me to come along?"

"Do you want to?"

"I'd rather keep digging for information on this place than encounter any spectral activity."

Sarah gripped her friend's hand and squeezed. "Stay here and find the answers we need to help with this investigation. I'll be fine. Besides, the guys will be there."

Half an hour later Garrett met the team at the cinder block house. Dewey welcomed them inside. Sarah rubbed her upper arms, trying to ward off the chill as she surveyed the cramped living room. A small sofa with two end tables faced a big screen TV that spanned most of the opposite wall. Sheer curtains covered the two front windows with an area rug centering the space. A Lowcountry scene of seagulls soaring over the marsh hung above the sofa. For a late-19th century structure, it was rather plain.

"What can you tell us about the place?" Harry asked.

"Not much," Dewey replied. "It was the local laundry until 1921. Then it became a small grocery and in the 50s it was converted into a single-family dwelling. I bought it a few years ago as a rental property."

"What sort of reports have you had about ghost activity?" Garrett asked.

"Most people complain about banging on the front door but when they open it no one is there," he replied. "Others talk about a woman moaning or the sound of jazz music coming from the back of the building. One couple moved out in less than a month because they were so freaked out over the noises. Said they couldn't take it anymore. The woman claimed she saw a ghost, but I think she was looking for a reason to break the lease."

Sarah looked around the room searching for any signs of otherworldly activity, but nothing showed itself. Reaching out, she rested her hand against the wall. All of a sudden, her head ached and the room began to spin. Men in uniforms crowded the space shouting for people to stay where they were. Women screamed and a man tried running out the rear exit until one of the uniformed officers snatched his collar and pulled him back into the room.

He did this, echoed in Sarah's mind.

"Who?" she muttered.

"What?" Dewey asked.

Aware that she'd spoken out loud, Sarah straightened. "Um...who do you think is haunting the place?"

"Don't know."

Sarah nodded. "Can we see the rest of the rooms?"

"Sure. I'm between renters right now. Feel free to look around."

"Do you mind if we film while we're here?" Harry asked.

"Go ahead. If it helps dispel this nonsense about ghosts, I'm all for it."

"You don't believe in ghosts?" Ralph asked.

"Generally, no," Dewey said. "If I hadn't had reports from previous renters, I still wouldn't believe it. Now, I suspect there may be something to the stories. I need to get this place rented out and the rumors of spectral activity are hindering that."

Good thing he didn't know how haunted the place really was, Sarah chuckled to herself. She entered the kitchen where a fridge, oven, and sink formed a triangular layout. A bistro table with four chairs anchored the space. Checkered curtains framed the window over the sink and a windowed door offered access to the back yard. Nothing here, she thought as she made her way down a short hallway to a small bath. From there, she started toward one of two bedrooms when mist puffed from her lips. Something was here. Bracing herself, Sarah prepared for an apparition to materialize. But nothing appeared.

Help them, tickled her ear.

"Who needs my help?" Sarah muttered under her breath.

He did this!

Sarah froze. Aggravation squeezed her chest. What was the ghost trying to tell her? Before she could ask, Harry entered the room holding his phone in front of him.

"The building is much different than it was in the early 1900s when it functioned as a laundry. Now there are complaints of voices and ghostly activity." Harry continued his dialogue as he made his way to the other bedroom.

"He's gone," Sarah whispered. "What are you trying to tell me?"

Silence ensued. Sarah rubbed her eyes with the heels of her hands. Why couldn't she ever get a straight answer? Then it struck her. Perhaps she wasn't asking the right question.

"Did someone hurt you?"

He did this reverberated off the walls.

"What did he do?"

A whisper as forceful as a hurricane swirled around Sarah.

Killed me.

Sarah had her answer. Someone killed Amelia. The question remained, who murdered her and why?

"I'll need more information if you want me to help you."

"Who are you talking to?" Garrett asked, walking up behind Sarah.

"Amelia," she replied. "It wasn't a simple drowning, she was murdered."

"She said that?" Garrett's brows arched.

"Turns out I wasn't asking the right questions. On the flip

113

side, she seems to have run out of energy because she didn't reveal any details. Unless your presence scared her off."

"I can leave," Garrett said, starting for the door.

Sarah grabbed his arm. "Wait. I want to apologize for this morning. I don't know why I took out my frustrations on you."

"It's okay. I'm sure it's getting tiresome with all the ghost hunting we've done the past few weeks, not to mention everything you went through at Borden House."

"Don't remind me." Sarah shuddered.

Garrett pulled her close, the warmth of his body melting against hers as he leaned in for a long kiss. She was breathless when he stepped back.

"We are definitely going to take a break when this case is done," he said, caressing her cheek. "Maybe we can go to the beach for a few days."

"Sounds good to me," she replied, fingering the charms around her neck. "Wish I knew more about this necklace. I get the feeling it could be useful if I understood how it works."

"I'd like some answers about that too. Like why Grams was buried in it and how it showed up in a book shaped box in my library."

Sarah grasped his hand and squeezed. "We'll figure it out," she said with a smile. Relief washed over her knowing they'd worked things out.

"You guys ready?" Harry asked, popping his head in the door.

"Yeah, let's get back to the house," Garrett said.

Garrett led Sarah from the room and out the front door where everyone had gathered. Cars whooshed past on Prince Street as the team huddled together.

"Now what?" Harry said.

"We do some more digging," Garrett replied.

They walked back to Hayden Place where Danni was

tapping away on her laptop. "I fixed a pot of coffee if anyone is interested," she said without looking up. "There's a cup of hot water on the counter for Sarah."

The guys poured coffee while Sarah dunked a tea bag in the mug of water and settled on one of the stools.

"Discover anything of significance?" Danni asked, straightening.

"Not really," Harry replied.

"I had a little encounter," Sarah said, bobbing the tea bag in her mug.

"What?" Harry and Ralph declared in unison, their eyes sparkling with anticipation. Danni groaned.

"Amelia showed up briefly and told me she was murdered."

"Who killed her?" Ralph asked.

"Don't know, she disappeared before I could get any information. At least we have an idea of why she's unsettled."

"Do you think she was killed at the laundry?" Harry queried.

"Not likely," Sarah replied. "It's obvious she drowned not to mention I've seen her here too."

"Sounds like she has a lot to tell you if she's following you around," Garrett added.

"No doubt," Sarah said. "I hope she's able to give me the information sooner than later."

"Agreed," Danni said with a roll of her eyes.

"You stayin' tonight?" Harry asked Danni.

"In a haunted house? Don't think so."

"Coward," Sarah said with a smirk. "You survived Borden House and it was much worse than this place."

Danni's shoulders slumped. "You make it sound so care-free. This haunted stuff is scary. I don't care how inconsequential you try to make it seem."

"You can stay with me, if that makes it less frightening," Sarah offered, gleaning a glare from Garrett.

"Ha! I'd rather be far from you. You're the one the ghosts are after."

"Which means better opportunity for information to help with your research," Sarah added.

Danni's eyes narrowed. "You know I'm not allowed to use anything you share from your dreams to win this bet."

"Doesn't mean you can't use your own experiences."

Sarah watched Danni mulling over the possibilities. Be haunted and possibly garner information to beat Walter or go home and sleep soundly without any spectral interference.

"You owe me," Danni grumbled, taking a sip of her coffee.

"Looks like you just got kicked out of your bed." Harry chuckled. "Where you gonna sleep, Dunc?"

"Guess I'm bunking with you," he replied.

"I don't want to stir up any trouble," Danni said, looking back and forth between Garrett and Sarah. "I'm more than happy to go home."

"Nope," Sarah interrupted. "You're staying."

"Joy," Danni groused. "But I didn't bring any..."

"I've got an extra set of pajamas. You can wear those."

After a couple of hours, the team had constructed a crude background of what they'd unearthed so far.

"We know from Sarah's dreams that Amelia Danbury was sent to live with her aunt and uncle after refusing to submit to a prearranged marriage. Her manner of death was drowning although we now suspect it was murder. Her aunt and uncle owned a mercantile and several cottages behind the house, one of which was rented to the Edwards family as a laundry business," Harry recited.

Sarah continued. "So far, Amelia's ghost has said a handful of phrases to include, *help them*, *he did this*, and *killed me*. Her ghost has appeared here, the Prohibition Museum, and now the old laundry building."

"Looks like we have a decent foundation," Garrett said. "Let's build on it."

Nightfall blanketed the house in a patchwork of doom. Old Victorian homes were magnificent in the light of day but gloomy after dark which made them the perfect place for fanciful imaginations and unexplainable occurrences.

Traipsing through the darkened front parlor, Sarah spied the massive crystal chandelier draped in a plastic sheath to protect it from the painters. In the dimness of twilight, it looked more like a misshapen ghost. She chuckled. As a child this would have been terrifying to her. She'd have expected something to pop out from behind the plastic or drop down on top of her. It would take more than that to raise her heartrate now.

Despite the eeriness of the space, there was also a comfort to it. Sarah was at home in old buildings, haunted or not. It was like a warm hug from a dear friend. Even when that friend housed spirits in all their corpselike fashion.

"Where you going to hang out?" Garrett asked, sauntering up behind her.

"I was thinking the bedroom," she replied. "If I can fall asleep, Amelia should have an easier time telling me who killed her."

Garrett nodded. "What about Grams?"

"Depending on my ability to focus, I'll call on her and ask about this necklace." Sarah ran her hand across the three charms dangling from her neck. "You know I can't take it off."

"I know," he replied, his voice apologetic. "I don't understand and I'm sorry you're stuck with it. Wish I knew more so I could help."

"Something tells me you're not supposed to understand it. That's why Ola never explained it to you."

Garrett looked away, a sour expression furrowing his brow.

"What's the matter?" Sarah asked.

"It's just..." He hesitated for a moment before meeting her gaze. "The necklace. It's part of our family. What if...?"

Sarah tensed. Was he actually inferring what she thought he was? "Go ahead and say it," she said. "What if we break up?"

Garrett's eyes widened. "That's not what I was trying to say."

"But it's what you meant," she snapped. "I suppose the blasted thing will fall off if that's what happens. After all, this is from your family line not mine. I wouldn't want us to be connected forever if you don't want us to be." Sarah tugged at the chain in an effort to rip it off but all it did was dig into her skin.

Garrett grabbed her hand. "Stop putting words in my mouth. This is confusing for me too. You're not the only one trying to make sense of all this."

Sarah yanked her hand away from him as Dallas came bolting into the room, whining as he ran to her side. She reached down to pet him, tears trickling across her cheeks. Dallas seemed to sense something was amiss and it broke her heart.

"Okay if he comes with me?" Sarah asked, her words clipped.

"You don't have to ask. You know he's allowed to go with you any time you want."

"This sounds like some sort of custody battle," Sarah groaned.

Looking up, Sarah noticed the flecks of pain emanating from Garrett's stare. She should say something to ease the tension flowing between them. Except she didn't know what to say. She was tired of having to deal with her haunted life and act as if she enjoyed helping him with his ghostly excursions. It was too much. How could she love someone and want to scream at him at the same time? He was only trying to help and yet she wanted to be left alone.

Garrett ran a hand through his hair. "I thought we worked things out this morning."

Sarah wanted to say something to mollify the situation but irritation prevented her from speaking. How could she possibly explain what she was feeling when she didn't understand it herself?

"You'd better get to work," she muttered. "Come on, Dallas. Let's go upstairs." Sarah left the room and jogged up the steps with Dallas on her heels. Danni was sitting on the bed in their room tapping away on the laptop. She slid the readers off her face when Sarah came in.

"You turnin' in already?" she asked.

"Figured I'd try to get some sleep. The sooner we get this over with, the quicker I can get back home." Sarah reclined on the bed and cuddled Dallas.

"What's going on?"

"I'm getting ready to be haunted," Sarah grumbled.

"This is more than communing with the dead," Danni replied. "Tell me what's wrong."

Rolling over, Sarah propped up on one elbow. "Garrett was being a jerk."

Danni's brows arched. "Not likely but tell me what he did."

Sarah told her friend about the argument, tears threatening to fall with each word.

"First, you're overreacting," Danni said. "He wasn't inferring you guys were going to break up. Second, every couple has spats which is what this is. You're stressed and taking it out on him."

Sarah shot up in bed. "You're taking his side again!" she exclaimed.

"I'm not taking sides. I'm telling you that you're out of line. Garrett isn't using you to further his ghost hunting career. He's trying to help you with this craziness that is your life and you're acting like a spoiled child."

"You *are* taking his side. And I'm not acting like a child! I'm just tired of all this!" Anger burned in Sarah's chest.

"If you need to take a break from him, go ahead. But don't push your internal struggles onto Garrett. Trust me, he's a great guy."

"Like you'd know the difference," Sarah snapped.

Danni stiffened, closed her laptop, and slid off the bed. "I'm going home."

"Don't be this way," Sarah pleaded, regretful for her attitude. "I'm sorry. I didn't mean it."

"I think you did mean it," Danni responded. "I don't know what's going on with you right now. I'm sure this dreamist stuff is difficult but I won't be your battering ram. I love you and I'm willing to give you some space to figure out whatever you're grappling with."

"Danni, don't go. It's too late to drive back to Beaufort. Please stay. I need you."

Danni hesitated. Dropping her head, she plopped onto the side of the bed. "I'll stay but you have to tone down this attitude toward Garrett. Give the guy a break. It can't be easy dating a haunted woman."

Remorse crawled up Sarah's throat and squeezed. Maybe she was out of line. But this wasn't the time to worry about it. For now, she needed to focus on solving Amelia's murder. That would help everyone involved. She'd apologize to Garrett later.

Slipping under the blanket, Sarah exhaled as Dallas burrowed under the covers and curled at her side. Something about the little dog always gave her peace.

"Will it bother you if I'm working on the computer?" Danni asked.

"You're good," Sarah said, closing her eyes. Within minutes she was asleep in a world of secrets and deception.

Bessie called Amelia to the front parlor for tea.

"There's some things of a delicate nature I need to discuss with you," Bessie said, tipping the silver tea pot to the cup. "As you know, your uncle and I have the mercantile on the riverfront along with some rental properties and the garage."

Amelia perched on the edge of her chair, the hem of her skirt brushing her calves as she crossed her left ankle over the right. "I'm aware."

"Recent alterations in our government have forced certain businesses underground, specifically liquor."

Amelia nodded, taking the steaming cup from her aunt.

"In our opinion, a small minority of religious zealots don't have the right to dictate what others do. This is a free country run by the majority, for those who are allowed to vote that is," she blustered. "Anyway, this is supposed to be a democracy where people have a choice in their religion, work, and opinions. Prohibition has wreaked havoc on those in the alcohol trade. Thousands are out of work because a few people felt liquor was causing the decline in society."

Amelia swallowed hard. Were they selling illegal liquor at the mercantile? Her stomach fluttered at the thought. Her father would lose his mind if he discovered such a thing. It was one of his greatest campaign pledges, the anti-alcohol train of thought. But Amelia knew the truth about all that nonsense. He kept his scotch hidden along with her mother who was generally passed out on brandy somewhere in the house.

Of course, his constituents were too stupid to realize any of this, even when one of the former maids told people in town. Her father denied it and accused the maid of trying to destroy him. Poor woman couldn't get work anywhere in the area and was forced to move to Alabama and stay with her sister. No one believed a word the maid said, despite the empty bottles as proof. Her father had that kind of hold on people. They liked him so much they refused to believe anything unsavory about him regardless of the evidence. His word was good enough for them, especially when it aligned with their narrow, controlling views of society.

Bessie continued. "We didn't want to inform you about this initially because we weren't sure how open-minded you'd be. Needless to say, we've been surprised at your ability to think rationally and independently. How you've survived your father's domineering manner is beyond me."

"I read a lot," Amelia replied. "It's amazing how seeing yourself in a book helps to broaden your perspective. Books gave me the courage to stand up for myself no matter how hard my father tried to crush me."

"Your mother was like that once. Carefree and joyful, but naïve. I think she truly believed your father was a gracious man. Of course, he was only interested in her money and her looks."

"The only mother I've ever known has been kind but absent. Our nanny raised me. My older brothers were permitted to do anything they wanted while I was forced to be prim and proper."

"Sounds like your father," Bessie said with a smirk. "Anyway, we have another business, one that's not openly advertised, if you get my meaning."

Amelia's eyes grew wide as she gasped, her hand covering her mouth. "Are you selling liquor?"

"Yes, but there's more."

The vision altered and Sarah found herself in what appeared to be the back room of the Miller's mercantile.

"What do you think?" Aunt Bessie asked, holding up a creamy silk dress with two layers of fringe at the hemline.

"It's lovely," Amelia declared, taking it from her aunt. "What's the occasion?"

A mischievous smile wrinkled her eyes. "I'm taking you somewhere special this evening. Someplace your father would deny access to if he knew about it."

"You don't like my father, do you?"

"That's a strong statement," Bessie answered. "I love him but can't stand his misogynic ways. I'm sick of men treating women like second class citizens."

Shaking her head, Amelia smiled. "You never cease to amaze me. I hope I'm as brave as you someday."

"You're braver than you think, my dear. Now try on the dress."

Moments later, Amelia emerged from behind a trifold screen, the fringe of the dress swaying with each step. She spun once, whirling the layers out like a merry-go-round.

"Beautiful!" Bessie exclaimed. She handed her niece a double strand of pearls and a cloche hat with an apricot hued velvet rose on the side. "These will complete the ensemble."

Amelia draped the waist length pearls around her neck and settled the cloche hat on her coffee brown locks. Glancing in the full-length mirror, she smiled. "I'm a flapper," she giggled. "Father would have a fit if he saw me dressed this way."

"You'll be a hit this evening. Every gentleman will want to dance with you."

"Where are we going?"

"That's a surprise," her aunt replied, waggling her brows.

Sarah startled when the vision changed abruptly. Her dreamscapes with Amelia were different than some of her previous experiences. Amelia's perspective was exceptionally clear and at times Sarah could feel the depth of her emotions.

Darkness permeated the scene. Amelia's heart beat faster as she held a candle in front of her, her shadow shifting across the wall. It was dark down here and she was having a hard time keeping up with her Aunt Bessie, who moved through the tunnels like a mouse in a maze. Amelia couldn't understand where they were going. Was this some sort of underground storage for the moonshine? If so, why did her aunt give her a new dress to wear?

Aunt Bessie's pace slowed, sending a shiver up Amelia's spine. The floors thumped and the walls vibrated. They climbed wooden plank steps that led straight to a trap door in the ceiling. Her Aunt Bessie rapped in a rhythmic fashion on the door. It swung open revealing a familiar face. Jackson Edwards.

"Hey, Mrs. Miller," Jackson said, helping her up and then grabbing Amelia's hand to do the same. "Good evening, Miss Amelia." The scent of cigar smoke and booze flooded the space.

"Jackson, I wasn't expecting you to be manning the door tonight," Bessie said.

"Thomas couldn't make it. Something wrong with his stomach."

"Well, it's good to see you."

"Good to see you," he said, with a tip of his head.

Amelia smiled as she took in her surroundings. A four-piece jazz ensemble belted out tunes from the far corner. Couples shimmied and swayed to the beat while others gathered at a bar where the liquor was flowing freely.

"Is this a speakeasy?" Amelia asked her aunt.

"Indeed. This and some other endeavors have funded the ongoing fight for the suffrage movement."

Amelia gave her aunt a puzzled look. "I thought women already earned the right to vote."

"Have you voted?"

"Well, no," she said, looking down. "Father won't allow it. He says women aren't savvy enough to be involved with politics."

"Well, I haven't either. The 19th Amendment was ratified in 1920 except for Georgia. They still don't allow us to vote. The rest of the country might be done with the fight but around here the battle continues."

"Is it really that important?" Amelia asked.

"Is being able to decide who you marry important? As women, we have as much right to vote and make our own decisions as men. Just like alcohol. No one should tell us what we can and cannot eat or drink because a few people have abused it."

A slow grin curled Amelia's lips. Her aunt was right. No wonder her father didn't speak to his sister except to pawn off his only daughter on her.

"Would you like a drink?" Bessie asked.

"Um...I don't know. I've never had alcohol before."

"If you decide you'd like to try something, just ask Benny at the bar. Otherwise, dance, have fun. You're young and free. Enjoy it before responsibilities anchor you to the daily drudgery of adult life."

Sarah jumped when Amelia screamed, *he did this*. Her dress altered to a tattered state and her face was scarred with wounds from where sea life had nibbled at her skin.

Swallowing the revulsion rising in her throat, Sarah spoke. "Who are you talking about?"

Over there! She screeched.

"Jackson?" Sarah thought. Before she could investigate further, someone grabbed her from behind and plunged her head beneath icy cold water. Brine burned her nose and her lungs felt as if they might explode for lack of air. Desperate to break free, Sarah clawed at the hand holding her under the murky water.

"Sarah!" Danni hollered, shaking her friend's shoulder. "Get up."

"Huh?" Rubbing her eyes, Sarah sat up. "What's going on?"

"You were thrashing about."

"Nightmare," she uttered, leaning against the head board. "Where's Dallas?"

"Garrett took him out for his nightly walk. Tell me what happened in your dream."

"It actually started out pleasantly. Amelia's Aunt Bessie gave her a flapper dress and took her to a speakeasy."

"Sounds like a pretty cool aunt," Danni snorted. "Reminds me of Aunt Millie."

"Seriously," Sarah agreed. "Anyway, Amelia seemed to be having fun until she morphed into her deceased state and said *he did this.*"

"Who did what?"

"Exactly. When I asked who, she nodded toward Jackson Edwards who was working the door that night."

"Who's Jackson again?"

"He worked for the Millers. Fixed cars in the garage behind the house."

"Possible love interest gone bad?" Danni queried.

"Unlikely. He's black."

"Got it. However, it was the Roaring Twenties and Amelia was in a speakeasy. If she was a flapper, she may not have cared about skin color."

"Good point," Sarah replied, chewing her lower lip.

"Did she identify him specifically?"

Sarah thought for a moment. "Not exactly. Like I said, she nodded in his direction. But Jackson doesn't give off a killer vibe."

"Sometimes they don't," Danni groused.

"Sorry," Sarah said. She wondered if Danni would ever heal from Brady's betrayal. It's not every day you fall in love with a guy only to discover he's a murderer. Although Danni had survived the heartbreak, Sarah could tell she was throwing herself into work and anything else to avoid facing the disgrace she felt. Danni wasn't one to show her emotions which meant the remnants of her regret were probably festering deep within her soul.

"Don't be. I'm only trying to make a point. A lot of violent men can be charming. Anything else in the dream?"

"I went from standing in the speakeasy to having my head plunged under the water. I was trying to fight off my attacker when you woke me up."

"Glad I was able to help."

"Me too, except I didn't get the chance to see who was holding me under, but I feel certain he's the one who killed Amelia."

"Do you think you could have seen who it was if I hadn't woken you?"

"Hard to say," Sarah said. "How about you? Any luck with the research?"

"Actually, yes. I found some info about Amelia's father, George Danbury. Apparently, he was an attorney before he turned politician."

"I'm not surprised he started out as a lawyer. Seems like most politicians do," Sarah said. "And then they promptly forget the law."

"Danbury had a lucrative law firm in Savannah when he switched to politics. That's why the family moved to Atlanta. They maintained the residence here but spent most of their time in Atlanta campaigning. He was running for the Senate when Amelia died."

"Did he win the race?" Sarah asked.

"Nope. It seems his constituents found his continuing to campaign after his daughter's death distasteful. The family stayed in Atlanta and Danbury went back to practicing law with two of his sons."

"Ouch. He lost his daughter and his political career," Sarah said. "Then again, from everything I've seen in my dreams, he was a hardcore man who sent his only daughter to live with an aunt she barely knew."

"Typical politician. He had no problem using his estranged sister when it suited his needs."

A soft knock on the door interrupted them. Garrett popped his head in as Dallas leapt onto the bed and snuggled with Sarah.

"Thought you might want him back," Garrett said quietly.

"Thanks," she replied, regret fingering her heart. The disappointment radiating from his gaze seeped into her soul. She wanted to say something, but Danni was there. Any personal conversations would have to wait for another time. "Get anything on tape tonight?"

"A few things. Of course, we won't know the significance until we go back through the footage." He yawned. "What about you? Anything notable in your dreams?"

"Kinda," she shrugged. "It's late. We can talk about it tomorrow. You look like you could use some sleep."

"Sorry to kick you out of your bed," Danni said.

"No worries. See you in the morning," he replied, closing the door behind him.

"He seemed a bit off," Danni stated.

"Probably because of me. I'll talk to him in the morning." Pulling the blanket over her shoulder, Sarah nestled her head against the pillow and cuddled with Dallas. "Goodnight."

"G'night," Danni replied as her fingers clicked across the keys.

The rhythmic clacking of Danni's typing lulled Sarah back to sleep where speakeasies and politics didn't mix well.

Chapter Nine

The roaring of a motor car rattled the front windows of the house as it parked at the curve. Amelia glanced through the curtains and groaned. Theodore Warren. What was he doing here? She watched as he emerged from the car and stared at the house with its two front entries, apparently puzzled by which door to use. Amusement at his dismay tickled Amelia's stomach. Which one would he choose?

After a moment, he chose the main entry on the Prince Street side. Amelia considered hiding in her room but thought better of it. She needed to know why he was here and if her father had sent him. Her pride still stung from being exiled like a common criminal from her own home.

Initially, Amelia had been fearful of what she'd encounter here. But her aunt and uncle treated her like a daughter and encouraged her independence. Her father's wicked scheme had backfired. Working at the mercantile wasn't hard labor. If anything, it was illuminating. It gave Amelia purpose.

Knocking reverberated from the entryway, interrupting

Amelia's ruminations. Smoothing her dress, she answered the door.

"Amelia," Theo said with a slight bow. "Please forgive my impertinence for arriving unannounced but I needed to speak with you."

Amelia stepped aside and motioned for him to enter.

His stout frame filled the doorway as he stepped inside. "Nice place," he said, removing his hat and fiddling with the brim.

"Follow me," Amelia said, leading him to the front parlor where a tray with tea rested on a center table. He must be here of his own accord, she thought. If her father had sent him, he'd not be reshaping the edge of his hat with his fidgeting. "I was just getting ready to have some tea if you'd like to join me."

"Thank you," he replied, taking a seat.

"Why are you here?" Her words were laced with contempt, and it felt good to be so bold, especially in front of Theo who would likely tell her father.

"I came to see how you were doing and to take you back to Atlanta. I only want what's best for us."

"Meaning marrying you?" Amelia poured some tea in a cup and handed it to him.

"Why are you so opposed to being my wife? I've never done anything untoward. Most women consider me a catch," he responded, sipping the tea.

"Then marry them," Amelia responded.

A crimson flush crawled up his neck and speckled his face. "You're rude, Amelia Danbury. And not very ladylike. I don't know why I even considered marrying you."

"To get in good with my father," she replied, matter-of-factly. "Perhaps you want to ride his coattails to congress."

The color in his cheeks deepened as his upper lip curled

into a sneer. "I shouldn't waste another minute trying to reason with someone as hardheaded as you."

"Then don't let me keep you," Amelia said, lifting her chin.

"How dare you?" he bellowed, spilling the tea as he leapt to his feet. "You're truly an ungrateful, spoilt child!"

"Everything okay?" a voice boomed. Jackson's towering form appeared in the doorway.

"Everything is fine, Jackson," she replied. "Mr. Warren was just leaving."

Theo's jaw tightened. "You can't dismiss me so casually! I'm your fiancée!"

"You're my father's employee, nothing more. Please leave," she repeated.

Jackson took another step closer, causing Theo to puff out his chest. "Stupid darkie, you'd best remember your place." Although he yelled the words, there was a quiver to his voice. Leaning into Amelia, he growled, "I'm going to tell your father about this. He won't like you sitting around this house doing nothing. You're supposed to be learning about hard work, not getting cozy with a colored man."

"Go ahead. Tell him," Amelia replied. "While you're at it, you can also explain why you're here trying to bring me back before he's directed me to return." A slow smile spread across her face, taunting Theo to challenge her. She knew full well her father would be furious if he knew Theo was here without his directive. Now Theo had no recourse but to leave.

At that moment she thought his head might explode as his lower lip quivered. Theo wasn't used to being told no, especially by a woman. Shoving his hat back on his head, he narrowed his eyes, wrinkled his upper lip, and stormed out. Pleased with her fortitude, Amelia listened as the engine of Theo's car roared and rambled down the road.

"You okay?" Jackson asked in a quiet voice.

Amelia nodded. Squaring her shoulders, she looked at him. "Never better."

The dream altered and Sarah found herself in an underground tunnel. The chilly air nipped at her skin as she rubbed her upper arms. The sound of dripping echoed through the darkened space adding an element of dread. Against her better judgement, Sarah decided to follow the sound. The tunnel twisted and turned, narrowing with every curve. Glancing over her shoulder, darkness swallowed the path she'd taken. Maybe she should go back.

He did this.

"Amelia?" Sarah called. "Are you saying Theodore Warren killed you?"

Silence.

Surely, the mystery behind Amelia's death wouldn't be as straightforward as this.

"Amelia, did Theodore murder you?"

A hand grabbed the back of Sarah's neck making her jump. A foul odor permeated the air as a voice moistened her ear.

Didn't deserve this.

Sarah wheeled around. In the shadowy dimness, a towering figure stood inches from her. From what she could see one eye was an empty socket and his skin had an ashen hue.

"Who are you?" Sarah muttered, her stomach churning at the disgusting stench emanating from the cadaver.

Blackened lips parted revealing missing teeth as the creature attempted a smile. "Leave here."

"That's no way to ask for help," Sarah goaded, proud of her gumption. "Now, tell me who you are."

The entity released a screech that caused the walls and floor to tremble. Bits of dirt rained down on Sarah's head as a rush of water echoed through the tunnel. Unsure which was more dangerous, the corpse in front of her or the thunderous noise reverberating from the walls, Sarah decided it was time to leave. Terror pulsed through her limbs. The last thing she wanted to discover was what this spirit was capable of doing. Staying calm was not something she could grasp at this moment. Shoving past the wicked creature, she bolted down the pathway, bumping against walls as she maneuvered her way through the shadowy space.

Music thumped in the distance. Was the speakeasy nearby? She continued around bends and sharp corners until she stood in front of wooden steps, the same ones she'd seen Bessie use in a previous dream. The sound of rushing water was gaining on her. Sarah dashed up the steps and banged on the trap door overhead shouting for someone to open it. The music grew louder but no one lifted the door. Then she recalled the rhythmic knock she'd seen Amelia's aunt use.

She repeated the knock as she remembered it and much to her relief, the door opened. On the other side was the corpse, the one from the tunnel with part of his head missing.

"We've been waiting for you," he croaked, reaching a bony hand toward her throat.

Sarah turned to run when a massive wall of water came crashing around the corner. Should she face the gruesome entity waiting to kill her or drown? With all her might, Sarah shoved the wraithlike creature back simultaneously pushing herself up through the trap door. Inside the speakeasy couples danced the Charleston while others sat at tables around the perimeter of the room sipping drinks.

As Sarah got to her feet, she noticed everyone in the room had stopped what they were doing. All eyes were trained on her. She watched as clothing deteriorated into tattered rags and faces melted into death masks. What was it the guy had said? We've been waiting for you? It was like watching Michael Jackson's *Thriller* video. Rotting corpses moving toward her, skeletal hands reaching her direction.

Paralyzed by fear, Sarah screamed, "Ola!"

Something touched her shoulder sending a wave of calm through her body. She spun around to see her mentor. "I'm so glad you're here," Sarah said, releasing the breath she'd been holding.

"You must remember, these spirits can do no harm so long as you remain calm."

"Remain calm? I thought they couldn't hurt me at all."

"When adrenaline courses through your body it lowers the threshold between the spirit world and the living. This is how some people end up with scratches or bruises. They panic, allowing the ghost to feed off their energy and cause injury."

"Why didn't you tell me this before?"

Ola smiled. "You're new to all this. It's difficult to stay calm when you're trying to remember too many things. Now that you've experienced a few hauntings you're better able to handle more information."

Sarah rubbed her temples. "It doesn't feel that way."

"You've done a marvelous job handling it all, especially since you've only been aware of your abilities for a couple of years."

Ola's praise warmed Sarah's chest. It was all so overwhelming and to get approval for her efforts helped. Something moved in the far corner, catching Sarah's attention. One of the corpses was sliding toward her.

Taking in a deep breath, she released it, and turned back to Ola.

"Can you tell me more about this necklace?" she asked, her eyes darting between Ola and the nearing cadaver.

"Perhaps another time. Right now, you have work to do."

"Wait!" Sarah yelled as Ola dissipated, leaving her in a

room filled with the dead. The bodies were reanimating and hobbling toward her as they chanted, *help them.*

Stay calm, Sarah told herself taking in deep breaths. The half-headed man's wicked smile dissolved into a sneer as he inched closer. Sarah's ability to stay calm was dissolving like sugar in a tea cup. The idea that she could be open to injury was adding to her fright. Why did Ola have to tell her that now?

The bodies drew nearer their chanting growing louder with each step. *Help them.*

"Help who?" Sarah yelled.

The half-headed man's shattered skull tilted back as laughter erupted from his blackened lips. His decaying hand reached for her throat.

Sarah slapped his hand away, crimson goo clinging to the palm of her hand.

Rage glowed from the eye socket that remained as he sprang toward her. His fingernails dug into her shoulder as she screamed in pain.

Panting, Sarah jolted awake. She ran her hand across her throbbing shoulder. Who was that guy? She thought she recognized him. With part of his head missing and the state of decomposition it was difficult to know where she'd seen him before. And why was he after her? He must realize she's a dreamist. Maybe he was trying to stop her from figuring out what happened to Amelia, which meant he was likely involved with her death.

Danni's back was to Sarah, her side rising and falling with each breath. Should she wake her friend or wait until morning? Better wait. Danni needed her sleep if she was going to be effective in helping with this mystery.

Sarah slid from bed and padded to the bathroom where she gazed in the mirror over the sink. Examining her shoulder, she noticed a slight red mark but nothing substantial. Ola was right. She was stronger than she thought.

She returned to bed and rested her head on the pillow. Staring at the ceiling, Sarah went over everything from the night's vision. The repeated phrase of 'help them' and the creepy man trying to get at her were the most prominent memories. Obviously, someone had blown part of the man's head off which suggested his glowing personality had probably led to his demise.

Touching the necklace, Sarah closed her eyes and tried to recall why this man was so familiar. Her breathing steadied as she ruminated over the image until she drifted back to dreamland.

A chilly breeze ruffled Sarah's hair. She stood in the back alley, the same one where she'd witnessed Theodore speaking with the mysterious man in a previous dream. Shadows appeared at the end of the alleyway just like before. A street-lamp glimmered as two men spoke. She couldn't hear what they were saying but she thought she recognized the one Theo was addressing. Was this the man who'd tried to kill her? It was hard to tell being that his face was intact. Who was this guy and what was his role in all of this?

A dog howled drawing Sarah's attention away from the two men. When she looked back, they were gone. The sound of wheels clattering along the pavement echoed down the narrow space as a gleaming automobile went by. Theodore was driving but the other man was nowhere to be seen.

Gonna pay, brushed against the back of her neck.

Spinning around, Sarah was face to face with the half-headed entity. Despite his close proximity, it was hard to discern his features in the darkened alley.

"Who did this to you?"

"Gonna pay," the man sneered. "Help me or you will too."

Instead of fear, anger pulsed through Sarah's veins. "Don't threaten me, especially if you want my help." Where was this brazenness coming from?

"Don't need you," he growled.

"You wouldn't be here otherwise."

The apparition's face crinkled, making him look like a rotted raisin.

"Stay away!" A voice bellowed down the alley.

Sarah turned to see Amelia's cadaverous form barreling toward her. Ducking, she could feel the whoosh of air as Amelia's spirit flew over. What she wasn't expecting was the sparks of light and what sounded like splintering bones as the two spirits collided. When Sarah raised her head, nothing was there. Only the buildings and a tabby cat scurrying behind a dented trash can remained. The air was heavy making it difficult to breathe.

What happened? And where were the ghosts?

He did this, skittered against Sarah's cheek, sending a wave of goosebumps across her skin.

The sound was so faint, Sarah almost thought she'd imagined it. Then the ground crashed into the salty current below. Struggling to the surface, Sarah gasped for air. Before she could catch her breath, something grabbed her hair and shoved her back under the water.

"Ola!" she screamed in her mind.

All of a sudden, the grip on her head loosened and the water began to recede. Sarah was back at the house as it was in the 1920s.

Amelia's Aunt Bessie entered the room in a mid-calf black dress. She wore a small pill box hat with a netted veil covering her face and a strand of ivory pearls draped about her neck.

"Are you ready, my dear?" Joe asked his wife as he stepped into the room. He wore a black suit with a crisp white shirt and a dark gray bowtie. A black band circled his bicep on the left side.

"No." She sniffled. "I'll never be ready for this. He's a monster and I'll never forgive him. How could he do such a thing? I should have done more to protect her."

"Bessie, you can't have this attitude. You've got to forgive him and move on."

Joe offered his arm and led his wife to the rumbling car waiting at the curb.

The scene changed and Sarah found herself standing in Colonial Park Cemetery. Joe and Bessie, along with several others, gathered around a tombstone. Their heads were bowed as a pastor led them in prayer.

Although she already knew the name that would be on the gravestone, Sarah stepped closer to confirm it.

Amelia Elizabeth Danbury

1903-1921

Nothing else was on there. That's odd, Sarah thought. Usually, families of Amelia's status created elaborate headstones with detailed information. This one was rather plain, an arched piece of marble with no embellishments.

When the pastor finished, the group dispersed except for Bessie who kneeled down, placing her hand on the cold marble.

"I'm so sorry, my dear. I won't rest until he pays for what he's done."

Standing, she turned and joined her husband who waited patiently. "At least he had the decency to stay away," she grumbled. "I might kill him myself if he ever shows his face here again."

Not here.

Sarah spun around to find Amelia, her soaked hair clinging to her bloated and discolored cheeks as a trickle of blood stained the right side of her face.

"Who's not here?"

Her head turned from side to side slowly before she repeated the words more forcefully. *Not here!*

"I don't understand!" Sarah shouted back. She was getting tired of all these cryptic messages. For once, she wanted the ghosts to use what little energy they possessed to say something meaningful. "Who's not here?"

Me, Amelia whispered as her form began to waver, and she vanished.

Sarah stirred when something shifted against her. Dallas was repositioning himself on the pillow next to her head. At some point during the night, he must have decided that was a better spot to snooze. Danni was still asleep. Sitting up, Sarah pondered all that had happened in her dreams. She'd bounced around like a ping pong ball from one scene to another.

First, the half-headed guy wanted Sarah's help but his request had been forceful. Amelia didn't seem to like him either and actually tried to intervene. After the two ghosts clashed, they disappeared. That was the most bizarre part. And then Amelia's strange message at the gravesite about someone not being there. None of it made sense.

Sarah thought about all the people in attendance. The only ones she recognized were Joe and Bessie and a few of the employees from the mercantile and speakeasy, except for Jackson. Now that she thought about it, the Danbury's weren't there either. Surely, they wouldn't miss their own daughter's funeral. No wonder Bessie was so upset. She must have been furious with her brother for not coming to say goodbye to his only daughter.

Danni rolled over with a groan and rubbed her eyes. "What time is it?"

"Time for you to get up," Sarah replied.

Opening one eye, Danni squinted at her friend. "If I find out it's before 7:00 a.m. you're gonna be in trouble."

"What are you going to do, haunt me?" Sarah huffed.

"No, but I might hide a Ouija board in your house."

"Aren't we cranky?" Sarah snorted. "Stop with the idle threats and get dressed. I need your research skills."

Danni sat up, her hair rumpled on one side. "This better be good," she groused, sliding from bed and trudging to the bathroom.

Sarah glanced at the clock that read 6:32 a.m. Oh well, by the time Danni got into research mode, she wouldn't care how early it was.

Chapter Ten

S arah heard the shower start and scooted downstairs to get a cup of coffee for her friend. Danni didn't function without an early morning shot of caffeine and Sarah needed her to be at her best. While pleased with the new information she'd garnered from her dreams, she was also perplexed. It seemed there were two entities seeking her assistance. One was confusing enough, but now she had multiple spirits vying for her attention. The obvious animosity between them would likely hinder an easy resolution.

When Sarah returned to the bedroom, Danni emerged from the bathroom in a cloud of steam, her wet hair combed straight. She grumbled a thank you as she took the coffee cup from her friend.

"What is so important you felt the need to wake me at this ungodly hour?"

"I've got some things for you to investigate."

"I thought you weren't supposed to give me an edge by sharing your dreamist visions."

"I'm not asking you to do this as part of your bet with

Walter. I need help figuring some of this out. I've got two ghosts haunting me which is making it difficult to decipher what each of them needs."

"You have two ghosts in need of assistance?" Danni's brows arched. "And you're asking me to help you but not let that filter into what I'm researching as part of the bet?"

Chewing her lower lip, Sarah hesitated. Now that she heard Danni say it, the idea did seem a bit preposterous. "I guess I didn't think it through."

"Well, you've piqued my interest so you might as well share your dream with me."

Sarah shared everything from the night's visions including the man with half a face to the repeated phrase of help them to Amelia's new statement, *not here.* "It's all so vague, I can't figure out what anyone is talking about."

"Didn't you tell me Amelia's father was angry with her and that's why she was sent to live with her aunt and uncle?"

"Yeah."

"Maybe her father discovered the speakeasy stuff, got angry, and did something to harm them."

"Makes sense," Sarah replied. All of a sudden, a thought popped into her head. "Oh my gosh, what if Amelia's father was the one who killed her?"

"Do you think he's really that coldhearted? Didn't you say she died by drowning?"

"Looks that way to me. She's bloated and has chunks of flesh missing where sea life nibbled on her." Sarah shuddered.

"Eww, didn't need that image this early."

"Sorry," Sarah replied.

Danni straightened. "Maybe we need to investigate Amelia's official manner of death."

"Like I said, it's obvious she died from drowning. Now that

I think about it, it couldn't have been her father. He was in Atlanta at the time."

"Let's check on her death." Danni grabbed the laptop, her fingers flying across the keyboard. Moments later, a ding brought a smile to her face. She turned her computer screen so Sarah could see it. "Voila, the official death certificate for Amelia Danbury."

"How did you get access to that?" Sarah asked.

"Friends in good places," she grinned.

Sarah read the brief report from the coroner's office. Amelia Danbury died from drowning, likely caused by an injury to the head rendering her unconscious. Police believed she had been walking along the water's edge on the riverfront, slipped, hit her head, fell into the water, and drowned.

"Seems fairly straightforward except she's inferred someone killed her," Sarah said.

"Unless you misinterpreted what she was trying to say."

"Not likely. We need to share this with the guys."

Thankfully, the men were awake and sitting around the center island sipping coffee when she and Danni entered the kitchen. Sarah explained everything from her dreams and the official cause of death for Amelia.

Ralph crossed his arms over his chest and addressed Danni. "You're not using information from Sarah's dreams to get ahead in the bet, are you?"

Danni stepped closer to Ralph and leaned into him. "I haven't had my second cup of coffee yet which means the filter on my mouth has yet to be established this morning. Be careful what you accuse me of because I *don't* cheat."

Ralph's face paled as he nodded his head. "Sorry."

Danni straightened and walked to the coffee pot for another cup.

"I'll get online with Walter and go over last night's footage.

Maybe we caught something on tape that aligns with Sarah's dreams," Ralph said. "I'm going to do this in the front parlor." He threw a sideways glance at Danni as he left the room.

"Harry and I can go to the library. There must be a newspaper article about Amelia's death somewhere," Garrett said. "Maybe we'll get lucky and find some new information while we're there."

With everyone's tasks declared, the team dispersed to do their jobs. Sarah hurried toward Garrett and touched his arm. "Can I talk to you for a moment?" she asked.

"Sure," he replied with a half-smile.

They started for the other room when his phone buzzed. With a quick glance at the screen, Garrett inhaled, his smile fading. "I need to take this. Can we talk later?"

"Of course." Sarah heard him answer the phone as he walked down the hall. This was the second time he'd received a call and wanted to speak in private which was unlike him. She looked down at Dallas who waited patiently at her feet, his tongue lolling to the side of his snout.

"I know, I'm being paranoid," she said to her furry companion. "I only want to make sure there's nothing I should be concerned about."

Yip!

Sarah giggled. "Thanks for the vote of confidence. I'm sure everything is fine between us." It felt good to say it, too bad she didn't feel it in her heart.

Chapter Eleven

Sarah was disappointed she didn't get a chance to speak with Garrett before he and Harry left for the public library. She'd have to wait until later. Sarah settled onto the stool next to Danni who was slouched in front of her computer at the kitchen island. Danni searched every site she could think of hoping to find something more about Amelia's life. After an hour they still hadn't found anything of significance.

"What else can you tell me about Amelia's death?" Danni asked, her fingers paused over the keyboard.

Then it hit Sarah. "Add the word prohibition and see what comes up," she suggested, sitting straighter.

"Huh?"

"Amelia died in 1921. We may not have found anything at the Prohibition Museum but we know there was a speakeasy somewhere around here and Amelia's ghost is wearing a flapper dress."

Danni typed in prohibition and gasped. "Oh my gosh, something came up."

"Are you serious?"

"It's not what you think."

Sarah leaned in closer and read the newspaper report from 1921 on Danni's screen.

November 19th, 1921.

Savannah, Georgia.

Police raided a laundry on Prince Street after receiving a tip about illegal alcohol distribution. Upon their arrival, police discovered a kitchen still as well as a speakeasy in the back section of the building. It appears the Edwards, a long standing and respected family in the area, fled before law enforcement arrived at the cinder block building where they found several cases of rum. Children scrambled to the scene with jugs to scoop up the liquor being dumped in the alley behind the laundry. Anyone with information as to the whereabouts of the Edwards family is encouraged to call the authorities.

"Did you pick up on anything when you were at the old laundry building the other day?"

"Kinda, but nothing specific." Sarah's stomach twisted. There was much more to this story than a police raid for booze. Did the Edwards family actually escape or did something sinister happen to them? As a black family during that time period, their punishment likely would have been more severe. Is this who Amelia was referring to when she said *help them?*

Harry and Garrett came in the back door grinning like two kids who'd just pulled a prank.

"Hey," Sarah said. "By the expression on your faces, I'm guessing you found something at the library."

"Indeed, we did," Harry said. "He handed Sarah a photocopy of a newspaper article from 1921.

A slow smile spread across Sarah's face. "It's the same one we just found."

"What?" Harry exclaimed.

"Danni found the same article online."

"You guys won't believe this!" Ralph declared, bolting into the room. "Walter found an article online about..."

"The raid," they all said in unison.

Ralph's shoulders slumped. "How'd you know?"

"Because I discovered it first!" Danni declared.

"Actually, I think we did," Harry added. "We stumbled across it while going through microfiche at the library."

"How do you know you found it first?" Danni asked.

Harry lifted his shoulders. "We found it about an hour ago, made copies, and drove back here. When did you find it?"

Danni's upper lip wrinkled as she groaned, "About ten minutes ago."

All eyes turned to Ralph. "I have no idea when Walter found it. He just told me."

"Let's call this one a draw," Garrett suggested.

"Fine," Danni grumbled. "But from now on, everyone has to record the time they find any significant information."

"Cut it out," Sarah said, nudging her friend's shoulder. "Did anyone discover anything besides the reason for the raid?"

The guys shook their heads.

"Does any of this tie in with your dreams?" Harry asked.

"Actually, it does. I've seen the speakeasy but didn't know its location until now."

"Anything else you can tell us?" Garrett queried.

"Not yet," Sarah replied, her head beginning to ache. "This extra knowledge will give me something to ask Amelia about. Hopefully, it will lead to more specific responses."

Sarah rubbed her temples. Even though they didn't have an official deadline for solving this mystery, she still felt the pressure. Garrett and the guys had missed a lot of work chasing their dream of being full time ghost hunters. But it was their dream, not hers. Her dreams were haunted enough without searching for specters. Right now, she felt like nothing more than a ghostly conduit and it annoyed her.

"Are you okay?" Garrett asked, touching Sarah's arm.

"As okay as a haunted person can be," she snapped.

He recoiled from her as if she'd thrown hot oil on him. Even Ralph and Harry seemed taken back. Danni shot her a warning glance. She was doing it again. Taking out her frustrations on everyone around her. It wasn't their fault and yet she wanted to scream at them to leave her alone and find the ghosts on their own.

"We've got to go back through some footage from last night," Garrett said gently. "Walter found something on the parlor camera."

Harry and Ralph nodded as they followed him from the room.

"What is wrong with you?" Danni asked, exasperation lacing her words.

"I don't know," Sarah replied, tears stinging her eyes. "I can't explain it. I feel...overwhelmed."

"Who doesn't?"

Sarah looked at her best friend, a tear streaking down her cheek as she spoke. "It's too much," she said. "I have all these spirits invading my mind at all hours of the day and night. I'm trying to maneuver a relationship that sadly revolves around the entities living in my head. To make matters worse, I don't feel like myself anymore. It's as if I'm a walking, breathing shell of who I used to be and it scares me."

Danni grasped Sarah's hand. "You've been through a lot the past couple of years. It would be enough to send anyone straight to a mental hospital. Maybe you need to take a break from it all."

Sarah snatched her hand from Danni's. "Take a break from it all? Do you hear yourself? I can't escape these spirits no matter where I go! I can't even sleep without them pestering me with their stupid short phrases and their disgusting faces!"

"Calm down," Danni said quietly. "I get this is hard for you. Major life changes are difficult. But you have a team of people helping you. You're not alone in this."

"I'm never alone, that's the problem." Sarah swiped at the tears.

"I can give you some space if you need it." Danni shut her laptop and stood up. "These constant attacks are starting to get old."

"Don't you understand?" Sarah pleaded. "I can't be alone. I'll never be alone as long as a spirit needs my help. As soon as I help one, another shows up and in this case two of them. If you thought I struggled to decipher the *Dreamist* book, try figuring out the back stories and meanings behind cryptic phrases of two ghosts at the same time."

"I don't know what to tell you. But I do know this. Garrett loves you and he's doing his best to help you so stop being mean to him."

"How convenient for him that his passion to hunt ghosts coincides with his girlfriend's freaky abilities."

"Stop it!" Danni declared. "He's been nothing but good to you. It's not his fault he fell in love with a dreamist any more than it's your fault for being one. I would think being surrounded by a group of ghost hunters would be a comfort. After all, they understand the ghost world from a different perspective which has helped you adapt to your haunted existence."

Burying her face in her hands, Sarah took in a deep breath. "You're right and yet I can't seem to reconcile it in my head." She looked up, her eyes puffy and her complexion pale. "I don't feel like myself anymore. What's happening to me?"

Danni sat back down. "Sounds like growing pains. Except

it isn't your body, it's your mind. You're having to shift everything you've ever known and restructure how you see the world."

Sarah rubbed her forehead. "My headache is getting worse. I'm gonna lie down for a bit."

"Holler if you need anything."

"Thanks, I will," Sarah replied, squeezing her friend's shoulder. "Sorry for being so cranky."

"It's okay," Danni said. "Go upstairs and get some rest."

Sarah trudged down the hall and heard the guys in the front parlor discussing something as she passed. Their voices were muddled but Garrett's stood out. She was being unfair to him. Deep in her heart she knew he wasn't using her. And yet, she felt used. Maybe it wasn't Garrett making her feel that way but the ghosts. Was it possible to transfer feelings from the dead to the living? Not wanting to speak to anyone, Sarah tiptoed upstairs to her room on the second floor.

Crawling into bed, she shivered. She pulled the blanket over her shoulders as her teeth began to chatter. Sarah squeezed her eyes shut and began taking deep breaths. That's when she heard it. The rushing of water. Except she was awake. Or was she?

Sarah floated down a river, the current pulling her under as the words, *he did this,* surged through her head. Sarah tried to think clearly but the lack of oxygen was jumbling her brain. She paddled her way to the surface only to be pushed back under by something. A hand? It had her by the hair and kept shoving her head under the water. No matter how hard she tried, she couldn't break free.

Fight him, echoed through her head from the watery expanse.

It felt as if her lungs were about to explode when something pulled her above the water's surface. Gasping for air, Sarah shook her head in an effort to clear her mind. She was bobbing in the river near the Savannah waterfront. A Model A was parked nearby as clouds gathered in the night sky shielding the moon. Something moved in the shadows by the car.

Sarah honed in on it. It appeared to be the lanky fellow from previous dreams, the one with half his head missing. Unfortunately, she couldn't make out his features in the darkness. He slipped into the vehicle and motored away.

He did this.

Sarah sloshed around to see Amelia in the water behind her, a trail of crimson trickling down her neck. Must be the head injury mentioned in the obituary Danni found online.

"You didn't die accidentally like the police report said?"

Amelia shook her head.

"Is the man who drove away the one who killed you?"

"Yes!" she bellowed, her voice rippling across the water making the tide choppier. Sarah swam to the river's edge and crawled onto the cobblestone walkway, her body shivering from the frigid water saturating her clothes. Despite being cold and exhausted, Sarah smiled. She'd done it. She'd managed to stay calm and get significant answers from Amelia.

Turning back toward the water, she searched for signs of Amelia's body but nothing was there. At least Sarah knew the truth behind her death. She was definitely murdered.

The ground beneath Sarah shifted and with it the scenery altered. She stood behind the laundry, aka, the speakeasy on Prince Street.

Didn't deserve this, a voice muttered behind her.

She turned abruptly but nothing was there. The voice had been gruff like a man. Unless decaying vocal cords could make a woman's voice sound scratchy.

"Amelia?" Sarah called out.

Silence.

Headlights flashed from the end of the street catching Sarah's attention. She started in that direction, her eyes darting around in case any spirits lingered nearby. Her body quivered from the damp clothes clinging to her clammy skin. But she was determined to find out what was transpiring at the end of the road. It's not like she'd get sick from wandering around in a dream wearing wet clothes.

That's when she noticed someone step from the shadows near the corner and lean into the passenger window of the idling car. Not wanting to be discovered, Sarah stayed close to the buildings and moved stealthily through the darkness. As she neared, she strained to hear the conversation.

"What's wrong with your hand?" the man in the car asked.

"Wench scratched me," the guy at the passenger side replied.

"Don't you dare speak of her in that manner! She's a lady!"

"Don't you mean a flapper?"

"I oughtta blow your head off for that!"

"You're beginning to bore me," the lanky man said. "Where's my cash?"

"Boy, you better remember your place," the driver growled. "You don't call the shots, I do."

"Listen, I did what you told me to do. Just give me my money."

The engine's rattling grew louder hindering Sarah's ability to hear what they were saying.

"Not until... frighten her. You'll need to keep... I'll pay you when she's learned her lesson."

The man outside of the vehicle rubbed the back of his neck. Thank goodness, he was easier to hear since he was standing outside of the car. "Don' think there's gonna be another time," he said. "She won't be comin' back. Ever."

"What do you mean?"

Sarah's heart was pounding so hard against her ribcage she was certain the men would hear it. She slinked closer hoping to catch more of the conversation when the ground below her crunched. The guy outside of the car turned her direction but the veil of night prevented her from seeing the details of his face.

A hand grabbed Sarah's shoulder catapulting her into a light filled room. Sitting up, she tried to get her bearings. Danni stood at the edge of the bed, concern masking her countenance.

"Sorry, didn't mean to scare you. How's your headache?"

Sarah rubbed her eyes. "Better, thanks."

"I know you don't like me waking you but the guys are getting ready to order lunch and sent me up to see if you wanted anything."

"Where are they going?"

"Some deli down the road. Typical stuff, sandwiches and chips."

"Got it," Sarah replied. She picked up her phone and texted Garrett.

Get me a ham and Swiss sandwich on pumpernickel with spicey mustard.

Dots paraded across the screen.

Any sides?

Salt and vinegar chips.

A thumbs up popped onto her screen before she set the phone back on the night table.

"Dream about anything significant?" Danni asked, sitting on the edge of the bed.

"You could say that."

Danni's eyes brightened. "What did you learn?"

"Amelia's death definitely wasn't an accident like the death certificate mentioned. I'm not sure of the circumstances that led to it but I think I know who's responsible."

"Seriously?" Danni exclaimed. "Who did it?"

"Don't know."

"But you just said..."

"I know who did it but not his identity," Sarah replied, her shoulders slumping.

"Tell me everything. Maybe we can figure it out together."

"Let's wait until the guys get back with lunch," Sarah said, sliding from bed. "We can discuss it while we eat."

Everyone gathered around the kitchen island eating sandwiches while Sarah filled them in about the two mysterious men in the car on the road behind the laundry.

"Fascinating," Ralph said, rubbing his chin. "And you don't have any idea who the men were?"

"Not at all. The voices sounded familiar but it was hard to hear with the clattering of the car engine. The guy at the passenger side seemed familiar. I know I've seen him before; I'm just trying to figure out where."

"What about the man in the car?" Ralph asked.

"Couldn't make out his features but I'm pretty sure it was Theodore Warren. The car was black like the one he drives."

"All cars were black back then," Garrett added.

"So, this probably didn't take place the night of the raid," Harry said. "I doubt anyone would have been hanging around after that."

Ralph's phone pinged. "It's Walter."

"What does the Internet wizard have to say?" Danni queried, her lips pursed as she crossed her arms over her chest.

"Says he's been doing some research on the Edwards' family."

"The ones who owned the laundry?" Sarah asked.

Ralph nodded before continuing. "They were successful

members of the community and lived in the neighborhood for more than a decade."

"We already know that," Danni said.

"There's more. After the raid on the laundry, they were never heard from again."

"As in they were killed?" Harry asked.

"He doesn't say. Only that they disappeared."

"I was afraid of that," Sarah said. "As black people, the justice system probably wasn't favorable to their situation." She sat for a moment. "I wonder why the police decided to raid the laundry in the first place."

"Maybe they suspected money laundering," Danni said with a snort.

Chills bumped along Sarah's arms. "It doesn't make sense," she muttered. "It's one thing to run an illegal bar but as a black family it seems like a huge risk given the time period.

"I'm only sharing what Walter found. I didn't say it made sense," Ralph replied.

"This has to be what Amelia is referring to when she says, *help them*. She must be referring to the Edwards. Unless..."

"What?" Harry and Ralph said in unison, excitement radiating from their eyes.

"The creepy man in my dreams with part of his head missing is tall and slender, like Jackson Edwards. I haven't been able to see his features clearly but it could be him."

"Are you saying Jackson killed Amelia?" Danni queried.

Sarah shook her head. "Don't know. Maybe."

"Have you had any more dreams about the speakeasy?" Harry asked.

"I've had a few where I followed Amelia through a tunnel to get there so I never knew the location until we found the article earlier."

"Tunnels?" Ralph asked. "Where did they originate?"

"Not sure. I've seen her in a dark passageway with her aunt and they ended up at a wooden trap door. She did some sort of secret knock like you'd see in old gangster movies."

"Perhaps it's a different speakeasy," Garrett said.

"It's possible, but what are the chances both the Millers and the Edwards were running speakeasies?" Sarah replied. "Wait a minute! I saw Jackson there. He was working one night because someone didn't show up."

"I thought he was a mechanic for the Millers," Danni said.

"He was. But in my dream, he was manning the door. He let Bessie and Amelia in."

"The garage was behind the house on the property layout we found," Danni said, pulling it up on her computer. "Right here." She pointed at a small yellow square behind the large one representing the house. "The Millers also owned the cottages and the cinder block building where the laundry was housed."

"This all has to be linked somehow," Harry said.

"What if the tunnels to the speakeasy originated at the garage?" Ralph suggested.

"The only problem is the garage is no longer standing," Sarah replied. "Which means the entry to the tunnel is long gone."

"What about Amelia's ghost?" Danni queried. "Any way you could ask her about it?"

Sarah blew out a long breath. "I've actually done fairly well the past few nights asking questions, when I'm not drowning," she said, rolling her eyes.

Ralph scrunched his face. "Ugh. That's my worst fear."

"You're the one who's always saying you wish you could do what I do. Facing things that terrify you is part of the package." Sarah huffed.

Ralph's eyebrows arched. "Well, I'll pass on the drowning

scenes but being able to speak with the dead would be pretty cool."

Sarah smiled. No matter what the subject, Ralph always had a positive attitude. It was one of the things she loved best about him.

"Looks like we still have a long way to go before figuring this out," Garrett said.

"There's definitely more here than we've uncovered," Danni added, heading for the doorway. "I'm going back to work."

"Did you guys capture anything on video last night?" Sarah asked.

"Actually, we caught a pretty weird image near the pantry off the kitchen." Harry motioned Sarah over to the laptop.

He queued up the footage and hit play. Sarah watched the grainy scene when a flash of light erupted from the floor.

"What was that?" she asked.

"We were hoping you could tell us," Harry replied. "Don't know what it is or why it showed up in that location unless Amelia was killed there? The death certificate mentioned a head injury."

"Makes sense. What if the person who hit her in the head panicked when they realized they killed her and dumped her body in the river?" Ralph said. "Whoever did it could have transported her via the tunnels to avoid being caught."

"Has anyone crawled under the house to see what's there?" Sarah queried.

The guys exchanged glances.

"Hadn't thought about that," Harry said. "Dunc, you're the contractor. Sounds like a good job for you."

"I don't think they would have risked connecting a secret tunnel to the house," Garrett replied. "The garage area would make more sense."

"Let's check it out," Ralph said.

Garrett headed for the back door in the kitchen with everyone following. He walked the perimeter of the property where the garage once stood, Dallas sniffing ahead of him. All of a sudden, Dallas growled and started digging. Crouching, Garrett nudged his dog and sifted the sand away. The team gathered around and watched.

"What's that?" Ralph asked.

"Looks like part of a foundation," he replied.

Sarah sucked in a breath when a stabbing pain zapped her temple sending stars dancing before her eyes as the words *didn't deserve this* echoed in her ear.

"What's wrong?" Garrett asked, standing.

"Sharp pain in my head at the same time someone whispered, *didn't deserve this.*"

Garrett glanced toward the foundation and back at Sarah. "Do you think there's a connection with this spot and the ghost?"

Blinking back the lingering ache in her head, Sarah nodded. "Definitely. I can feel it."

Chapter Twelve

Sarah walked over to the area where the chunk of foundation jutted from the sandy soil. Leaning over, she ran her fingers across it. As if receiving a jolt of electricity, Sarah stumbled backwards, a quick image flashing through her mind.

"Are you okay?" Garrett asked, steadying her.

"I think so," she responded, trying to get her bearings. "That was weird."

"Did you see something?" Harry asked.

"It was only a snippet but I think it was the half-headed guy."

"What?" Harry said.

"I've seen him several times," Sarah responded. "Sadly, I haven't gotten a good look at him. All I know is that he's missing part of his skull."

"As in someone shot him?" Ralph asked.

"Considering the gore, I'd say yes," Sarah replied.

"But you don't know who he is?" Ralph said.

"Not sure because I can't get a good look at his face. He's

always in the dark. But I think it may be Jackson Edwards. He has the same build," she replied, unease wrinkling her brow.

"What's wrong?" Garrett asked.

"Don't know how to explain it," Sarah said. "Jackson seems like such a good person. I don't want to believe he killed Amelia."

"At least we have someone to focus on," Harry said.

"Until we know the ghost's exact identity, we can call him Half-Headed Fred," Ralph chuckled.

Sarah grinned at Ralph's comic relief. It helped alleviate some of the tension she felt about Jackson Edwards possibly being a murderer. Then again, many of the ghosts in her dreams seemed affable in the beginning. Until they ended up being psychopathic killers. Was that the message Amelia was trying to convey? Jackson was dangerous and her aunt and uncle needed help? If his family was running the speakeasy at the back of their laundry it would have been hazardous for the Millers as well. Police raids, stray bullets, thugs in and around the establishment at all hours of the night."

"What are you thinking?" Garrett asked.

"I feel like I'm missing something," Sarah said. "My dreams about Jackson have been positive so far. There's no reason for Amelia to be afraid of him."

"Maybe he started out as a friend and then turned into a killer," Harry suggested.

"What if you kept your hand on the foundation?" Ralph asked. "Would you get a more detailed vision?"

"No," Garrett interrupted. "You saw what happened to her. She nearly fell from touching it the first time."

Sarah's chest tightened. How dare he speak on her behalf. She was perfectly capable of deciding what she could and couldn't do. "I appreciate your concern," she said boldly. "But I can do this."

Or so she hoped. Considering what just happened, touching the remnants of the foundation could cause serious discomfort. Why was she being so stubborn? Because she needed to prove she could make her own decisions, even if she suffered a bit in the process.

Sarah stepped closer and reached down when Garrett grabbed her wrist. "Maybe it would be better to wait and see what Amelia reveals in your dreams. No sense clouding your thoughts with disturbing images. It could interfere with your ability to decipher the ghost's message."

Sarah shot him a warning look. "I'm sure I can handle it," she said through gritted teeth.Now she was definitely doing it.

Wrenching her hand free, Sarah rested her palm on the rotting board and closed her eyes. This time she was able to keep her hand there without any pain to her head or jolts of electricity. Opening her eyes, she stood. "Nothing. Sorry guys."

"Thanks for trying,' Ralph said, heading back inside with Harry.

Garrett gave Sarah a questioning look. "I'm trying to support you in all of this but you're making it really hard," he said, marching up the steps and into the kitchen before she had a chance to respond.

At least Danni hadn't been here to see what had happened. She would've lectured Sarah about her attitude. Sarah hesitated in the brisk air. Why had she openly defied Garrett like that? He was only trying to protect her.

Frustration squeezed her chest as tears threatened to fall. She felt like she was stuck on a Ferris wheel spinning out of control. On the flip side, she was a grown woman and capable of taking care of herself. Sarah took in a deep breath and released it as she started for the back door. No sense dwelling on it now. She couldn't take it back so she might as well address the entity in the room. Once she helped Amelia move on, she could fix things with Garrett. At least, that's what she wanted to believe.

The afternoon passed quickly with everyone either surfing the Internet for more information or editing video clips from the previous night. Sarah avoided Garrett, unsure what to say, especially since she didn't understand it herself. Danni had said all couples have arguments so maybe this was typical stuff.

Day faded to night shrouding the house in darkened shadows and green lights glowing from the cameras.

"Okay if I hang with you this evening?" Sarah asked Garrett, hoping this would be something of a peace offering without having to discuss anything in detail.

"If you're sure you want to," he replied, fiddling with the settings on the camera in the front parlor.

"I'm sorry about earlier. I know you were only trying to keep me safe. I don't know why I snapped at you like that."

He looked up, disappointment emanating from his stare. "No need to apologize. You have a right to make your own decisions without my interference."

Sarah reached out to touch his arm when his phone pinged. He glanced at the screen and sighed. "I need to take this. I'll be right back."

Who was texting him this late? she wondered. He'd been getting a lot of calls and texts lately. He returned a few minutes later and resumed adjusting the settings on the camera.

"Everything alright?" she asked.

"Huh? Yeah, everything's fine."

"You've been getting a lot of messages lately."

"Got a lot going on and some big decisions to make," he responded, avoiding her gaze.

"Anything you want to talk about?"

His eyes met hers. "Not yet."

His curt response wasn't lost on her. Something *was* wrong.

If they were in a committed relationship, wouldn't he share any pressing news? Or was he just focused on the job at hand? She had been snippy lately. That's probably all it was.

Dallas plunked at her feet and stared at her with his deep brown eyes. When she reached down to scratch behind his ears, he rolled onto his back with all four legs in the air which was his way of saying, *scratch my belly.*

"Why don't you take him out?" Garrett said. "He needs a break before we start filming."

"Sure," she replied. "Come on buddy, let's go outside."

With a resounding 'woof,' he rushed out of the room, through the dining room, and stood at the back door in the kitchen, his stubby tail wagging furiously.

They stepped into the frigid night air, Sarah wishing she'd grabbed her jacket as she wrapped her arms around her body. Stars glittered against an inky backdrop and a nearly full moon illuminated the six-foot fence behind the house. Dallas sniffed around the perimeter of the yard as Sarah tried to imagine what it must have looked like a hundred years before. From what she could remember from her dreams, there was an alley that ran behind the house and the neighboring homes. The cottages and cinder block building where the laundry-slash-speakeasy had been still lined the road perpendicular to this property.

Sarah stared at the remnants of what had been the foundation of the garage. Something inside her wanted to know more about what had happened here and if there was a connection to the speakeasy. And yet, she didn't have the courage to reach down and touch it again.

If the Edwards' family was running liquor from their laundry establishment, it made sense that Jackson could have been helping his parents by making use of the alleyway for secreting liquor into the establishment. It would have been well shielded from public view. This area hadn't been a prominent neighborhood at the time meaning a strong police presence wasn't likely. If that was the case, how did the cops learn about the illegal enterprise? Raids were usually well planned with a great deal of prior knowledge about the suspected activities.

Dallas growled pulling Sarah's attention from her ruminations. The hair at the base of her neck bristled. Something was there.

"Hello?" she called. "Is there something you want to tell me?"

The fur on Dallas's back rose as his growling grew in volume.

Inhaling, Sarah walked over to where Dallas stood.

"Is that you, Amelia?"

The scent of decaying flesh permeated Sarah's nose making her gag. It was the other ghost, the man with the threatening demeanor.

"If you have something to say, do so," she commanded, pleased with her fortitude.

Did me wrong, the voice muttered.

Turning slowly, Sarah braced for what she might see. A misty figure wavered, part of its skull missing. It appeared to be Half-Headed Fred, the tall man she'd seen in her dream speaking to the gent in the car. Sarah studied the apparition, trying to stay calm at the revolting sight. It was difficult to tell but his skin seemed to be dark. Was it Jackson Edwards? The entity was in such a state of decay it was hard to tell.

"What happened?" she asked, trying to maintain her composure.

The ghost's remaining eye bobbled in its socket as it tried to focus on her. Before he could respond, a warm draft brushed against Sarah's cheek.

Get away.

Sarah watched as Amelia's translucent frame materialized.

Despite Amellia's warning, Sarah was able to harvest some fortitude. She needed answers and was determined to get them. "You killed Amelia," Sarah stated to Half-Headed Fred, hoping to force a response from him. Maybe if she agitated him, he'd reveal his secrets, specifically why he killed Amelia.

Apparently, her accusation infuriated the murderous corpse. His remaining eye glowed red and his lips wrinkled as he hissed obscenities through rotting gums. Sarah ducked as the gruesome creature flew over her. Dallas whizzed past, chasing the apparition into the darkness. When Sarah stood, both ghosts were gone. Dallas waddled back, his nose in the air triumphantly.

"Good boy," she said, patting his head.

"Everything okay?" Garrett asked.

Grabbing her chest, Sarah sucked in a breath. "You startled me."

"Sorry about that. I heard Dallas carrying on and decided to check on you."

"I'm fine but there were two spirits here vying for my attention."

"Amelia and?"

"The man."

"Still don't know who he is?"

"As much as I hate to say it, I think it may have been Jackson Edwards."

Garrett rubbed his forehead. "We haven't had much luck getting details on him."

"All I know is he worked for Amelia's aunt and uncle as a mechanic in the garage behind the house."

"So, the question we need to answer is why did he kill her?" Garrett said.

"Something tells me the only way to get those answers is in my dreams," Sarah replied with a sigh. "I tried to aggravate him into giving me a response but all he did was cuss me out and fly at me. Dallas chased him away."

Garrett leaned in, his lips meeting hers as he pulled her close. She returned the kiss, the warmth of his body dissolving the chill encapsulating her.

"Dunc?" Harry called, breaking them apart. "You need to come in here. Walter found something."

Sarah stepped back, her head still spinning from the kiss. How could she have doubted his feelings for her? Of course, he loved her. He wasn't using her for her haunted proclivities to further his ghost hunting ambitions. The two aspects of their lives were intertwined. There was no way to pull them apart. So, why had she been so sensitive lately?

"Let's go inside and find out what Walter discovered. Danni is probably stewing and will need some reassurance, or a stiff drink depending on how juicy the tidbit is," Sarah said.

Garrett took Sarah's hand and led her inside with Dallas running ahead of them.

The overhead kitchen light illuminated the space where the team gathered. Ralph was grinning like a mischievous child who'd just pulled a prank and gotten away with it. Harry stood by Danni who was sulking, her brows furrowed.

"What did Walter find?" Garrett asked, sidling up to the kitchen island with Sarah.

"He found the person responsible for the raid," Ralph said. "Theodore Warren called police and reported he'd seen whiskey barrels being loaded onto a wagon behind the laundry at midnight."

Sarah's hand flew to her mouth. "Theodore Warren was the man Amelia was supposed to marry. He's been in several of my dreams." Her father had arranged the match but she refused him. It's how she ended up in Savannah."

"Walter said he was able to locate some old records in a

database about political history in Georgia. According to what he read, Theodore was working for George Danbury, Amelia's father who was a stout proponent of prohibition. I assume Mr. Danbury's political ambitions prompted him to send Theodore to the authorities with the information," Ralph said.

"How'd Walter learn about that?" Danni asked, her hands folded over her chest. "I have a friend in the records department here and he hasn't shared that with me."

Ralph shrugged. "I don't ask how my brother gets the information; I only use what I'm given. It's better if I don't know."

Sarah pondered the new evidence and how it related to what she'd dreamt. If Theodore was trying to impress his boss and eliminate things he believed were preventing Amelia from committing to him, it made sense he'd try to destroy the speakeasy. It couldn't have been pleasant knowing his fiancée was involved in such scandalous endeavors, especially if he thought she was involved with a black man. Which made Sarah wonder how much Ameila's father knew about her life in Savannah.

"Is it possible the dead guy in your dreams is Theodore?" Garrett asked Sarah.

"Maybe he was murdered by rum runners for snitching,"

"It's not probable given what I've seen so far. When Theodore has appeared in my dreams, he's fully intact. No sign of death or decomposition. And I've witnessed him speaking with the decaying guy."

"Eww..." Danni moaned, wrinkling her upper lip. "I don't know how you do this."

"Don't have a choice," Sarah replied. "Either I help them or they haunt me. The sooner I help them, the quicker I get rid of them."

"Which leads us back to what you saw in the back yard," Garrett added.

"You saw something outside?" Ralph exclaimed.

Sarah described the scene and the bizarre interactions that ensued.

"You still aren't sure who the dead man is?" Harry said.

"After the latest encounter I was beginning to believe it might be Jackson Edwards. Now, I'm questioning that."

"Why?" Harry asked.

"I don't think Jackson would've risked his family's welfare."

"Maybe Amelia is referring to the Edwards when she says 'help them,'" Danni suggested.

Sarah massaged her temples. This was getting more complicated.

"We were getting ready to start filming when Walter called," Ralph said. "Any possibility you'll be going upstairs to lie down?"

"Not yet," Sarah responded. "I'm still a bit wired from my ghostly confrontation in the backyard."

"Why don't you stay with me in the front parlor?" Garrett offered. "Last night's clip was fraught with orbs but we aren't certain if they're actual ghosts or light reflecting on dust particles from the streetlamp in front of the house. I made some adjustments to the window coverings to block any extraneous glare."

Sarah inhaled. Spending time with Garrett was probably a good idea given she'd been so snarky with him as of late. "I'll hang out with you for a little while. If I get tired, I'll go upstairs and lie down."

Sarah perched on a stool in the corner of the front parlor with Dallas snoring at her feet. Leaning her head against the newly plastered wall, she contemplated all she'd learned thus far.

Amelia had died by drowning. The coroner's report claimed it was an accident although Amelia's spirit had revealed it was murder. Otherwise, Amelia wouldn't be seeking Sarah's help. Theodore Warren, Amelia's wannabe fiancée, reported the illegal liquor activities at the Edwards' place of business resulting in their disappearance. Did they disappear or were they eliminated? Theodore had the connections to get rid of them which would explain Amelia's repeated phrase of *help them*.

With the footage and newfound information about the home's history, it was clear there was a lot more to this story than a liquor trade gone wrong. There were secrets, scandalous ones, that needed to be addressed if the spirits were ever going to rest. Shutting her eyes, Sarah crossed her arms over her chest and took in a few deep breaths. Her body relaxed as her mind drifted off.

The tittering of heels against cobblestones caught Sarah's attention. She looked around but didn't recognize where she was. Had she actually fallen asleep? Obviously, she had or she wouldn't be watching Amelia clattering along the waterfront, whisps of hair crawling across her face as she rushed toward the water's edge.

What on earth was Amelia doing on the waterfront after dark? This was no place for a lady. Sarah watched as the heel of Amelia's shoe caught between the cobblestones, dropping her down, her head thwacking against the pavement. For a moment she was still but then pushed herself up with one hand while rubbing the side of her head. That's when Sarah caught sight of something moving toward her. A shadowy figure appeared from nowhere, his hat flying off as he hurried to Amelia's side.

A scream erupted from her lips as she swatted at the figure whose face was obscured by the darkness. Unfazed by her efforts, the man yanked her up by the hair and shoved her toward the river. Amelia stumbled along, her steps like a drunken sailor. Instinct prompted Sarah to intervene until it hit her. This was a dream. There was nothing she could do to alter the past. Only help bring the truth to light.

As they approached the water's edge, the man pushed Amelia forward, causing her to stumble into the river. With the swiftness of a lion on its prey, the man jumped in, grabbed Amelia's head, and plunged it beneath the water. Thrashing, she clawed at his hand. He yelped as her nails dug into his skin. His rage seemed to increase as he used both hands to hold her under. Moments later, her creamy flapper dress with its silky fringe dipped below the murky water and disappeared from sight.

Help them, gurgled in Sarah's ear.

Sarah's stomach churned as she watched the male figure emerge from the water, pick up his hat, and disappear behind a building as if killing someone was a regular thing. This removed any doubt about Amelia's demise. The head injury had nothing to do with her death. At least Sarah knew what really happened. But why was Amelia at the waterfront after dark? More importantly, was this the same man Sarah had seen leaning against the car at the end of the alleyway in previous visions?

If it was Jackson Edwards, why would he want to harm Amelia? They seemed to be good friends. Perhaps Amelia and Jackson's friendship became something more for one of them, which wouldn't bode well for the times. A black man with a white woman would have been frowned upon in the 20s. Was Amelia referring to the Edwards family when she said 'help them?' So far, the team hadn't uncovered anything about the Edwards family after the raid. Only that they'd vanished without a trace. Did Jackson kill his family too?

You're wrong, tickled Sarah's ear.

Looking over her shoulder, Sarah inhaled sharply at Amelia's festering image. Water streamed from her coffee brown tresses and her sodden dress clung to her slender figure like saran wrap.

"What do I have wrong?" Sarah asked as the briny odor of the river infiltrated her senses.

His fault! the spirit screamed, her lips turning a deep plum as her jaw dropped to an unnatural level.

Sarah cupped her hands over her ears as the ghost's screams increased in intensity shattering the windows of surrounding buildings. Stooping down to avoid the flying shards of glass, Sarah closed her eyes and waited for everything to settle.

The ground below her shifted and she began to fall. Sucking in a breath, Sarah jolted awake. She was in the parlor with Garrett. She must've dozed off and started to topple from the stool. Garrett glanced her way, his head tilted. With a shake of her head, she mouthed, "Tell you later." Sleepiness clung to her limbs and fogged her brain. She wanted to process what she'd seen before discussing it.

Apparently, he didn't want to wait and strode toward her. Leaning over, he whispered in her ear. "What's going on?"

"Drifted off and had a dream," she replied in a hushed tone. Ugh. Why couldn't he just wait like she'd asked?

His eyes widened. "What happened?"

"Saw Amelia's death. I can share this with the team later." Her words were clipped. Hopefully, he'd take the hint.

His smile broadened telling Sarah something was up. "Why so happy?" she asked.

"Saw something on tape a few moments ago."

"Do you think there's a connection?"

"Yes." Excitement radiated from his broad smile.

Crash!

Dallas scurried from the room, barking like mad with Sarah

and Garrett following. The noise seemed to come from the back of the hallway. When they got there, Ralph stood in the doorway between the kitchen and the butler's pantry staring into the hall.

Harry's voice buzzed over the radio. "Everything okay down there?"

"Not sure yet," Garrett replied.

"Need me to help out?"

"Stay put. We've got it."

Dallas stared at the wall, his nubby tail straight and the fur at the base of his neck bristled. A low rumble emanated from his throat.

Ralph and Garrett searched the area but nothing had fallen. "Whatever was here is gone now. Hopefully, something will show up on one of the camera feeds," Garrett said.

Ralph nodded and returned to the monitors in the kitchen while Sarah, Garrett, and Dallas went back to the front parlor.

"Hope you don't mind, but I'm going to turn in," Sarah said, rubbing her eyes. The adrenaline that fueled her burst of energy when they heard the crash had dissolved leaving her feeling as if a vampire had sucked the life from her body.

"Go ahead," he replied, giving her a quick peck on the lips.

Sarah padded up the stairs to the bedroom where Danni was tapping away on her laptop.

"Calling it quits for the night?" Danni asked without looking up.

"Yup. Figured it was safer up here."

"Huh?" Danni grunted, glancing at her friend. "What prompted this?"

"Ghost encounter of the bizarre kind," Sarah replied, going to the bathroom to wash up and change into her pajamas.

Danni got up and leaned against the doorway. "You can't

come up here, drop a line about bizarre ghost encounters, and then walk away. What happened?"

"I'll tell you after I get ready for bed," Sarah replied.

Danni went back into the bedroom as Sarah changed into her pj's and brushed her teeth. A few minutes later, she slipped into bed.

"What's going on?" Danni asked.

Sarah filled her in on her dream about Amelia's murder and the crash downstairs. "Garrett said something showed up on video about the same time I had the dream. The crash occurred shortly thereafter suggesting it may be connected since we didn't find evidence of anything falling."

Danni shook her head. "Don't know how I get myself into these situations," she muttered. "Decaying corpses speaking to you, unexplainable things on camera, and invisible items crashing to the ground. Can't believe I'm still here."

"You know you love it," Sarah teased.

Glaring at her friend, Danni cocked her head. "I love you, not the spirits. Trust me, there are times I long for a ghost-free friend."

Sarah chuckled and rolled over. "Love you too," she snickered.

With a few deep breaths, Sarah felt her body melt into the mattress. Exhaustion weighted her eyelids while her mind buzzed with possibilities about Amelia's demise, most importantly, the circumstances surrounding her death. By all accounts, she was well-liked. So, what would possess someone to kill her? While puzzling the facts she'd garnered thus far, Sarah drifted off to dreamland where the mysteries multiplied.

Chapter Thirteen

Sarah found herself in a dingy room with bricked walls and a dirt floor in what appeared to be a basement. Several women perched on wooden chairs, their hair neatly coifed in updos reminiscent of the early twentieth century.

"Welcome ladies," a voice boomed. A slender woman dressed in black silk stood at a lectern. "Today's meeting is one of promise. We're one step closer to getting the vote in Georgia."

The vote? Sarah thought. How had she gone from prohibition in the 1920s to the suffragette movement? The suffragette movement ended when prohibition began. There was no connection between the two. Or was there?

"Fortunately, all this prohibition nonsense is distracting the authorities from looking for those of us fighting for the vote. It seems our government will never stop trying to deny us our freedoms whether to vote or partake of alcohol."

A round of laughter tittered through the room. Sarah noticed a familiar face in the front row. Bessie Miller. Was there anything this woman wasn't involved in? She seemed to have a proclivity for the controversial and illegal. Amelia was sitting beside her. Was that what Amelia was trying to convey? Had her aunt's need to fight for the right to vote cost Amelia her life?

"Ladies, we have our work cut out for us. This state doesn't have the right to deny us what the rest of the country has ratified. We must stand firm and fight, no matter how arduous a battle it may be. I can assure you it will not be pleasant so prepare yourselves. Others have been beaten and killed. We cannot be deterred."

A round of cheers rose from the group reverberating off the brick walls.

Maybe this was the group Amelia kept referring to when she said 'help them.'

Before Sarah could contemplate further, the scene shifted to Colonial Park Cemetery. Tombstones littered the area beneath towering live oaks and barren Camillia bushes. She'd already dreamt about Amelia's burial so why was she back here again? Glancing around, Sarah caught sight of Amelia's funeral. Sarah could hear the pastor's words as Bessie's shoulders shook.

"Amelia was a fine girl with great potential who will be missed by all who loved her..."

Behind a nearby tree was a figure, one Sarah recognized. Jackson Edwards. Why was he hiding in the shadows instead of standing with the family? Granted, segregation was enforced at this time unless he was hiding because he murdered Amelia and returned to see his victim laid to rest.

Sarah looked around. She could see Amelia's headstone but there was no freshly dug earth or mound of dirt. They were having a funeral but it seemed there was no grave.

. . .

Sarah stirred from the dream, her mind cluttered as she brushed the sleep from her eyes. Danni wasn't there. She glanced at the clock on the night table, 6:37 a.m. Where was Danni? She wouldn't be up at this hour, not on purpose anyway.

Sarah slid from bed and grabbed a pad of paper and a pencil. She jotted down a few notes about her dream and went to the bathroom to dress. After changing, she padded down the stairs and found the team, along with Danni, gathered around the kitchen island discussing the video from the night before.

"Good morning," Sarah said, joining the group. "By the happy expressions, I assume you had some luck last night."

"You won't believe it!" Ralph declared.

He turned the laptop toward Sarah and hit play. She watched as a flash of light flared at the same time a crash resounded from the pantry.

"Can you play that back?" she asked.

Ralph nodded as he reset the segment. Sarah leaned in, fiddling with the necklace as she watched the replay. Something was there.

"Can you play it again but in slow motion?"

"Sure," he replied, clicking a few keys.

Squinting, Sarah watched the light particles explode across the screen. In the center was something familiar. A faint outline hovered in that split second and it resembled Amelia. "I think it's Amelia," she announced.

"You can see that?" Harry declared, staring at the screen.

"It's fuzzy," Sarah said, "but I can see the contour of a woman's face. "I'm assuming it's her."

"Any idea why she'd show up in the pantry?" Garrett asked.

"Nope. In my dreams last night, I saw her at some sort of meeting with her Aunt Bessie about women winning the vote."

"That doesn't make sense," Ralph responded. "Prohibition started after the 19th Amendment was ratified."

"That was my thought too," Sarah said. "The other part of my dream was at Colonial Park Cemetery. Everyone was there for Amelia's funeral. Oddly, Jackson Edwards was watching it from behind a tree." Sarah shared her new theory that perhaps Amelia was killed because she was involved with suffragettes.

"Nothing would surprise me," Garrett added. "What now?"

"There are some things I want to check out," Sarah said. "I need to learn more about the suffrage movement in Georgia. I'm confused about the discrepancies in the timelines between the ratification of the 19th Amendment and prohibition. I also need to find the location of Amelia's grave marker in Colonial Park Cemetery."

"We can go with you. Probably a good idea to go back and get shots of her tombstone for the final project," Harry suggested.

"When we toured the cemetery with Willow I didn't pick up on Amelia which is odd," Sarah said. "If her remains were there, she'd have made herself known to me."

"Is it possible she might have been elusive because all of us were there?" Ralph asked.

Sarah shook her head. "If I'd been that close to her body, she would have let me know. I can't explain it but anytime I'm close to where one of the spirits is buried, they get more active."

"Are you certain it was her funeral you saw in your dreams?" Garrett asked.

"I heard the pastor say her name. It was strange, there was no evidence of a recent burial, only the tombstone." Sarah said. "I've dreamt about her funeral once before but this was more detailed and it showed Jackson watching from a distance. Don't know if he was hiding due to segregation or because he was the one who killed her."

"What makes you believe he's the killer?" Harry queried.

"I keep seeing a tall, lanky fellow in my dreams. So far, I've seen him talking to Theo in his car, slinking around a back alley, and murdering Amelia."

"You're positive it's him?" Garrett asked.

"Pretty sure," she replied. "I can't get a clear look at him but he fits the image that keeps showing up."

"How much do we know about Jackson?" Ralph said.

"Only that he worked for the Millers and occasionally at the speakeasy located at the Edwards laundry establishment."

"We need to do some more research." Harry said.

"Got something!" Danni exclaimed. "It's about the suffragette movement in Georgia. Although the country ratified the 19th amendment in 1920 giving women the vote, Georgia didn't allow ladies to vote in the national election until 1922. Get this, Georgia didn't ratify the 19th amendment until February 20, 1970!"

"That explains the overlap between the suffragette movement in Georgia and the start of prohibition in 1920," Sarah replied. "Now we need to figure out how this applies to Amelia's death and where she's buried in the cemetery."

"And whether Jackson murdered her," Ralph said.

"Finding more about Amelia's burial will probably be easier than figuring out whether Jackson killed her," Garrett said.

"I think we need to contact Willow," Harry suggested. "Her knowledge about the cemetery is pretty deep. Maybe she knows where Amelia is buried."

"You guys won't believe this!" Danni hollered.

"What?" Harry queried, craning his neck to see her screen.

"Apparently, someone researched the Miller family years ago and put the info on a blog."

"How reliable can it be?" Ralph snorted. "Blogs are generally personal opinions, not factual."

Danni straightened in her seat, a scowl crinkling her eyes. "The blog was written by Willow Knightly so I'm going to take it as fact."

"Willow did the research?" Ralph exclaimed. "Why didn't she say something when we took the tour?"

"Did she know what we were looking for?" Danni asked. "Or did you just book a tour?"

Ralph slouched. "All we did was book the tour."

"Looks like we need to talk to her again," Garrett said.

"I think this counts as a point for Danni," Sarah giggled as Ralph rolled his eyes.

Harry pulled out his phone and sent Willow a text. She responded quickly and the two of them went back and forth, Harry's thumbs flying over the screen. He looked up with a broad smile. "She's on her way over."

Twenty minutes later, Willow was sitting at the kitchen island with coffee from Java City. Dallas was plopped at her feet enjoying head scratches.

"Didn't realize you all were staying at the Miller house," she smiled, her eyes scanning the room. Her brown hair was pulled back revealing tiny skulls dangling from her earlobes. "The place is looking good. Last time I was here the wood floors were dull, the plaster was chipping, and the kitchen was twenty years out of date."

"The homeowner has invested a substantial amount in the house which is why we're trying to help her out," Harry said. "What can you tell us about this place?"

"A lot," Willow grinned. "Do you want the basic history or the haunted part?"

"Both," Garrett replied.

Willow shifted on her stool. "The Miller family was one of the wealthiest in the region. They owned a huge mercantile store on East Bay Street."

She paused to sip her coffee. "The Millers seemed to have it all; a thriving business, a beautiful home, and respect from the locals. But then things changed."

"What happened?" Ralph asked.

"Not sure exactly. From what I could find in the archives and newspapers of the time, there was another family in the neighborhood who ran a laundry in the building a block back from this place." Willow continued. "The Edwards' family rented the space from the Millers and lived in the cottage across the street from this house. It's the museum with all the gingerbread."

"I went there the other day," Sarah added. "I didn't get much information except that the Edwards' were prosperous with their laundry service and that their son, Jackson, worked for the Miller's as a mechanic."

"They try not to share the seedier side of the story," Willow said. "Apparently, Jackson was a genius with automobiles and people from all over town would bring their vehicles to him for repairs. Of course, the Millers couldn't socialize with the Edwards due to their ethnicity; however, that didn't stop them from renting space to them and employing their son.

"Anyway, the Millers had a reputation for being kind-hearted people, including their niece, Amelia. Their business was thriving and things looked pretty good for them until Amelia died."

Sarah chewed her lower lip. Did Willow know Amelia was murdered and that Jackson might have been the one to kill her?

"What happened?" Harry asked.

"That's where things get weird. Supposedly, Amelia was

down at the riverfront late one night which didn't make sense since the mercantile closed at 6:00 every evening. A lady of her standing wouldn't have been down there after dark, especially alone.

"When her body was found, there was a wound to her skull. The death certificate cited the cause of death as drowning after falling and hitting her head. The strange part is the disappearance of the Edwards family shortly thereafter."

"Do people consider the two instances connected?" Garrett asked.

"It's hard to say but there's a strong possibility. The Edwards' place of business was raided a few days later where authorities found a speakeasy in the back of the building. By that time, they were gone with no trace of their whereabouts. Most people concluded they were tipped off about the raid and left town. Back then it was harder to track people."

"Or they were murdered," Sarah muttered.

Willow cocked her head. "That's a new theory. Never crossed my mind that the cops made them disappear. No one would have questioned the disappearance of a black family, especially if they were running a speakeasy."

"And no one ever suspected the Edwards' family was connected to Amelia's death?" Danni queried.

"There's been some speculation," Willow answered. "Amelia was found wearing a flapper dress which made some believe she was part of the speakeasy crowd."

The group sat in silence as Willow patted Dallas on the head.

"Do you have any more questions?" Willow asked. "I have a tour in an hour and need to get ready."

"None that I can think of," Garrett replied. "Thanks for coming over. We really appreciate it."

"No problem," she responded. "I love sharing local stories. Give me a call if you think of any other questions."

Willow scooted out the back door leaving the team pondering all she'd shared.

"Do you still think Jackson killed Amelia?" Danni asked.

"It's possible," Sarah said.

"Maybe Amelia was the one who told the police what was going on at the laundry. It would give Jackson motive to get rid of her," Ralph suggested.

"I don't think so," Sarah replied, shaking her head. "I've seen Amelia and her Aunt Bessie going to the speakeasy. They wouldn't go there and then report it. At this point, we don't know who was running it, the Millers or the Edwards. Both families were definitely involved."

"And Amelia and Jackson were friends?" Harry asked.

"Seemed like it. Now I'm questioning that theory," Sarah said.

"Didn't you say you've seen Jackson talking to what's his name, the fiancée?" Ralph queried.

"Theo," Sarah replied. "It's strange how I can recognize him but not the other guy. Like I said, the mystery man has the same build as Jackson and appears to have dark skin. Granted, I've only seen him in the dark."

"You also said this mystery man was in a state of decay," Garrett said.

"Definitely," Sarah replied, wrinkling her upper lip.

"That can cause an alteration in skin tone. Are you certain this entity has dark skin or could it be decomposition making it appear that way?" Garrett asked.

"That's a possibility too," Sarah replied, rubbing her forehead. "This is getting complicated."

"It would be great if we knew who Amelia's spirit is referring to when she says 'help them,'" Danni said. "It could be the Edwards family or the Millers."

"Exactly. I need to go back to the Edwards' house museum across the street and speak with Tilda. She was getting ready to share something scandalous that wasn't part of the tour but another couple walked in and she had to stop. I suspect this might be it," Sarah said, standing.

"I'll keep searching online," Danni said.

"I'll share all of this with Walter," Ralph stated, garnering a nasty look from Danni.

Sarah hurried across the street to the gingerbread trimmed cottage. Stepping inside, she took in the aromatic essence of an old house. Hayden Place lacked that glorious scent with all of the new plaster and paint smells.

A lovely woman with mocha skin and a broad smile appeared from the back room. "Welcome to Hayden Street Neighborhood Museum. I'm Shunta. How can I help you today?"

"Is Tilda here?"

"She's out of town. Is there something I can help you with?"

Sarah contemplated the offer for a moment. Tilda had been getting ready to share information outside of the tour script. Maybe this woman knew something too.

"Actually, do you know anything about the Edwards family that's not covered in the general tour?"

Shunta hesitated. "The museum has a script about the history to make sure everything is accurate. I'm afraid that's all I can tell you."

"Thanks anyway," Sarah replied. She left the museum and walked back across the street, her mind racing with possibilities. Obviously, the museum didn't want to discuss the seedier side of what happened with the Edwards family. Looks like the team would have to rely on other sources regarding the speakeasy.

Afternoon faded into evening. Sarah and Danni continued researching online with little success while the guys watched and rewatched segments from the previous night. With Danni's help, they managed to polish off a bottle of wine leaving Sarah feeling like a slug. After her third yawn, Sarah rubbed her eyes and slumped against the countertop.

"You look tired," Danni said.

"I am," Sarah mumbled.

"Why don't you take a walk? That'll perk you up."

"Good idea," Sarah replied. She shoved her phone in her pocket and started for the back door. "Be back in a little while."

Sarah stepped into the chilly air, a shiver rattling her frame. Pulling her jacket tighter around her, she made her way down Prince Street, past the line of cottages behind the house, and stopped at the cinder block building that once housed the laundry. A 'For Rent' sign was still perched in the front window with the home's stats and a number to call if interested. Vibrant ribbons of mango and deep purple reflected from the windows as the sun slipped behind the horizon. An oval bronze placard by the front door read 1892.

Walking to the back yard, Sarah studied the structure. There wasn't anything distinctive or special about the late 19th century building. Other than functioning as a laundry business in the twenties and being the location of an illegal speakeasy, the building had nothing of architectural significance. Even when the team had walked through it a few days prior, nothing about its original use stood out.

Sarah moved closer to the back door and stared at the antique doorknob with elaborate designs embossed on the brass surface. A deadbolt had been added for security purposes. Perhaps if she touched the knob something would appear. Sarah reached for it, jumping back when it rotated and the door creaked open. Taking a deep breath, she waited for someone to step out. Except no one did.

Sarah poked her head in the door and hollered, "Hello!" Dusk painted the walls in shadowy hues adding a layer of eeriness to the space. Stepping inside, she called out once more. "Is anyone here?"

Help them, brushed her ear.

"Who do I need to help?" Sarah asked, whirling around.

The faint sound of a saxophone wafted through the space along with the scent of cigar smoke. Sarah gasped when something grabbed her shoulder. Turning, she found a tall figure looming before her. He reeked of brine and rot making her shrink back from the offensive odor. This wasn't a living person; this was the man from her dreams. As he tilted his head, the light from the street lamp outside the window shimmered against the side of his skull where bits of flesh and bone clung. Based on the damage, there was no doubt a gunshot wound had ended his life.

Sarah's heart thumped against her ribcage as she swallowed the angst rising in her throat. Stay calm, she told herself even though her instincts screamed for her to run.

"What do you want to tell me?" she murmured, trying not to gag on the foul odor emanating from the creature.

Did me wrong! He wailed.

"Who?"

War on!

Before Sarah could ask another question, the entity lunged at her. She turned to bolt through the door when his hand caught her hair. In her haste to get away, she lurched forward and slammed the door behind her. She heard a cracking sound and turned to see the remnants of the creature's hand lying on the ground with a few strands of her hair entwined in its rotting flesh. When the fingers began to move, Sarah ran down Prince Street, around the corner, and up the back stairs into Hayden Place. Safely inside the kitchen, she leaned over with her hands on her knees. Dallas dashed toward her planting his paws on her hands.

"What's going on?" Garrett asked.

Straightening, Sarah looked up and exhaled. "Kinda ran into one of the ghosts," she replied.

"Let's get you something to drink and you can share what happened."

Everyone had stopped talking and stared at Sarah.

"What the heck happened?" Danni asked.

"Had a run in with Half-Headed Fred," Sarah said, accepting a glass of wine from Garrett. She took a swig and settled on one of the bar stools.

"Judging by the look on your face, it wasn't a pleasant encounter," Danni responded.

"Don't think there's anything pleasant about this one," Sarah grumbled, taking another sip. "I don't know what's worse, his half-headed appearance or the disgusting odor he emits. Either way, he's angry and keeps trying to take it out on me."

Sarah shared everything that had happened, including severing his hand when she slammed the door on it.

"Do you think it's still there?" Harry asked with excitement.

"I have no idea," Sarah grimaced. "Didn't hang around."

"Let's check it out," Ralph said to Harry, grabbing his phone.

The two men rushed out the back door leaving Garrett, Danni, and Sarah staring at each other.

"Glad someone is happy about all this," Sarah huffed.

Garrett rubbed her shoulders as he kissed the top of her head. "They'll be even happier if they find the severed hand."

Danni's upper lip wrinkled into a sneer. "You guys aren't right."

"Aside from being scared half to death, did you garner any information?" Garrett queried.

"He repeated the phrase 'did me wrong' and also said 'war on.' Except there wasn't a war in the 20s."

"That is bizarre," Danni said. "Is it possible he's a random spirit from another time who also needs a dreamist to help him?"

Sarah sighed. "I feel like he's affiliated with this case. He's been showing up in my dreams almost as frequently as Amelia."

"Which leads to the question, which ghost is doing the haunting?" Garrett said.

Sarah shrugged and took another sip of wine.

A few minutes later, Harry and Ralph trudged through the back door.

"Nothing," Ralph announced, his face sullen.

"You didn't actually believe it would still be there?" Danni asked.

"In our line of work, you have to hope," Harry replied.

A dull ache squeezed Sarah's skull. "My head hurts," she announced. "I'm going upstairs to lie down for a little while."

"Do you want to take Dallas in case the ghost returns?" Garrett asked.

"That would be great," she said. "Come on, little fella"

Dallas followed Sarah upstairs and hopped onto the bed as she rested her head against the pillow. Stroking his soft coat, she closed her eyes and took in a few deep breaths in an effort to calm herself. The pounding in her head began to subside as Dallas curled closer. Within minutes she drifted off.

. . .

Two shadowy figures stood at the end of the street arguing. A nearby gas lamp flickered, throwing light onto one man's face. Theodore Warren. Inching closer, Sarah leaned in, hoping to hear what the two men were discussing. There must be something relevant about it or the ghost wouldn't have brought her here.

"It was an accident!" the taller one proclaimed. "I was just trying to scare her like you said. How was I to know she'd drown?" He rubbed the scratches on his hand as he said the words. Amelia had clawed at whoever had killed her, Sarah thought. It's a shame they didn't have DNA testing back then. Of course, her being underwater probably would have washed the evidence from under her nails.

"Nevertheless, you did kill her and now her father is trying to keep things quiet until after the election. So don't go bragging about it to your buddies."

The lanky man straightened. "What's it worth to ya?"

"Excuse me?" Theo growled.

"You heard me. How much is my silence worth?"

"Are you threatening me?"

"Not at all," he replied sarcastically. "Consider it more of a business transaction. I have something of great value to you. Occurs to me it might be worth a little cash to keep my mouth shut."

"What do you plan to do? Tell the cops you murdered Amelia Danbury?" Theo's head tilted back in a laugh. "They'll arrest you on the spot."

"I'll tell 'em you told me to do it," the other man shot back.

"And you think they'd believe you? Someone of your *type* wouldn't be taken seriously? The authorities always believe men like me. People like you are worthless in the eyes of the law."

The gangly one balled his fist and drew back his arm. Theo grabbed him by the wrist and twisted a yelp out of him. "Don't even think of hitting me. I'll have you thrown in jail for assault."

"And I'll tell 'em everything," he sputtered, wrenching his arm free.

"Go ahead," Theo retorted. "I'm not giving you another cent. You botched up the job with Amelia."

"Little tramp got what she deserved, if you ask me."

A loud thwack echoed down the alleyway as Theo's hand landed across the man's face. "Don't ever speak of her in that manner."

"Fine," he muttered, rubbing his jaw. "But I can't promise to keep my mouth shut about the other stuff. I'll expect payment tomorrow. A thousand is a good start. Meet me at the riverfront after midnight. Place is pretty dead at that hour," he snickered as he skulked away.

Other dealings? Sarah thought. Had he killed someone else? He definitely had the same build as the ghost who'd been haunting her. The one with part of his head blown off. Sarah shivered as the air turned frigid, making her teeth chatter. Looking around, she realized Theo and the other man were gone.

Why was she still here? Rubbing her upper arms, she turned to find the half-headed man standing behind her, a devious smile wrinkling his remaining eye. Sarah squinted, trying to make out what remained of his features. Night's veil made it difficult to tell if it was Jackson or if the corpse's skin was darkened from the decay and lack of light.

"What do you want to tell me?" she asked.

"Didn't deserve this," he uttered, his raspy voice and fetid odor making Sarah cringe.

Maybe if she reasoned with him, he'd reveal more. "No one deserves to be killed," she responded.

"Stupid wench deserved it!" he screamed, bits of putrid spittle sprinkling Sarah's face.

Recoiling, she stepped back and released the breath she'd been holding. She needed to stay calm and get his name. "Who are you?"

"Your greatest fear," he growled, stepping closer.

Sarah jolted from her sleep and glanced at the time. An hour had passed yet it felt like only a few minutes. She hadn't meant to fall asleep. Dallas stirred and stretched. Sitting up, Sarah smoothed her hair and glanced around the room. All she needed was a simple name, something to solidify what was happening in her dreams. Just once she wanted to get the answers necessary to put the spirits to rest. Aggravated, she slid from bed.

"Come on Dallas. We need to tell the others what I dreamed. Maybe they can figure this out because my mind is mush." He answered with a 'woof' and scooted out the door with Sarah in tow.

"How are you feeling?" Danni asked, as Sarah entered the kitchen.

"Annoyed," Sarah replied, grabbing a water bottle. "Fell asleep."

"Any good dreams?" Harry asked.

"Not exactly. Half-Headed Fred definitely killed Amelia, not that we had any doubts."

"Was it Jackson?" Danni said.

"All I know is the guy with half his head missing definitely did it. I woke up before I could determine his identity."

"So, same problem as before," Ralph said.

"Pretty much. But I heard the conversation between him

and Theo. It seems Theo employed this man which means he's involved too."

"Except Amelia's death was ruled an accident by the coroner. We won't be able to find any evidence of foul play," Danni said. "Especially after all these years."

"We don't need hard evidence," Sarah replied. "If I can figure out the identity of the ghost who murdered Amelia and any information about why he's haunting me too, we'll be able to wrap up this case."

"We've caught a few things on video but nothing substantial. Let me go back through it and see if something makes more sense now," Ralph said, tapping the keys on his laptop.

The evening whizzed by with everyone looking for evidence online about the haunting of Sarah's dreams and Hayden Place. Bits and pieces popped up but nothing that pulled the information together. After losing the election, Danbury returned to his law practice and didn't pursue politics again. Basically, he disappeared from public view. No investigation was conducted regarding Amelia's death due to the coroner's ruling. Nothing more was available except the raid on the Edwards' place of business with the illegal speakeasy found in the back of the laundry.

Sarah was beginning to believe Amelia's repeated phrase, 'help them' referred to the Edwards' family. Who else could it be? They disappeared before the raid and were never heard from again. The only person from the family to appear was Jackson at Amelia's funeral. This, and the apparition in her dreams, led Sarah to the conclusion Jackson was responsible for Amelia's demise and possibly his family's disappearance.

Eventide wrapped the house in sinewy shadows while the guys prepared for another night of filming. Sarah's head was beginning to ache.

"I'm going upstairs," she said to Garrett. "My head is hurting again."

Leaning in, he planted a kiss on her lips. "Hope you feel better."

Sarah flashed a smile and jaunted up the stairs to her room. She found her friend tapping away on the computer. Danni stopped typing and peered over her dollar store spectacles.

"You're not staying with the guys?"

"My head hurts," Sarah replied. "I just want to lie down."

"You've been complaining of headaches a lot lately. Do you think it's the double haunting?"

Sarah shook her head. "Probably all the construction dust."

After washing up and changing into her pj's, Sarah crawled into bed and pulled the covers over her shoulders.

"G'night," she said, closing her eyes.

"Sweet dreams," Danni replied as her fingers tapped the keys.

"Humph," Sarah grunted. "Not likely but thanks anyway."

Despite the pounding in her skull, Sarah managed to drift off to the back alley of her mind.

A street lamp flickered from the corner, casting shadows across the face of the lanky fellow. Sarah craned her neck to see him clearly but to no avail. His face was dark and his build was that of Jackson Edwards.

He did this, reverberated in Sarah's ear. Turning, she saw Amelia hovering behind her, her expression shrouded in doom.

"Are you saying Jackson murdered you?"

Amelia's head shifted from left to right as if she was moving in slow motion.

"If it wasn't Jackson Edwards, who killed you?"

Amelia's bloated arm rose, shreds of sodden skin flaking

from her flesh. Her finger pointed in the direction of the man. Why couldn't Sarah make out his features? Perhaps Amelia didn't have the energy needed to accurately portray the images.

Sarah started to speak when fingernails dug into her shoulder from behind. With a screech, she whirled around to see a shadowy form towering over her. The fetid odor of rotting flesh let Sarah know it was the half-headed guy. Holding her breath, she tried to step away but he held her there.

"Didn't deserve this," he growled.

"What happened?" Sarah managed to mutter.

There was either a great deal of power or hate for a spirit to have enough energy to hold her in place. Sarah feared the latter was fueling his strength which didn't bode well for her.

"Did me wrong!" the entity bellowed, sending Sarah tumbling backwards, her head smacking against the ground.

Blinking away the stars parading across her vision, Sarah found herself in Colonial Park Cemetery. Bessie and Joe stood at the spot where the funeral had taken place.

"Scoundrel," Bessie sniffled. "Won't even tell us where she's buried so we can visit her."

Joe patted Bessie's hand that rested in the crook of his elbow. "Your brother has his reasons, I'm sure."

"Joseph Miller, don't patronize me! You know he blames us for her death even though it was an accident. And having her body buried without the benefit of her family in attendance..." A sob choked back Bessie's ability to finish her sentence.

"I don't mean to upset you my dear, but George and Sophia are her parents. I'm certain her brothers were at the private memorial too."

"They might be her family by blood but none of them ever gave two bits about her. If they had, she would've been given more opportunities as an independent woman instead of being forced into an arranged marriage to that dolt,

Theodore Warren. We're more family to her than they ever were."

"All that matters is that we hold her memory in our hearts. Her body might not be here but we have a tombstone in her honor. We can visit as often as we like and pay tribute to her life."

Bessie dabbed her eyes with a black rimmed hankie. "It's still not right but I suppose it's all we have."

"Let's head home. We have much to do if we're going to keep things from getting worse."

"Please don't remind me. I dread what awaits us. I'll never forgive that wretched brother of mine for causing all of this."

Sarah watched as they made their way along the brick pathway, through the iron gates with the eagle perched overhead, and down the street toward their automobile. She could feel the weight of their despair over the loss of their beloved niece and yet there was something more. A foreboding seemed to override their grief.

Sarah wanted to follow them but they motored down the street in a cloud of dust. Amelia's words rang out in her head. *Help them.* So, it *was* her aunt and uncle she was referring to. The question was, why did they need help? Were they in danger?

The scene shifted again. Sarah was standing in a lavishly decorated space replete with silk curtains and a large mahogany desk centered in the room. Shelves of books towered against one wall while paintings of pastoral scenes in gilded frames covered the others. Cigar smoke wafted through the room. Touching her necklace, a memory played across Sarah's mind. She'd been in this room before. This was George Danbury's office. The one where he scolded Amelia about her refusal to wed Theodore.

Danbury paced back and forth, the cigar dangling from his

mouth. A knock at the door halted him as he removed the cigar and called out, "Come in."

Theodore entered the room, his hair slicked neatly across his head and a confident grin on his face.

"Good afternoon, sir," he said with a nod.

"Don't know that I'd call it good," Danbury replied, placing the cigar in a polished stone ashtray on the desk. "Sit down, Theodore."

The two men sat across from each other as a thin trail of smoke snaked between them. George leaned his elbows on the desk and folded his hands together.

"I don't know how else to say this so I'll be blunt. Amelia is dead."

"Sir?" Theodore responded, trying to act surprised. "When? How?"

"Accident. She fell into the river and drowned. Never was much of a swimmer."

Theo slumped back in his chair and rubbed his forehead feigning sorrow. "When is the funeral?" he mumbled.

"There won't be one," he replied, gruffly. "Elections are coming up soon. I can't afford to be away from the campaign trail."

"She's your daughter," Theo said, furrowing his brow. "This could be a boost for votes. Nobody wants a grieving father to lose his bid for congress so soon after the death of his child."

"I disagree," he retorted. "Don't need any bad press this close to election day. She was found in the Savannah River. There'd be too many questions about why she was there and how she drowned. You're in charge of my campaign and I expect you to keep this quiet until after the polls have closed. Do I make myself clear?"

"Yes, sir," Theo replied in a hushed tone.

"You may go," Mr. Danbury said, dismissing him.

Theodore rose from the chair and walked to the door, a slight smile creeping across his face. The idiot was none the wiser to the circumstances surrounding Amelia's death. Danbury needed the Warrens as much as they needed him. If he tried to fire Theo, he'd reveal his secrets. If all went well, he wouldn't have to use that information. He'd be able to keep it buried along with his involvement in Amelia's demise. This was turning out better than if he'd married her.

Sarah shuddered when sticky fingers grasped the back of her neck. By the scent of decay, she knew it was the mysterious spirit.

"Did me wrong," he groaned.

The clammy feel of his rotting skin against her own made her want to wretch. Ducking, she was able to break his hold and spin around. Blood was splattered across his sallow skin and his remaining eye practically dangled from its socket. Repulsed, Sarah screamed, wrenching her from the dream.

Sweat covered her body as she sat up in bed, the feel of the corpse's touch still adhering to her body.

"Ugh," Danni moaned as she stirred. "How can it be morning already?"

"I'm glad for it," Sarah grumbled, massaging the back of her neck.

"Anything new in your dreams?"

"Other than a decomposing corpse that wreaks of rot and wants me dead, nope."

"Eww...that's gross."

"Which is why I'm getting in the shower. He also has a tendency to spit when he speaks and I need to wash it off. My skin is crawling."

Danni's upper lip crinkled in disgust. "Thanks for the

imagery," she said. "I'm going downstairs for coffee. I need to erase that image from my mind."

"Good luck," Sarah replied, closing the bathroom door behind her.

Danni had it easy. Images from someone else's description were much milder than witnessing the gore yourself. Turning the shower knobs, Sarah waited for the water to heat before stepping beneath the spray. Pricklets of hot water cascaded across her skin, washing away the feel of the corpse's touch.

This was the hardest part of being a dreamist. The gruesome scenes, the stench of death, the tacky feel of decomposing flesh against her skin. Even though it all took place in her head, the effects lingered long after waking.

When she felt as clean as she could get, Sarah turned off the water and wrapped a towel around her. The shower curtain fluttered. Her chest seized as she waited to see if it was a heating vent causing the ripple or something undead. When her breath puffed before her, she knew it was the latter.

Inhaling, Sarah grabbed the edge of the shower curtain. Before she could pull it aside, a hand with graying skin clinging loosely to its bones wrapped around her wrist. A scream escaped her lips as she slipped backwards, fell against the shower wall and to the floor. Seconds later, the bathroom door opened.

"Sarah!" Garrett yelled. "Are you okay?" he drew the shower curtain back and reached in to help her up.

Her knees shook as she rose to her feet still clasping the towel around her.

"Are you hurt?" he asked.

"Only my pride which is as bruised as my hip will be," she grumbled, kneading the area where she'd landed.

"What happened?"

"Let me get dressed and I'll fill you in when I get

downstairs."

"I'll fix you some tea," he said, concern radiating from his stare.

"Add a splash of something to it. I get the feeling it's going to be a busy day."

"You're getting close to the answers, aren't you?"

Sarah nodded. "I'm getting close to something but I'm not sure it makes sense."

Ten minutes later, Sarah sat at the kitchen island sipping a cup of steaming Earl Gray while the team gathered around her wide-eyed and anxious to hear what secrets she had to reveal. After filling them in, she sighed.

"A rotting hand grabbed you in the shower?" Danni asked, her expression sour. "Gives a whole new feel to the Psycho shower scene. Think I'll wait until I get home before I bathe."

"Don't be silly," Sarah scolded. "The ghosts aren't after you. They're trying to get my attention and doing a pretty good job."

"We have something special to share that might shed some light on all of this," Ralph said.

Sarah cocked her head as he turned the laptop around and pressed play. The previous night's footage from the front parlor flashed across the screen. Sarah gasped when a grainy figure in the far corner emerged, droplets of water falling from the scraps of fringe hanging from the hem of her dress as she floated toward the camera's lens.

"Oh my gosh," Sarah muttered. "It's Amelia."

"Seriously?" Ralph exclaimed, craning his neck to look. "You can tell?"

"Yes. It's grainy and a bit distorted but I recognize the dress. She was wearing it the night she was murdered."

"Looks like a shadow to me," Danni added.

"I agree." Harry said. "But it's a distinct shadow which is

significant. The viewers will be able to identify it as something supernatural."

"You guys can't see the details?" Sarah asked.

They all shook their heads as Ralph backed the video up and hit play. Sarah watched as a very distinctive Amelia drifted across the camera's path. How could they not see her? Without warning, a spectral face popped up sending Sarah stumbling off the stool.

"What the heck was that?" she asked.

"You mean the flash?" Ralph said with an impish smile. "We were excited about that too. It indicates a burst of energy which means spirit activity."

"But the face was...alarming."

"What face?" Garrett asked.

"The one that popped up on the screen. Don't tell me you didn't see that either."

Ralph replayed it.

The same ghastly visage with its sallow skin and rotting lips flashed on the screen. "There," Sarah pointed. "It's a man."

Everyone stared at her as if she had two heads.

"It's only a burst of light," Harry said.

Sarah buried her face in her hands. Was her imagination causing her to see images from her dreams on the film clips? Now more than ever, she wanted to speak with Ola. And she wanted straightforward answers, not riddles.

"Are you alright?" Garrett whispered in her ear as he rubbed her back.

"No, I'm not," Sarah spat. "I'm sick of all this! I need explanations and all I get are ambiguities."

Everyone was silent until Danni spoke. "Please don't get angry with me, but you probably need to consult the book."

"I want answers not brainteasers!"

"The answers are there and we're all here to help decipher

the meaning," Danni said calmly. "Go get the book. Maybe we can figure out why you're seeing things on the screen the rest of us can't."

"Fine," Sarah grumbled. She dashed up the stairs, retrieved her *Dreamist* book with its worn brown cover and gilded lettering, and returned to the kitchen.

"Anyone want to give it a go?" she asked, tossing it on the marble surface of the island.

"I'll have a look," Harry said, gently lifting the brown leather tome.

He flipped through, scanning several pages. Dallas plopped at Sarah's feet; his brown eyes fixed on her. She reached down to pet him when Harry gasped.

"Think I found something."

"Already?" Sarah and Danni said in unison.

"You've told us you get images from touching things that belonged to the deceased. Does this apply?"

Each dreamist has her own skills, tis true,
Give heed to the things that can help you,
Note the charms and baubles that in lieu,
Can conquer fear and see you through.

Garrett and Sarah exchanged glances. How had Harry found that particular passage so quickly? And did it say what Sarah thought it did? Was it referring to the necklace Ola gifted her? She still didn't understand the specific meanings behind the charms but hopefully she'd discover that sooner than later.

"What's going on?" Harry asked. "You two look like you just saw a ghost."

"In a sense," Sarah replied, pulling the chain from under her sweatshirt.

"What's that?" Harry asked.

"A necklace that belonged to Grams," Garrett replied. "She wore it every day."

"That's sweet of you to give it to Sarah," Ralph said.

"He didn't," Sarah responded. "Ola did."

"Huh?" Ralph grunted.

Garrett blew out a long breath. "Grams never took that necklace off. She was buried in it."

Shocked expressions spread through the room like gale force winds across the ocean.

"If she was buried in it, how come Sarah's wearing it?" Ralph asked.

"We don't understand how it happened," Garrett said. "We found it at the house before we left to come here."

Sarah fingered the charms, goosebumps parading across her skin. "The strange part is, I can't take it off."

"That is seriously weird," Ralph groaned.

"I'm wondering if that passage has some connection to the necklace," Sarah said.

Harry reread the quote again. "Possibly."

"Maybe some of the other passages will make more sense now that we know about the necklace," Danni said.

"There's a problem." Sarah replied. "This is my *Dreamist* book so why would there be something about a necklace from another dreamist's family?"

Danni shook her head. "You got me on that one. Maybe all dreamists have a necklace that's passed down and since you don't have one from your family, Ola gave you hers."

"I don't mean to dismiss this topic, but we should focus on what the ghosts are trying to tell us," Harry said. "Cheryl needs answers about why they're haunting the place. We're getting great footage and Sarah's dreams are providing valuable information but there still aren't any concrete correlations."

"Harry's right. We have to focus on the ghosts, not the mystery behind the necklace or why I can see details on film clips you guys can't." Sarah added. "Let me view the footage again from last night. Maybe it will trigger something from my dreams."

They cued the video and hit play. Sarah scrutinized every aspect of it. Once again, Amelia appeared in a state of decay, her ragged flapper dress clinging to her soggy corpse. That's when Sarah noticed it. A second shadow hovering right behind Amelia's image.

"What's that?" she asked, pointing at the screen.

The guys leaned in to look.

"Oh my gosh," Harry muttered. "How did we miss that?"

"Looks like another figure but it could be a shard of light from the streetlamp outside," Ralph offered.

Garrett shook his head. "Nope. After the first night of filming, I made sure the windows were completely covered. No way any exterior lights could have infiltrated that space."

"Can you make this bigger?" Sarah queried.

"Sure." Ralph clicked a few buttons and the computer enlarged the section of the video.

Sarah gasped. "That's him. That's the guy I keep seeing in my dreams."

"Who is he?" Ralph asked.

"Not sure, I've only seen him in the shadows. Up to this point I believed it was Jackson Edwards. He has the same build and height. But now I can see this man is Caucasian."

"You couldn't decipher that before now?" Harry said.

"No," Sarah replied, sitting straighter. "The few times I got a decent look at him; his skin appeared to be dark which led me to believe it was Jackson. Granted, I usually encountered him at night or in dark spaces. Sarah fiddled with the charms when an image popped into her head. "Just remembered something! In my dream, when I asked Amelia if Jackson was the one who murdered her, she shook her head no."

"If the other ghost isn't Jackson, who is he?" Harry asked.

203

"If we can answer that, we'll likely solve this mystery," Sarah replied.

"I'll get online and see what I can find about anyone affiliated with the Millers," Danni offered.

"Check into the Edwards family as well," Harry added. "From all accounts, they disappeared before the raid. When the feds arrived, the place was empty with only the liquor and the furnishings in the building."

"Where'd you get that tidbit of information?" Danni queried.

Harry looked at Ralph and then back at Danni before answering. "Walter shared it with us."

Danni crossed her arms over her chest, a scowl rumpling her face. "And when were you planning on telling me?"

"Didn't know we were supposed to," Ralph said timidly.

Danni narrowed her eyes as she spoke. "All information is to be shared with the team."

"But your wager with..." Ralph started when Danni cut him off.

"The bet between Walter and me doesn't allow for withholding information.

"Got it," Ralph said. "Share everything."

With a nod, Danni snatched her laptop and left the room.

"Now what?" Harry asked.

"I'd like to view more of the videos," Sarah offered. "Maybe something else will trigger images from my dreams."

"I know we said we should focus on the haunting and not the necklace but what if the necklace is the key to solving this quicker?" Garrett said.

"Do you really think that's wise?" Sarah queried. "I know we don't have an official time limit on this project but you guys have to get back to work at some point. Figuring this out should be a priority for everyone involved."

The guys exchanged looks.

"She's right," Ralph said.

"I have to agree with her on this one, Dunc."

"What about the quote from the book? Sounds as if it's related to the necklace," Garrett said.

"Why do you keep harping on the necklace?" Sarah exclaimed. "Whatever is written in my *Dreamist* book obviously has nothing to do with the necklace. It's only a coincidence. When Ola's ready she'll let me know what it means." Sarah closed her eyes and exhaled. "I'm sorry. I didn't mean to yell at you. This house has so many secrets and I can't focus on one long enough to figure out what's going on. Add in the nonsense with this blasted necklace and I feel like a merry-go-round for the dead."

Sarah's chest constricted. Garret looked like a wounded child. What possessed her to go off on him like that? Then again, he'd latched on to this necklace nonsense when he should be focusing on the ghosts. Maybe her little scene helped get him back on track. The idea made her feel better whether it was accurate or not.

Pushing back from the island, she slid from the stool. "I'm going for a walk. Maybe if I spend some time in the neighborhood something will reveal itself."

"Take Dallas with you," Garrett suggested.

"Thanks," she replied with a slight smile. "Come on buddy, let's go for a walk."

Dallas scurried ahead of her to the front door and waited, his tail wagging. They made their way down the street lined with townhouses in the same architectural style of the original Victorian homes on the block. A cool wind ruffled Sarah's hair and crept down her jacket and shirt. Dallas trotted at her side gazing up at her every so often as if waiting for a command.

Her head was beginning to ache again. Probably the stress.

She was so tired of having to deal with the mysteries in her dreams and Garrett's need to know about everything related to them. The battle raging between her heart and her mind was interfering with her ability to focus on what the spirits were trying to reveal. Deep down she knew Garrett loved her yet she felt as if she was nothing more than a cell tower for the undead. How was she supposed to reconcile all of this and help two different ghosts move on?

Sarah and Dallas curved around to the street behind Hayden Place. More townhomes lined both sides of the road like soldiers in formation. These buildings were newer. What a shame, she thought. The original structures had probably been torn down to make way for modern construction.

Dallas sniffed a stray branch stretching from a hedge of boxwoods edging the sidewalk. A low growl pierced the air as his fur bristled. Sarah tensed. Was there a rodent in the bushes or something else? Without thinking her hand went to the chain around her neck, gently brushing the charms.

That's when she noticed it. For a split second, the houses before her vacillated into an empty lot and then reappeared. It was more of a hiccup of the brain than an actual vision except Dallas was still focused on whatever was hiding in the hedge.

"Hello?" she called out.

Silence encompassed her. Looking around, she realized they were the only ones on the street. No people, no cars driving past, not even a bird chirping. Then it occurred to her. This hadn't been a road in the 1920s, it was the alleyway behind the Edwards' laundry business. Without warning, the stray boxwood branch morphed into a skeletal hand and latched onto Sarah's ankle, its razorlike nails cutting into her skin. She screeched in pain as Dallas lunged for the thing, teeth bared. As soon as his jaws locked onto the decomposing limb, it vanished.

Did me wrong, wafted on the autumn breeze chilling Sarah to the bone.

Terrified, she raced toward Prince Street. As if sensing where she was going, Dallas ran ahead of her and stopped behind the former laundry building where the Edwards once did business. She half expected to see the disembodied hand crawling across the gravel parking area.

The sage green exterior with black shutters and white trim emphasized the lack of architectural glamor seen on so many of the surrounding homes. The property was nothing more than a postage stamp lot with the front porch edging the road. How the Edwards had managed to run a speakeasy and a laundry business in such a small place was baffling. Reaching out, Sarah touched the corner of the house.

A pulse of electricity ran up her arm, knocking her to the ground. Dallas ran to her side, his velvety tongue lapping her cheek.

"I'm okay, buddy. Just lost my balance is all," she mumbled, pushing herself up. An image had accompanied the shock. It lingered in her mind like an etching on glass. Jackson Edwards was dressed in coveralls holding a large wrench in his hand. He was talking to another fellow, one just as tall and lean. The image had flashed quickly, and although the other man was familiar, she wasn't sure who he was.

"Just once, I'd like a haunting to be easy," she groaned. "Come on, Dallas. I've had enough fresh air. Let's go share this with the others."

Sarah hurried back to the house, frustrated she couldn't even escape the entities on a walk. Most of her dreamist encounters happened while she was sleeping. Now they seemed to come out of nowhere. But why?

She stood before Hayden Place and studied the intricacy of the fretwork and architectural details. It was like layers of decorative icing on a three-tier box cake. Movement in the third-floor window caught her eye. Must be one of the guys, she thought as she waved. Except Dallas charged up the porch stairs, barking and scratching at the front door. Something was amiss. Garrett opened it and the little dog dashed inside, his barks echoing from the staircase in the hallway. Her chest tightened. It wasn't one of the men she'd seen in the window, it was something ethereal.

Sarah rushed past Garrett and up the steps to the third floor, her lungs screaming from the sprint to the upstairs landing. She really needed to get back to her running regimen. Sarah found Dallas snarling at the baseboards below the window in the third-floor bedroom that used to be Amelia's.

"What is it?" Garrett asked, appearing in the doorway. "Do you see anything?"

Her heart thumped in her ears as she noticed a shimmering spot on the floor next to Dallas. Kneeling down, she ran her hand across it.

"It's wet," Sarah said.

Garrett looked up at the ceiling. "No sign of a leak."

"Amelia," Sarah muttered. "She was here."

"You saw her?"

"When I was standing outside. I thought it was one of you guys. Then Dallas went crazy and bolted inside when you opened the door."

"What does the water on the floor have to do with it?"

"She drowned, remember?"

"And she's manifesting in a physical way?" Garret shook his head. "This is definitely an intense haunting. No wonder Cheryl couldn't brush it off as faulty plumbing."

"Hadn't thought about the ghost turning on faucets. Makes more sense now."

"We should go downstairs and tell the others."

They started down the steps. As they passed Sarah's room on the second floor, Danni popped her head out. "Everything okay?" she asked.

"Wanna join us in the kitchen while I share my latest ghost encounters?" Sarah asked.

"Not particularly, but I have a bet to win so I don't have much choice," Danni moaned.

Danni followed them to the kitchen where Harry and Ralph were huddled around the computer screen.

"Thanks, Walter," Ralph said.

Danni scowled. "What did he want?"

"Found some more info on the Edwards' family," Ralph replied. "Apparently, they relocated to Colorado under a different name."

"That couldn't have been cheap," Garrett said.

"Especially with new identities. Not sure how they worked it out but they set up a neighborhood grocery in a little town near Boulder."

"I'm surprised Walter was able to locate that kind of information," Danni said, sarcastically. "How reliable is his source?"

"Don't ask me," Ralph replied. "All I know is he's rarely wrong."

"But he is wrong sometimes," Danni retorted.

"Did he give you any information to help us with the haunted aspect of all this?" Sarah asked. "We already knew the Edwards disappeared and now we know where. But that doesn't resolve the reason behind the haunting."

"The only thing he said was they moved to Colorado, opened a new business, and their son Jackson went on to own a couple of garages. He married and had two kids."

"Looks like we still have some work to do but we're getting closer," Garrett said. "By the way, we had a visitor upstairs."

"Who?" Harry asked.

"I saw someone in the window when I was standing outside," Sarah replied. "Dallas must have sensed it and went darting to the third floor. When Garrett and I got there, we found a wet spot on the floor beneath the window where I'd seen the figure standing."

"Do you know who it was?" Harry queried.

"It had to be Amelia since there was water on the floor," Sarah responded. "Makes sense," Ralph said.

"I had another bizarre occurrence while I was walking," Sarah continued. She talked about the skeletal hand grabbing her ankle and how it disappeared when Dallas grabbed it. "Then I went to the old laundry building. When I touched it, I got a quick flash of Jackson Edwards and another fellow."

"Do you know who the other guy was?" Harry asked.

"Not exactly, but I recognized him."

Danni cleared her throat. "I found something that might add to this new information. Well, my friend, Dave found it, but still, it counts for me."

"What is it?" Sarah asked.

"Apparently, the records office has archives with files of miscellaneous documents. There was a transfer of ten thousand dollars from Joseph Miller to Jared Edwards, Jackson's father."

"Are you serious?" Ralph said.

"What was it for?" Garrett queried.

"It doesn't say but it's dated the day before the police raid on the Edwards' laundry."

"Let me get this straight," Ralph said. "Amelia's body was found floating in the river. Then the Millers gave the Edwards ten grand and they disappeared before their business was raided for illegal liquor."

"That's the timeline," Danni responded.

"But I saw Jackson hiding behind a tree during Amelia's memorial at Colonial Park Cemetery which was after the raid.

He must have stayed behind for the service and joined his family later," Sarah said.

"Unless he really was the murderer," Danni suggested. "What if the Millers didn't know he killed Amelia? Just because he joined his family later in Colorado doesn't mean he didn't do it. Especially, if he was still in town for the memorial. Maybe this unidentified man in your dreams knew about it so Jackson killed him too."

"Except Amelia indicated in my last dream that he didn't kill her." Sarah rubbed her eyes with the heels of her hands. She hated the idea of Jackson's guilt resurfacing. "This is getting more complicated instead of leading us to the truth."

"Maybe not," Harry replied. "We know there was a raid and the Millers and Edwards must have known it was coming. Otherwise, they wouldn't have made arrangements for the Edwards' to leave town. Jackson wasn't the killer according to your most recent dreamscape. Sounds like he hung around to say goodbye to his friend before starting a new life in Colorado."

"If we can identify the mystery corpse in my dreams, we'll unravel the truth of what happened to Amelia and finally put this thing to rest," Sarah said with a shiver.

"What do we do now?" Ralph asked.

"I don't know about you guys but I'm chilled from being outside," Sarah replied. "I'm going upstairs to soak in the tub."

"Take your time. We'll keep looking for more info on the Edwards family," Garrett said.

With a nod, Sarah left the room. Climbing the stairs, she went into the bathroom and searched the vanity. Sure enough, a bottle of lavender bubble bath was stashed behind a few rolls of toilet paper and an extra bottle of shampoo. The nickel-plated knobs squealed as Sarah turned them. Steam wafted through the air as she filled the tub and added the lavender scented suds. Waves of bubbles topped the water like meringue on a pie.

Slipping into the steaming water, Sarah leaned her head against the edge, and closed her eyes. Nothing like a long soak in a bubble crested claw foot tub. The hot water encapsulated her body, easing the tension from her muscles and consciousness from her mind.

Theodore Warren stood in an office lavishly furnished with leather chairs, a burled walnut desk, and a spectacular view of Savannah.

"She is to be frightened, not harmed. Do you understand?" Theo told the man standing in front of him.

"Yeah, I got it," the man spat. He was tall and slender like a pine tree. A scar zigzagged beneath his left eye and above his beak-like nose which had obviously been broken at some point in his life.

"Eddie, don't screw this up or I'll have your head," Theo called out as the man turned to leave.

Rolling his eyes, Eddie smirked. "I heard you. No need to worry. All I gotta do is scare the girl. No problem."

Theo eased into his chair as Eddie left the room. Hopefully, he hadn't made a mistake involving him in this. But Theo needed someone ruthless right now. At least if something did go wrong, Eddie would take the fall for it. No one would ever connect a man like him to Theodore Warren. A wicked smile curled his lips. Once Amelia realized life with him was safer than living with her aunt and uncle, she'd come running back. Even better, Mr. Danbury, would be impressed he'd won Amelia's heart. It would secure a position for him in the D.C. office when Danbury won the election. Theo's plan was foolproof. When his marriage to Amelia

Danbury was secured, his future would be one of prosperity and success.

After Eddie got the job done, Theo would visit Amelia. No doubt, she'd listen to reason and agree to his proposal. Everyone would attribute her initial refusal as nothing more than nerves.

Sarah blinked and found herself at the riverfront. A symphony of crickets blended with the baritone serenade of bullfrogs in a cacophony of late-night clatter. Two men emerged from an automobile parked by the edge of the woods. Squinting, Sarah tried to determine their identities but they were too far away. A flash of light accompanied by a pop made her jump. The taller figure crumpled to the ground.

Moving closer, Sarah hid behind a small building and watched as the man grabbed the shoulders of the guy lying in the dirt. He lugged the form into the backseat of the vehicle, got behind the wheel, and motored off.

War on, echoed through her mind.

Sarah stirred. She was in the tub. The water had grown tepid and her neck ached. Brushing the hair from her face, she fidgeted with the key charm around her neck. An image of the automobile popped into her head. It was the same one she'd seen in the alleyway and also at Hayden Place. Theodore's car.

He was the one who shot the guy in her dream! Unless someone else was driving his car. Not likely. Which led to the question, who did he kill and why? It was obvious Theo was a self-absorbed louse, but a murderer? He didn't seem to have the gumption to do something that significant. Sarah got out of the tub and dressed. She hurried to the bedside table and jotted down a few notes. A name flashed in her mind. Eddie. She knew the name. She'd heard it in one of her other dreamscapes.

Perhaps the team could find out if Theo had ever been convicted of a crime. She smiled. This might be the bit of information they'd been waiting for.

Chapter Fourteen

"**Y**ou saw a man shoot someone and put the body in his car?" Danni asked.

"I recognized the vehicle. I'm pretty sure it's the one I've seen Theo driving. It was too dark to see who the men were so I'm assuming it was Theo," Sarah said. "Earlier in the dream I saw Theo talking to a guy named Eddie. He wanted him to scare Amelia so she'd agree to his proposal." Sarah's eyes widened as a memory from a previous dreamscape popped into her head. "Just remembered something else. I've seen Jackson working on Eddie's car at the garage."

"We need to find out more about this Eddie fellow," Ralph said.

"Wait a minute!" Sarah declared. "The ghost said 'war on' in my dream upstairs. He's said it before. Except he wasn't speaking of an actual war; he was saying Warren!"

"Now we have something to go on," Garrett said.

Danni hunched over her computer, determination furrowing her brow. Sarah could tell her friend had an idea. Hopefully, it would lead to the answers they needed.

Afternoon faded to nightfall, leaving everyone on edge from a day of editing video clips and researching. Between the complexity of this haunting, the ongoing questions about the necklace, and her annoyance with everyone wanting her to solve anything ghost related, Sarah was mentally worn out. At least they were getting closer to the answers regarding what happened to Amelia.

Not wanting to delay the inevitable, Sarah bid goodnight to the guys and joined Danni in their room.

"Are you tired?" Danni asked as Sarah slid beneath the covers.

"Exhausted."

"Will my typing bother you?"

"Nope," Sarah responded, closing her eyes. "Whatever you do, don't wake me unless the world is ending. I'm ready to finish this haunting."

"Got it," Danni replied.

Sarah listened to the rhythmic tapping of the computer keys until it lulled her into a troubled slumber.

"Sir," Theo said. "I came as soon as I received your message."

A scowl masked Danbury's face as he towered over Theo.

"You ruined me. I'll never be able to make another run for congress," Danbury said, stepping closer to Theo. "I offered you my daughter and an opportunity to serve me in D.C. Your incompetence cost me the election and I'll not forget it."

"How is this my fault?" he demanded.

Danbury leaned closer, his nose only inches from Theo's. "You were supposed to keep an eye on Amelia. Make sure she stayed busy at the mercantile. Marrying you should have been an incentive to leave that miserable place. It wasn't a difficult task. Now she's dead and I've lost my bid for congress."

Theo's upper lip twitched at the innuendo. Of course, he botched the job by trusting that idiot, Eddie. But that was his only complicity in the situation. A slight smile curled his mouth. At least, he'd disposed of Eddie in fine fashion. No one even missed him.

"What are you smiling about?" Danbury growled, obviously incensed by Theo's arrogant grin.

"I...um...wasn't smiling at you, sir," Theo replied.

"Thanks to you, my political career is over. I've lost the house in Savannah and will have to go back to work as an attorney. Get out of my office and don't ever show your face here again or I'll make sure you end up like that miscreant, Eddie Porter."

The color drained from Theo's face. How did Danbury know? Eddie's body had never been found. Swallowing hard, he decided it wasn't prudent to question the man further. If Danbury knew the truth behind Eddie's death, Theo's best course of action was to do as he was told. He understood the magnitude of the threat and decided it was time to return to Savannah. The last thing he needed was his own father discovering what he'd done. He wasn't one to suffer fools, even his own son.

Didn't deserve it, brushed Sarah's ear.

She spun around to see Eddie standing behind her, brain matter seeping from the missing portion of his skull as he dripped blood onto the rug in Danbury's office.

"I know Theo killed you," she said, hoping to ward him off. "You can move on now."

"Need revenge," he sputtered.

"Everyone is dead," Sarah replied. "There's no revenge to be had."

His black tongue licked moldering lips as his remaining eye widened. "You'll do," he said, reaching for her neck.

Dumbstruck by his gruesome appearance and rancid stench, Sarah's chest constricted, her legs refusing to move. Without thinking, she reached for her throat, her fingers grazing one of the charms. All of a sudden, Eddie was gone. Ola stood before her.

"What happened?" Sarah uttered, her eyes darting from side to side for any sign of Eddie.

Ola smiled. "You touched the thistle charm on the necklace."

"What does that mean?" Sarah asked.

"Each charm boosts your dreamist skills. The key fob unlocks memories from previous visions. The peridot gives clarity. And the thistle charm can shield you from predators. Granted, it doesn't give you much time, maybe a second or two, but enough to get away or decide on a course of action."

"Why not tell me this before?"

"Because I wasn't sure how the necklace would respond to you," she replied, her blue eyes sparkling.

"Garrett said you were wearing this when you were buried."

"Indeed. I wore it every day of my adult life. My mother gifted it to me upon her death."

"Then how did you get it from..." Sarah hesitated, unsure she wanted to know the answer. A small part of her hoped there was a duplicate necklace and that Ola's body still wore the original.

"My grave to the house?" Ola finished for her. "As a dreamist I have certain abilities in the afterlife, one of which is moving things around."

"But why me? We aren't related."

"You and I have a bond, my dear, despite our lack of a biological connection. Trust me. This necklace will help as you develop your skills. You're a gifted dreamist."

"I'm glad you have confidence in me. I don't feel special at all. In fact, I feel more lost now than ever. Did you ever feel that way?"

"Many times," Ola responded. "The difference being, I had my mother and grandmother to guide me. And my abilities weren't nearly as complex as yours."

"What do you mean?"

"You have skills well beyond most dreamists. Between your mother's line and that of your paternal great-grandmother, you have a double dose as you discovered last Christmas. But there's more to it than that. You have a depth of understanding that exceeds the human realm. You have the ability to sense the residual memories imprinted on inanimate objects."

Sarah rolled her eyes. "Great, I'm the super freak of the dreamist world."

Ola laughed. "My dear, you're blessed with an abundant gift, one that allows you to understand a variety of issues on multiple levels."

"Might be a blessing in your mind but it's frustrating to me."

Ola's expression softened. "I know it's difficult which is why I left you the necklace."

"Why did you wait to explain this to me? Why not tell me what the charms could do before now?"

"As I said, I wasn't' sure how the necklace would respond to your specific dreamist DNA, or even if it would help at all."

"Do all dreamists have a talisman of some sort?"

Ola nodded. "This was something special, gifted to my great-grandmother before she left Ireland. It's been passed down through the generations. When my daughter didn't inherit the dreamist gene, I had no one to pass it on to, until now."

Sarah fingered the tiny gems. "Why now?"

"I suspect you'll need it in the near future."

"Is something going to happen?" Sarah asked, panic gripping her chest.

"You'll be fine. Just remember, stay calm..." Ola's image began to waver.

"What if I need you?" Sarah hollered.

"I'm...only..."

She vanished, leaving Sarah standing in the cold, still fidgeting with the charms dangling from the chain around her neck. What was Ola trying to tell her? It seemed as if summoning Ola was getting more difficult.

Glancing around, Sarah realized she was in the alley behind Hayden Place. A feeling of dread prickled her skin as a chill slithered down her spine. Something was waiting, something that wanted to harm her. She sensed there was a battle waiting, one she'd have to engage in if she wanted to solve this mystery and help the spirits move on.

Stirring, Sarah opened her eyes. Darkness encapsulated the room and her shirt clung to her sweat dampened skin. Ugh, she thought. Why did she always wake up when she was on the verge of discovering something big?

Danni was snoring softly next to her and the clock showed 6:07 in the morning. She reached for the journal on the night table and scribbled a few notes about her dreams, especially the one with Ola about the necklace.

They were getting closer to the answers, she could feel it. Once she helped Amelia move on and was able to get Eddie to do the same, she'd be able to relax a bit. At least for a while until the next ghost needed her help.

Exhaling, Sarah touched the chain of the necklace. There was so much to consider. While she was grateful for Ola's guidance, there was something unusual about the depth of Ola's trust. When Ola was alive, she hadn't known Sarah and yet she'd chosen to gift Sarah with an heirloom that had been in her family for generations. It didn't make sense but then again, nothing about being a dreamist did. At least, Ola was a kind spirit.

Unable to go back to sleep, Sarah slipped from bed with her journal and padded downstairs to fix a cup of tea. She needed to revisit all she'd learned and figure out how it fit in with everything the spirits had revealed so far.

Sitting at the kitchen island, Sarah looked through her journal and jotted notes in the margins. Somehow Bessie and Joe Miller were involved with the speakeasy that was housed in the back part of the Edwards' laundry. The cops believed the Edwards family were the sole proprietors of the speakeasy but now Sarah wondered if it was a joint endeavor with the Millers. By all accounts, the Edwards were well-liked but vanished right before the raid on the illegal liquor establishment. Their son, Jackson, worked as a mechanic for the Millers and sometimes as a bouncer at the speakeasy. Amelia was killed by Eddie who was only supposed to frighten her enough to go running back to Theodore Warren. Theo wanted to marry into her family and was helping Amelia's father with his campaign for congress. When Theo learned that Eddie had killed Amelia, he shot him dead. This entire situation was more twisted than a Maurie Povich paternity episode.

In addition to the bizarre aspects of this haunting as well as having two ghosts vying for her attention, Sarah was truly puzzled by Amelia and Bessie using underground tunnels to transport liquor and access the speakeasy. This seemed unlikely given Savannah was like Beaufort. If you dug too deep, you hit water. Maybe Danni could find something more about that.

"Good morning," Garrett said, kissing Sarah's cheek. "How'd you sleep?"

Sarah's eyes narrowed as she smiled playfully. "That's a nice way of asking if I had any informative dreams."

"Why would you think that?" he asked, placing his hand on his heart as if hurt by her words. "I may have been genuinely concerned that you slept well."

Dallas barked.

"Even the dog knows that's a crock," Sarah chuckled, feeling a bit like her old self. "Not to mention, Harry and Ralph are standing in the doorway looking at me like I'm Santa Claus," Sarah said.

Harry started the coffee while Ralph and Garrett sat.

"What did you dream about?" Ralph queried.

"Let's wait for Danni to join us," Sarah replied. "There's a lot to discuss."

A collective groan made its way around the kitchen island. While they waited for Danni to join them, Ralph cued up the footage from the night before. Nothing significant had shown up, only the typical orbs and an occasional shifting shadow.

A short while later, Danni trudged into the kitchen, went straight for the coffee pot, and filled a mug. All eyes shifted to her as she lifted the coffee cup to her lips.

"What?" she croaked.

"We've been waiting for you," Ralph said. "Sarah has info to share."

Danni trudged to the island and plunked onto a stool, her eyes still droopy with sleep.

Sarah proceeded to tell them everything from her dreams. "It doesn't make sense," she sighed. "I've never heard of an underground anything in the Lowcountry. Yet these tunnels keep showing up in my dreams."

"Sounds like more research," Ralph said, pulling his phone from his pocket to text Walter.

Danni lowered her cup and grinned. "Looks like proximity

will play a role in my discovering the answers first." She headed for the doorway and stopped. "You comin'?" she asked Sarah.

"Where?"

"To get dressed. I'm off to do some sleuthing and you're coming with me."

"I've been summoned," Sarah said, giving Garrett a quick peck on the cheek. She leaned in and whispered in his ear. "I have information about the necklace from Ola that I'll share with you later."

His eyes glimmered as a slow smile lifted his lips.

* * *

Danni drove down the tree lined streets of Savannah past Colonial Park Cemetery. Sarah shivered as she spied the bronze eagle over the archway leading to the graveyard. Something niggled at her nerves, or someone. Shaking off the unease, Sarah turned to her friend.

"Have you been in touch with Walter?"

"Uh-huh. He's being tight lipped about what he's found so far. I suspect he's not sharing everything with the guys either."

"I think you're being paranoid," Sarah chuckled.

"Maybe so, but I'm not going to let down my guard on this one."

They pulled into the parking lot of an old house with a sign designating it as the local historical society. The clean lines and expansive staircase of the Neoclassical structure gave it an imperious feel. Arched windows held court on either side of the portico with its rounded columns.

"When did you find this place?" Sarah asked.

"A few days ago. I was waiting for a reason requiring a local visit. Something Walter can't do," she replied with a mischievous grin as they entered the mansion. A young woman with flaxen hair in a bobbed style greeted them.

"Hi, I'm Emi. Welcome to the Historical Society. How can I help you today?"

"We're looking for information about underground passageways in the area," Danni said.

"The Cluskey Embankment Vaults are a good place to start," Emi said, smiling. "Follow me."

Danni and Sarah exchanged glances. There were actually underground vaults and they had a name?

Emi led them to a room at the back of the building with a section dedicated to the Cluskey Embankment Vaults.

"These files talk about the contractual agreements with the architect as well as drawings and a few photos. If you have any questions, let me know," she said, leaving the room.

Sarah and Danni paged through several articles aghast at what they were seeing.

"Sounds like government spending on unfinished construction goes all the way back to the early 19th century," Danni snorted. "Can't believe the architect kept stringing them along for four years with promises to complete the project."

"And that the locals dubbed the incomplete vaults, *The Tombs*."

"Of course, you'd focus on that part," Danni grimaced.

"While this has been fascinating, these vaults are above ground," Sarah said with a sigh.

"And near the mercantile building where Amelia worked for her aunt and uncle," Danni replied.

"That's the only link. If these vaults had an underground connection someone would have discovered it by now."

"Are you sure?" Danni asked. "How many times have we discredited a theory only to later discover it was legitimate?"

Sarah's brow wrinkled. "Even if there were underground tunnels, how do we prove it?"

"This isn't a court case. We don't need to prove anything beyond a reasonable doubt. All we have to do is find out if there are any tunnels below ground and if they run near the old laundry building."

Emi peeked into the room. "Having any luck?"

"Not exactly," Danni replied, her shoulders slumping. "The Cluskey Vaults are fascinating, but we're more interested in tunnels that actually run underground."

Emi's smile broadened. "The hidden tunnels."

"Hidden tunnels?" Sarah and Danni said in unison.

"Let me show you," she replied, booting up the computer next to the file cabinets.Spooky scenes appeared on the screen, causing Sarah to shudder. This looked more like what she'd witnessed in her dreams except these were much wider, like sewage tunnels.

"What were these used for?" Danni asked.

"Escaping slaves, kidnappings by pirates, carrying dead bodies, that sort of thing. Supposedly, one of them runs below the Pirate's House restaurant and another underneath the First African Baptist Church. I think one is located under Forsythe Park. I don't believe there's any kind of layout, at least none I'm aware of."

"Are they still accessible?" Sarah queried.

"Goodness, no. Even if they were, I'm sure they're structurally unsound after all these years."

"Thanks anyway," Danni said.

For more than an hour Danni and Sarah searched the Internet but the only information they could garner was what Emi had shared. The Cluskey Vaults were partially below ground and the alleged underground caverns were located in the areas she'd mentioned.

"None of these tunnels appear to go anywhere near Hayden Place." Danni moaned "Looks like another dead end."

"Poor choice of phrases," Sarah grumbled, leaning back in the chair. "Without some sort of map there's no way to verify if the tunnels in my dreams are the same ones Emi told us about."

"What if we found the entrance to the tunnels?" Danni said.

Sarah chewed her lower lip. Danni was right. The proximity of the Cluskey Embankment Vaults to the Miller's mercantile on the waterfront wasn't a coincidence. Neither was the idea of tunnels being used for illegal liquor distribution. There had to be a connection. All she had to do was find it.

They headed back to the house with the few facts they'd garnered at the historical society, but nothing directly related to the haunting.

"I wonder if Walter found anything," Sarah said as they drove across town to the house.

Danni shot her a stern look. "Doubtful since we didn't find anything of substance online. The best info we got was from Emi."

They pulled into the drive behind Hayden Place and started up the backstairs. Sarah stopped, glancing around. The backyard was nothing more than piles of sand bordered by a six-foot privacy fence. They'd already discovered what they believed was the foundation where the garage would have been located in the far corner. So, where did the tunnels originate that she'd seen Bessie and Amelia walking through?

"You comin'?" Danni called out.

"Yeah," Sarah replied, following her friend to the back door.

As they stepped inside, Dallas greeted Sarah with an enthusiastic *woof.*

"Find anything useful?" Garrett asked, looking up from his laptop.

"Kinda," Sarah replied. She shared what they'd learned about the Cluskey vaults and the underground tunnels.

"Anything related to what you've dreamed so far?" Garrett asked.

"Not exactly," Sarah replied. "But it might help me ask the right questions next time I'm asleep. How about you? Anything notable on tape?"

"Actually, yes." He turned the laptop to show a filmy image of what appeared to be a young woman standing at the pantry door in the kitchen. "Any idea who she is?"

Sarah leaned in and studied the figure, her stomach twisting at the sight. She knew exactly who it was. "That's Amelia."

"Do you have any idea why she would appear in the kitchen?"

"No," Sarah replied. "The only places I've encountered her in my dreams have been the front parlor, her room on the third floor, the tunnels, the speakeasy, and the waterfront where she was killed."

"I suppose it's feasible she'd have been in the kitchen while she lived here," Garrett said. "Usually spirits frequent areas where they spent most of their time or where something significant occurred."

"Maybe she liked to cook," Danni offered.

"Not likely," Sarah answered. "I'm sure the Millers had someone to do that. They were wealthy. There has to be another reason for her to be there."

"Has anyone heard from Walter?" Danni queried.

"Nope. Looks like you'll get credit for the information about the tunnels," Garrett chortled.

"Where are Ralph and Harry?" Sarah asked.

"Out scouting the neighborhood for additional footage."

"When was the last time Dallas went outside?" Sarah said.

"Been a while," Garrett replied. "You can take him out if you want."

"Come on, buddy," she called, walking out the back door. Dallas frolicked around the yard for a few moments, then seemed to sense something, his nose surfing the ground. Sarah inhaled, the crisp air sending a chill fluttering across her scalp. If only they could find a connection to the tunnels, perhaps they could put this haunting to rest.

A strong breeze picked up, cutting through Sarah's coat like an icy scalpel. Dallas sniffed the air, his ears pinned back. Something was wrong, she could sense it and obviously Dallas could too. The fur at the base of his neck bristled as he made his way toward the side yard, a low growl rumbling from his throat.

Sarah followed as he crept around the brick foundation of the house and started digging. The little dog's determination to get at whatever he was sensing was intense. Sarah stepped closer, her eyes trained on the ground where Dallas was digging. What was he after? Within seconds, the only thing she could see was his backend jutting out from the small crater he'd dug. Moments later, his head popped up from the ground, flecks of dirt clinging to his snout. Something glinted in his mouth. Sarah reached out her hand and spoke to him.

"Give," she commanded like she'd seen Garrett do before.

The dog growled.

"Give," she repeated, snapping her fingers.

This time he dropped the item into the palm of her hand. A skeleton key, its edges corroded from years of being buried in the sandy soil, tingled against her skin as she turned it over. Sarah studied the delicate scroll at one end of the barrel and the key bit to open a lock at the other. She shuddered when an image of Amelia in a state of decay flashed through her mind. Tossing the key to the ground, she took a step back, her heart thrumming against her ribcage.

Dallas snatched the key, bolted around the house and up the back stairs with Sarah in pursuit. When she opened the door he raced inside, dropping the key at Garrett's feet.

"What's this?" Garrett asked, retrieving the treasure from the floor.

"He dug it up at the side of the house," Sarah said, breathlessly. "It's connected to Amelia."

Garrett examined the key. "What's the connection?" he asked.

"Not sure," Sarah replied.

"Wonder what this went to?" Garrett said.

"Maybe there was a doorway there years ago and this was the key," Danni suggested.

"A doorway in that location would have led below the house," Garrett replied. "This place never had a basement so there's no logical reason for an entry."

Below the house, Sarah thought. "What about tunnels?" she asked. "We know they existed. What if they started here and ran all the way to the waterfront? Since the Miller's mercantile was located there they may have used the passages to transport liquor."

"It's a bit if a stretch but I suppose it's possible," he said.

"Perhaps the Millers discovered the underground passages while building the house and tapped into them," Danni added.

A cold blast of air rushed through the space as Harry and Ralph stepped in the back door.

"Get anything good?" Garrett asked.

Harry nodded. "Got some great shots of the neighborhood for the opening and closing scenes. How about you guys, find anything significant?"

"We learned about underground passageways in the city but nothing concrete about a layout or where they begin," Danni replied.

"I wonder if Willow would know about the tunnels in Savannah?" Sarah said.

"You could contact her," Ralph responded. "She seems to know a lot about this city, especially the haunted aspects."

Sarah texted Willow about Savannah's underground passageways and slid the phone back into her pocket.

"Check this out," Garrett said, handing Harry the key. "Dallas dug it up near the foundation at the side of the house."

"Any idea what it's for?" Harry asked.

"Not yet but Sarah had a vision when she handled it."

"What did you see?" Ralph queried.

"Just a quick flash of Amelia in a state of decomposition. Hopefully, Willow will get back to me soon with information about the tunnels. Something tells me there's a connection between the key and whatever is below this house."

"While you wait to hear from her, I'm going upstairs to do some research of my own. There has to be more info about these tunnels," Danni said, scooting from the room.

Sighing, Sarah leaned against the counter.

"Everything okay?" Garrett asked.

"Yeah, just trying to figure out what to do while I wait to hear from Willow."

"You can look at last night's footage with us," Harry offered.

"Sure," she said with a nod. Sarah slid onto a stool at the kitchen island and shared the laptop with Garrett. They watched the front parlor video from the previous night while Harry watched one on his tablet from the third floor and Ralph viewed one on his computer from the entry hall. Quietude blanketed the atmosphere in anticipation. For Sarah, this was the tedious part. Sitting in front of a computer screen looking for any sort of anomaly that could be classified as supernatural was mind numbing. But the guys were dedicated to it and she wanted to help. Especially after they lost the bid for their own ghost hunting show. Even though it wasn't technically her fault, her relationship with Garrett had played a role in the team losing the contract and she still felt guilty.

Sarah's phone rang. "It's Willow," she announced, pressing the green button as Danni walked back in for a bottle of water.

The men stopped what they were doing and watched her.

"Hey, Willow. Thanks for getting back to me so fast. Do you mind if I put you on speaker? The guys are here. Great." Sarah tapped a button and held the phone out for everyone to hear.

"How's the ghost hunt going?" Willow asked.

"We're making progress," Sarah replied. "Earlier today, Danni and I stumbled across some information about underground tunnels in Savannah. Do you know anything about them?"

"Everyone in the ghost tour community knows about the tunnels. Sadly, none of them are accessible anymore," Willow said. "Except for the one in the basement of the Pirate's House. That place is one of the most haunted locations in Savannah."

Danni stepped closer to Sarah and mouthed "pirates?"

Sarah nodded before resuming her phone conversation. "Does the place allow people to enter the tunnel?"

"Nope. Too dangerous. It's boarded up. They store supplies and liquor in the basement of the building but it's only open to staff."

"So, it's a bar?" Danni queried, a slow smile spreading across her face.

"Yup, and one of the best restaurants in town. You guys should go."

Danni's brows arched as she looked at the group.

"Thanks for the info, Willow," Sarah said.

"No problem," Willow replied. "If you do go, tell Johnny at the bar I said hello."

"We will," Sarah said. "Bye."

"Happy haunting," Willow declared before she disconnected from the call.

"Sounds like we're going out to eat," Danni announced, her eyes glimmering.

"I could use a break from this place," Harry stated.

Garrett exhaled. "Maybe if we get away for a while, we'll be able to see things clearer when we get back."

"Sounds good to me," Sarah answered, relieved to be escaping the house for a bit. Turning to Danni, she asked, "Why are you so excited about going to a haunted restaurant?"

Danni's eyes widened. "Pirates! You know I love that kind of stuff."

"For someone who is so adamant about the law, I'm shocked you like people who violated it on a daily basis."

"It's a Jack Sparrow thing," Danni said. "Where's the rum? Argh!"

Sarah shook her head and chuckled as everyone headed to their rooms to get ready.

Twenty minutes later, the group drove across town and parked behind a grey, clapboard structure located at the edge of the road, its windows glowing in the darkness.

Sarah swallowed hard. Something told her this wouldn't be the enjoyable dining experience she was hoping for.

They stepped inside the two-hundred-year-old building and looked around. Wall sconces washed the space in a soft light. The floor slanted slightly from age giving a feeling of vertigo depending on where you stood. The hairs on Sarah's neck stood on end. She could feel the spirits gathering.

Garrett squeezed her hand and gave a sly smile, settling some of the trepidation building in her chest. She'd be fine. The team was here. Nothing serious could happen.

"Welcome to the Pirate's House, I'm Jo," the hostess chirped. She wore a puffy white shirt with a long black skirt. Her sandy brown hair was twisted in a knot on top of her head. "Six for dinner?" she asked.

The team exchanged confused glances while Sarah stood still. She could feel a spirit right behind her, its breath tickling the back of her skull.

"There's only five of us," Garrett corrected.

"Sorry," Jo said. "Sometimes the candlelight casts shadows that make it look like someone else is there. Follow me."

Garrett and Sarah lagged behind as Jo led the group to a room towards the back of the restaurant.

"What was that about?" Garrett whispered in Sarah's ear.

"Not sure, but she didn't miscount. I could feel something behind me but I was too scared to turn around and see what it was."

"Probably a good idea," he replied. "Do you think it was Amelia or Eddie?"

Sarah shook her head. "This ghost had a different vibe to it."

"Will this be alright?" Jo asked, pointing at a round table with six ladder back chairs.

"Sure," Harry said.

Jo handed everyone menus and smiled. "Ariel will be your server this evening. She'll share the dinner specials and take your drink orders," Jo said before leaving the room.

The room was intimate with only one other table and two chairs near the entryway. Deep set six-over-six windows filled the back wall and a darkened doorway with stairs was nestled in the corner. A simple hearth with brick surround showed years of built-up soot and the floor was worn from chairs scraping across the surface. Sarah sat at the back of the table near the staircase with Danni on her left and Garrett to her right.

A perky blond entered, her eyes dancing as she approached the table.

"Good evening, I'm Ariel, I'll be your server this evening. Can I get you started with some drinks?"

Everyone ordered a mixed drink from the specialty menu, not something they did ordinarily but being in an old pirate establishment it seemed fitting. A short time later, the waitress returned with a round tray filled with colorful cocktails sporting small plastic animals. After taking their food orders, Ariel scooted off.

"What on earth is this?" Danni asked, pulling a green parrot from her drink.

"Not sure," Sarah said, looking at the orange monkey floating near her straw.

Ralph smiled as he plucked a blue giraffe from his glass. "It's kinda fun," he said, placing the plastic creature on the table.

"What'd you get, Dunc?" Harry asked.

Garrett shook his head and smiled. "I think it's a purple rhino."

A herd of colorful plastic animals sparkled in the candle light as it paraded across the table top. The conversation was lively and devoid of haunted topics. They'd been at this ghost hunting thing for several weeks. Right before the trip to Borden House, Harry had left the genealogical library which meant all the guys were now self-employed and able to control their schedules. As a contractor, Garrett could check in with his crew and run most things from a distance. All were frugal with their money so they could take time off to hunt ghosts. The men talked about returning to their jobs and the upcoming Christmas holiday. Sarah felt the tension draining from her body. It was good to be away from the house and the constant need to be on alert for impending messages from the dead.

But her relief was short lived. An icy breeze traced the back of her neck, ruffling her hair and sending goosebumps skittering across her skin. Something was nearby. Before she could say something, the waitress came in and served their food.

The guys dined on New York strip while Danni enjoyed crab cakes with broiled shrimp. Sarah went with her standard shrimp and grits. The aroma of grilled steaks intermingled with the garlic mashed potatoes and sauteed veggies making Sarah's mouth water. For a moment, she forgot about the cold spot in the stairway behind her. The waitress brought another round of drinks and the herd of plastic animals increased.

Sarah sipped the tangy mango margarita when a cold breath blew against her ear followed by a harsh grip on her right shoulder like icicles jabbing at her skin. Lowering her drink to the table, she took in a deep breath, held for a count of five, and released. The jovial conversation around the table ceased as everyone seemed to notice Sarah's sudden silence.

"What's going on?" Danni asked Sarah, touching her arm.

"Not sure," she said in a hushed tone. "There's something behind me."

Danni's face paled as she looked toward the staircase behind her friend. Harry took out his phone to record and Ralph's eyes twinkled with anticipation.

"Everything okay in here?" Ariel's voice chimed causing them all to jump.

"Great," Harry responded, putting the phone down. "Best steak I've had in a while."

"Where do those stairs lead?" Ralph asked.

Sarah rolled her eyes. Count on Ralph to focus on the ghosts and not his meal.

"They lead to the old cellar," Ariel said with a dimpled smile.

"Could we take a peek?" Harry asked.

"Sorry, it's not open to patrons. Once a year the owner of the place allows the local ghost tour guides to go down there but that's as far as he's willing to go with public visits. There's really nothing to see. It's a cramped little room with a wooden gate blocking entry to the old tunnels." Ariel shuddered. "It's actually pretty creepy."

"Thanks anyway," Garrett said.

As soon as Ariel left the room, Ralph leaned forward and whispered. "We need to see what's down there. Maybe we could contact the owner and ask for a private showing."

"We really don't have time, especially if it's not related to the haunting at Hayden Place," Garrett said, turning to Sarah. "Unless you're sensing something from Amelia or Eddie."

"Nothing from them," she replied. "But there's a lot going on."

"Maybe I should sneak down there," Harry offered. "I'll snap a few pics and come right back."

Sarah shook her head. "No. If anyone is going down there, it should be me. If there's any connection to the ghosts at Hayden Place, I'll know."

"Are you crazy?" Danni exclaimed. "The waitress just told us it's off limits. You're going to get us kicked out of this place."

"Since when are you against a little adventure?" Sarah asked. "You spent half your high school years protesting on land you weren't supposed to be on."

"I wasn't an attorney at the time. Besides, these crabcakes

are fabulous and I'd like to finish them before we get hauled off on trespassing charges."

"Finish your meal," Sarah replied. "I'm the only one who'll get in trouble."

Garrett grabbed Sarah's wrist as she stood. "I'm not sure this is such a good idea."

Sarah inhaled. She needed to know what was down there. Not to mention, Ralph and Harry looked as if they were about to jump from their seats with excitement.

"I'll be fine," Sarah reassured him. "If Ariel comes back, tell her I went to the restroom. I'll go down the stairs and see if anything shows up. I won't stay long, promise."

Danni downed her drink and placed her napkin on the table. "Can't believe you're doing this," she said.

Puffing her chest, Sarah looked at her friend. "If I can find a link between these tunnels and the house, maybe we can finally help Amelia and Eddie move on." Where was this bravado coming from? Sarah thought. Regardless, she needed to act on it before fear took over.

Sarah got up and walked to the doorway. A red velvet rope like the ones from movie theaters was draped across the opening letting patrons know the area was off limits. Glancing over her shoulder, she checked to make sure none of the servers were around. The team watched as she ducked under the rope. Darkness enveloped the space so only a couple of stairs were visible. It was like looking into a black hole.

Chewing her lower lip, Sarah went down three steps and halted. The scent of the two-hundred-year-old structure mingled with the stale air of the underground space. Her lungs constricted. Was it mildew or something otherworldly? Only one way to find out. Sarah turned on her cell phone flashlight and lowered her foot down to the next step when a gurgling sound echoed in her ear.

You can do this, she told herself, descending several more steps until she reached the bottom. She scanned the space. Nothing but stone walls and an arched exit on the opposite side. Several boxes of booze lined the wall to her right.

Sarah made her way across the dank cellar, her heart thumping in her ears with each step. Creaks and groans from the floorboards overhead intensified her angst as she approached the opening. The wooden gate blocking access to the passageway was rickety. Leaning over it to get a better look, Sarah wondered if this was one of the hidden tunnels.

A shadowy face emerged from the darkness, its glowing eyes and skeletal form causing her to stumble back. She bumped into something and whirled around to find a corpse in a black hat and tattered clothing standing behind her. She gasped and stepped past him only to be met by another more gruesome creature, scraps of hair crowning its skull and its left arm dangling by a few bloodied ligaments. Panic took hold as she spun around where a torso, its head missing, swayed to and fro.

Her throat burned as the cadavers moved closer, trapping her in place. Unable to breathe, Sarah grabbed the thistle charm. Instantly, the entities vanished leaving her alone in the shadowy space. Sarah bolted up the stairs, ducked under the rope, and plopped onto the chair, her breathing labored.

"Oh my gosh," Danni said, her brows furrowing. "What happened? You're as pale as a..."

Sarah shot her friend a warning look.

Garrett gripped Sarah's quivering hand. "Are you alright?"

Nodding, Sarah grabbed her drink and downed it. "I think I found one of the tunnels," she said, breathlessly. "Along with every pirate that ever frequented the place."

"Ghost pirates?" Danni queried, her forehead wrinkling.

"More like zombie pirates. They surrounded me down there."

"How'd you escape?" Harry asked.

Sarah fingered the charms around her neck. "I touched the thistle charm. It repels spirits so I can get away."

"That is so cool!" Ralph declared with a broad smile.

"It sure is," Sarah agreed, her heart rate beginning to slow.

"Did you discover any connections to Amelia and Eddie?" Harry asked.

"Nope. Neither of them showed up down there," Sarah replied. "If it's alright with you guys, I'd like to leave."

"Of course," Garrett said.

They paid the bill and headed back to Hayden Place beneath the shimmering street lamps of old Savannah. There was nothing more serene than the glimmer of light reflecting from tufts of Spanish moss under an inky night sky. All of a sudden, Sarah felt drained. Now more than ever, she wanted to wrap up in a blanket and sleep without ghostly intrusions. Unfortunately, that wouldn't be the case until she could help Amelia and Eddie move on.

When they got back to the house, Danni went upstairs to do more research while the men discussed their plans for the evening's filming. Even though Sarah was exhausted, she wasn't ready to face the entities battling for her attention in dreamland. Besides, it was only 8:00 in the evening. The guys wouldn't start filming for another hour.

Sarah's back ached and her vision blurred. Yawning, she rubbed her eyes. "I'm going upstairs to rest," she said, standing. "And before you get too excited, I'm not going to sleep."

Garrett gave a sly smile, making Sarah's insides flutter. She really did love him. Trudging up the stairs, Sarah padded to her room and plopped onto the bed.

"Everything alright?" Danni asked, not looking up from her computer.

"Just needed to take a break." Closing her eyes, Sarah snuggled against the pillow relieved to get away from conversations about the undead. Her breathing steadied as her mind drifted to another time. That's when it happened. Something wrapped around her throat and squeezed. Sarah opened her mouth to scream but nothing came out. Thrashing, she tried to free herself from the invisible force crushing her trachea except nothing was there. Terror ripped through her body. What was happening? And where was Danni?

All of a sudden, whatever was choking her stopped. She jumped from the bed, holding her throat. Looking around, her chest seized. She wasn't in the room.

She was at the waterfront where two men were arguing. Eddie stood by the car, a snarl on his face as he stared at the man pointing a gun at his head. Theodore Warren.

How did she get here? Had she fallen asleep? Theo's voice jarred her from her ruminations.

"You were only supposed to scare her, not kill her," Theo grumbled. "You've ruined everything you dolt. Danbury has lost all confidence in me not to mention I won't be his son-in-law now. Everything hinged on that."

"Can't help it if the wench got what she deserved," Eddie retorted. "Took a chunk out of my skin when she clawed me." He rubbed the back of his hand where the wound was healing.

"What kinda wimp are you? Can't handle a scratch so you kill a woman! You're an idiot. You'll not get a penny from me."

"You'll pay up or I'll tell everyone about you funding my stills."

Theo sneered. "Pretty brazen for a man with a gun pointed at his head."

"Ha! You don't have the guts to shoot me. Your pampered self wouldn't last a day in prison."

Sarah jumped as the bullet burst from the pistol in a flash of light. Eddie crumpled to the ground, bits of his skull splattered across the grass. Theo ran his tongue across his teeth as he wiped blood spots from his face, a spit of smoke lingering near the barrel of the gun. "Stupid hick," Theo growled.

He stuffed the pistol in his waistband, grabbed Eddie by the shoulders, and pulled him a few feet to the car. Theo opened the door and with a heave and a grunt, maneuvered the body into the back seat. Sliding behind the wheel, he cranked the engine, and drove away.

Sarah exhaled. This entire situation was the culmination of greed and a series of tragic decisions by men trying to make their way to notoriety. Amelia was the true victim. Her only crime was being the oppressed daughter of an ambitious man who cared solely about his career.

A stinging sensation cut into Sarah's shoulder. She spun around to find Eddie glaring at her, bits of bone and blood clinging to what was left of his face.

"I know your secret," Sarah said. Her insides shook like jelly despite her brave façade. "Theodore Warren killed you and was never charged. You can move on now."

"Didn't deserve this," he growled.

"Maybe not, but you did murder Amelia Danbury."

"Wench scratched me!" he screeched.

"If you hadn't been holding her head under the water she wouldn't have done it," Sarah retorted.

Eddie's cadaver stepped closer, rage glowing from his hollow eye socket as his sinewy fingers gripped Sarah's throat. Her lungs screamed for air as everything around her began to fade.

"Sarah!" Danni called.

"Huh?" she moaned, rolling over.

"You fell asleep."

Pushing herself to a sitting position, Sarah rubbed her forehead. Her heart was still pounding. "I don't remember dozing off. Someone was choking me. It's almost like I passed out."

Danni's face paled as her eyes widened. "Seriously? I was absorbed in my research and heard you mumbling. That's when I realized you were asleep."

"How long was I out?"

"Dunno." Danni shrugged.

"Could you tell what I was saying?"

"Not really."

Sarah nodded, her hands still trembling as she fidgeted with the charms on the necklace. The scenes from her dreams flashed through her head like an old-fashioned home movie. She'd seen Eddie's murder and knew the circumstances surrounding it. The information could bring the haunting to a close, although the depth of Eddie's rage could prove to be a hindrance.

"I know who murdered Eddie and why," Sarah announced.

"Oh my gosh!" Danni exclaimed, sitting straighter.

"Let's go downstairs and share this with the guys."

They found the men in the front parlor working on camera placement. Ralph and Harry's eyes widened as Sarah regaled them with her latest dream. Garrett ran his hand through his hair.

"What's the matter, Dunc?" Harry asked.

"Knowing the manner of Amelia and Eddie's death should end the haunting." Garrett stated, scratching his head.

"That's my concern," Sarah said. "Is knowing going to be enough for both ghosts to move on?"

"We weren't able to prove to the world what really

happened at the Borden House or Virginia Intermont," Danni said. "Knowing the truth was enough in those cases."

"And both places are likely still haunted," Sarah responded. "We're here to help Cheryl get these ghosts out of her house. If we can't make that happen, she'll bring in an outsider who might scam her. She doesn't have the money for that sort of thing."

"Could you speak with her?" Ralph asked.

"Cheryl?" Sarah said.

"No, Amelia. Why can't you just ask her to leave. If what you're saying is true, we know the truth behind her death. She didn't slip, hit her head, and drown. She was murdered. And now we know that Theo murdered Eddie."

BAM!

The front doors along with the back doors flew open sending a gust of wind moaning through the space. Dallas started barking ferociously. Dust and bits of loose plaster formed mini cyclones before coming to rest at Sarah's feet. As suddenly as it began, it ended, leaving behind a silence that bore straight through to her soul. The men stood frozen while Danni leaned against a wall, her eyes as big as marbles.

"What the heck was that?" Danni muttered.

"Amelia?" Garrett asked Sarah.

"Not sure," she replied, staring at the mound of plaster dust at her feet.

Danni inched away from the wall and started for the kitchen.

"Where are you going?" Sarah asked.

"Anywhere but here," she breathed.

"You're going to help with this," Sarah commanded, stopping her friend from scooting through the doorway.

Danni stayed where she was. Harry was filming while Ralph snapped pictures. Dallas sniffed the air.

"What's happening?" Garrett asked.

"Not sure," Sarah said. "Something tells me the ghosts aren't ready to leave yet."

"Now what?" Danni muttered, still standing in the doorway.

Harry smiled. "Take a look at this," he said, holding out his phone. "I started videoing as soon as the doors flew open."

Sarah, Garrett, and Ralph leaned in to watch. Sarah shrieked when the funnel of dust formed an outline that resembled Amelia.

"You saw it too," Harry said.

Nodding, Sarah touched the phone's screen to replay the clip. "It's her," Sarah said. "Danni, come over here and see this."

"No, thank you," she replied.

"Let's download this to the computer and see if we can enhance the image a bit more," Harry said, walking to the kitchen where the laptops rested on the center island. After downloading it, everyone except Danni gathered round to watch the images.

"There!" Sarah called out, pointing at the screen. "There's another funnel behind Amelia. Can you zoom in closer?"

Ralph tapped a few keys enlarging the image.

"It's him," Sarah mumbled. "That's Eddie."

"I don't see anything but dust floating in the air," Ralph said. "Let's send this to Walter. Maybe he can bring out the form like he did with the other video."

"Do it," Garrett said.

Ralph forwarded the clip to Walter while Sarah rewatched it. Thirty minutes later, Sarah's eyes were beginning to blur from staring at the grainy images on the screen.

"What are we missing?" Sarah moaned. "Maybe Amelia can't move on until Eddie is pacified."

"Joy," Danni replied, rolling her eyes.

A round of chuckles echoed through the room. It was obvious Danni didn't want any part of the haunted stuff but her loyalty to Sarah kept her engaged.

Ralph's computer pinged.

"It's from Walter," he announced. "Whoa! Check this out."

Everyone gathered round, including Danni.

On the screen were two very clear outlines of a woman and a tall man.

"That's them," Sarah said. "Amelia and Eddie."

"What do you think it will take to get them out of here?" Ralph queried.

"That's what I've got to figure out," Sarah grumbled. "The two have been haunting me simultaneously. What's strange is that I know how they died yet they're still here."

"We might have to consult your book on this one."

Sarah groaned.

"Let's go upstairs and take a look," Danni offered. "I'll help you."

Sarah plodded up the steps behind Danni, a mild ache building in her head. By all accounts, the hauntings should be over. In previous cases, Sarah had helped her great-grand-mother, a murder victim, Lizzie Borden, and a jilted college student move on once she discovered the manner of their demise. The team now knew that Eddie drowned Amelia when he lost his temper with her and that Theo shot Eddie. So, why were they still lingering? More importantly, what was Sarah missing?

They sat on the bed and started going through the book, Sarah leaning in to read alongside her friend. After jumping around from one chapter to another, Sarah gasped.

"That's it!"

"The first passage?" Danni asked.

"Yes," Sarah replied, sitting straighter as she read.

When one spirit steps forward with another behind,
  The dreamist must break the ties that bind,
  Or the haunting continues as you will find.

"Oh my gosh, you're right!" Danni declared. "Good job. You figured it out on your own. You're getting better at this."

"According to this passage, I have to separate the spirits in order to stop the haunting. The problem is, Eddie's energy seems to be fueled by his need for revenge. I think that's why he's able to hold on and speak as much as he does. He uses more phrases than Amelia."

"Then how are you going to get rid of him?" Danni asked, consternation furrowing her brow.

"Not sure," Sarah replied, chewing her thumb nail. "The guys have more experience with ghosts. Maybe they can come up with an idea."

"Did Ola mention anything like this?" Sarah asked Garrett after she and Danni shared what they'd found in the *Dreamist* book.

"Not specifically, but now that you mention it, I remember something about a dual haunting. It took her much longer to resolve it because she had to separate them before they could move on."

"Which is exactly the problem I'm facing," Sarah said.

"Do you recall what Ola did?" Harry asked.

Garrett rubbed his chin. "I think she asked the primary ghost to help."

"It can't be that obvious," Sarah said.

"Have you asked Amelia about Eddie?" Harry queried.

"No," Sarah replied, softly.

"Next time you see Amelia, ask if she can tell you how to get rid of Eddie," Ralph suggested.

"Sounds easy enough but once I get into the dreamscape, it's not always that simple."

"What can we do to help?" Harry asked.

"I'm afraid there's nothing you can do. I'll concentrate on it all before going to sleep. Hopefully, I can communicate with Amelia and find a way to split them."

"Let's get started," Garrett said, rubbing his hands together.

Danni went back to the bedroom, Harry headed to the third floor, and Ralph made his way to the kitchen. Sarah joined Garrett in the front parlor. She sat on the floor and leaned against the wall with Dallas snuggled beside her while Garrett manned the camera in the far corner. Darkness crept through the house like a thick fog. Sarah felt as if a hundred spirits were milling about sucking all the oxygen from the room.

Worn out from the emotional roller coaster she'd been riding for the past few days, Sarah closed her eyes and began her deep breathing exercises. They were so close to solving this mystery and she wanted to clear her mind of any doubts or misgivings.

Her body relaxed as she continued taking deep breaths. Her fingers brushed against the necklace when she scratched her neck. A vision began to form in her mind. Was she asleep? No. Not wanting to interrupt the image, she kept her eyes shut and concentrated on what was appearing.

Amelia held a flashlight in one hand and pulled at a panel in the floor of the pantry off the kitchen with the other.

Sarah released the breath she'd been holding as she watched Amelia slip through the opening with the covertness of a spy. How had Sarah and the guys missed this? Then again, the panel had probably been covered over during the remodel.

Sarah followed Amelia down a narrow flight of stairs, the glow of the flashlight licking at the inky blackness. Crudely constructed floor to ceiling shelves lined three of the four walls in the tiny underground room. Each shelf held bottles of liquor. Amelia grabbed a couple of bottles, placed them in a basket, and slipped through a thick wooden door into a corridor.

Sarah had never been claustrophobic but the air was dense in the tight space, making it difficult to breathe. The passage was so narrow her shoulders brushed against its walls. Amelia climbed a set of stairs that ended where the ceiling began. It was the entrance to the speakeasy. She knocked three times in a succinct rhythm. The clicking of a lock followed by the screeching of rusty hinges echoed through the cramped area.

A burly gent wearing a plaid shirt and suspenders smiled. He was missing a couple of teeth but his eyes twinkled with delight as he looked down at Amelia.

"Is Jackson here yet?" she asked the man towering over her.

"Haven't seen 'im."

Amelia gave a quick nod and handed the man the bottles of liquor. Then he reached down, took Amelia's hand, and helped her up. Thus far, Amelia seemed oblivious to Sarah's presence. Was she purposefully ignoring her in order to show Sarah these events?

Sarah took in the setting, her lips curling into a smile. Women with bobbed haircuts and knee length dresses swiveled and hopped with gentlemen in suits to the upbeat music of a jazz ensemble.

Her heart leapt. If only Garrett could be here with her. Sadly, she'd have to enjoy this from the sidelines since she wasn't actually in the scene but observing from the ghost's perspective. Nevertheless, this was without a doubt the most enjoyable experience in all of her haunted visions. Until she realized something terrible might happen. Sarah tensed at the idea. Speakeasies were known for violence, especially if they were raided and according to the records, this one had been. But the raid happened after Amelia's death so why show her all this?

Then Sarah saw him. A scrawny man in denim pants and a ragged plaid shirt stood to the far right of the bar. Eddie. He threw back a drink and watched Amelia approach.

"Hey, Eddie," Amelia said with a smile. "Have you seen Jackson? He sent me a note asking me to meet him here."

"Jackson told me to pick you up," Eddie said, a wicked grin sweeping across his face.

"Where is he?"

"Down at the riverfront. Asked me to bring you there. Something about some hooch."

"He must've gotten an unexpected shipment," she muttered. "My aunt usually handles that but she's out of town this evening."

"Guess that's why he said to bring you along."

"Alright," she replied, heading for the door to the tunnels.

"Can't go that way," he said. "Gotta take the car."

"Must be a big delivery," Amelia added, following Eddie to the back door where the guests came in.

Even though Sarah knew what was going to happen, she desperately wanted to warn Amelia not to go with him. Sarah's stomach twisted. Sadly, this was only a vision, a reflection of things that had already happened.

The scene shifted and Sarah found herself standing at the waterfront. Cicadas trilled as the clattering of automobile wheels reverberated through the nightly serenade. The car parked at the river's edge and Eddie and Amelia exited the vehicle.

"Why are we stopping here?" Amelia asked, looking around in the darkness.

"This is where Jackson said to meet," he replied. "Just doin' what I was told."

Amelia nodded.

"I'll go check the warehouse," he said.

Amelia didn't question him further. Instead, she made her way to the edge of the water and stared out at the moon sparkling across the choppy tide.

Eddie made his way into the shadows and disappeared as Sarah watched Amelia standing innocently by the river. So, this is how it happened, Sarah thought. Amelia wanted Sarah to see her death and everything that led to it. Maybe this was her way of severing the connection between them.

Eddie circled around and approached Amelia from the shadows. Swinging his arm around her neck from behind, he pulled her against him. She struggled to free herself but his grip only tightened around her throat cutting off her ability to breathe.

"Stop fighting," he grumbled, altering his voice. "Do what I say and nothin' will happen to ya."

Amelia froze. "What do you want from me?" she croaked.

"You're dressed awful nice," he said. "Got any money on ya?"

"No," she whimpered. "Please let me go. My friend will be right back."

"Don't believe ya."

At that moment, Amelia managed to shift her head, biting down on his forearm.

Eddie let out a yelp as Amelia broke free and spun around.

"Eddie! What are you doing?" she declared.

"You little wench!" he hollered, looking at the drops of blood forming where her teeth had latched onto his skin.

Drawing back his other arm, he landed a slap against her cheek knocking her off balance. Amelia started to run but her heel caught in one of the cobblestones sending her to the ground. Her head smacked against the pavement sending stars scattering across her vision. Before she could recover, Eddie grabbed her by the hair, and dragged her into the water, shoving her head beneath the surface. Clawing at his arm, she managed to scrape a chunk out of his hand.

"Owww!" he hollered. Fury pulsed through his veins, strengthening his grip as he held her under. Moments later, her thrashing stopped. Eddie pulled her head from the water and inhaled. Her lifeless expression stared at the starlit sky overhead.

"Blasted wench! Look what you gone and made me do!"

Eddie released her and made his way to the cobblestone walkway edging the river. He watched as her head bumped against the seawall several times before disappearing beneath the watery expanse.

Scrutinizing Eddie, Sarah realized why she'd confused him so many times for Jackson. They were about the same height and had a similar build. In the shadow of night, Eddie's skin appeared darker than it actually was. A hand latched onto Sarah's shoulder making her jump.

"Sarah?" Garrett said.

Sitting up, Sarah rubbed the back of her neck. "I saw Amelia's murder," she muttered.

"You were asleep?"

"I guess I was," she replied. "I saw Eddie kill Amelia."

"And?"

"It was horrible," Sarah replied. "Eddie wasn't supposed to kill her. He was trying to scare her by making it seem like a random mugging. Except Amelia fought back."

"Do you think this is why they're connected?"

"It can't be," Sarah replied. "None of the other ghosts I've helped have been attached to the murderer."

Garrett ran his hand through his hair as he exhaled. "There's got to be a reason. We'll look into that later. At least we're getting more answers."

A smile spread across Sarah's face. Garrett had a way of finding the positive aspects in what seemed like an impossible situation. She loved that about him.

"I almost forgot," Sarah said in a hushed tone. "In one of my dreams, I saw Amelia enter a small storage area with shelves of liquor beneath the floor in the kitchen pantry. There was a tunnel leading from it to the speakeasy. That must be how they snuck the liquor in without being seen."

"Incredible!" he muttered. "We'll check it out in the daylight and revisit some of the footage we've captured in that area."

The night seemed to slog on like a zombie dragging a rotting foot as it walked. Sarah's mind pinged with all the possibilities of why the two entities were still attached. As she fidgeted with the charms around her neck, the nightly visions started to resurface. Mr. Danbury dismissing Theo, preventing Joe and Bessie from attending Amelia's actual burial, his disdain regarding his daughter's death, and his disgust at losing the election. The man was a heartless, power grabbing monster who cared only about his own reputation and prestige.

Still didn't explain why Amelia wasn't able to move on yet. Then it hit her. The tombstone in Colonial Park Cemetery. It was nothing more than a marker. Joe and Bessie were only paying tribute to their beloved niece. Amelia's body wasn't there. So, where was it? Closing her eyes, Sarah blew out a long breath. There was still more to Amelia's story, specifically her final resting place.

"I think I know why Amelia's still lingering," Sarah said.

"Why?"

"We know who killed her and how she died, but we don't know where her body is. That may be why Eddie is still here too."

Even in the dark, Sarah could see Garrett's complexion pale. It was one thing to discover the circumstances surrounding a spirit's death. It was another thing to locate a body with no record of its burial location. Despite all their progress, something told Sarah they were far from unraveling the mystery behind this haunting.

Chapter Fifteen

Sarah's hips ached from sitting on the parlor floor for hours. Changing into her night clothes, she was relieved to slip into bed. Danni was already sound asleep, her laptop on the night table. Sarah grabbed her small journal and made a note about not being completely asleep earlier but being able to witness dream-like visions. Just what she needed, another aspect of her skillset to investigate. She wasn't sure what was worse, trying to solve the mystery of the hauntings or figure out her emerging dreamist abilities.

Resting her head on the pillow, Sarah stared up at the ceiling where shadows danced in the light from the street lamp outside. She'd dreamt so much since arriving in Savannah. Almost too much. Was that because there were two ghosts seeking her help?

Now that Sarah knew what she was looking for, she concentrated on what she'd ask when she saw Amelia again. Maybe she could relax and watch the scenes without falling completely asleep like she had in the parlor earlier that evening. That would make it easier to ask questions and maybe escape any attacks from Eddie. With a few deep breaths, she felt her body melt into the mattress as consciousness faded into the past.

Sarah yelped when a hand grabbed her shoulder, the fingernails digging into her flesh. Turning quickly, her eyes rested on Eddie, part of his head missing and his remaining eye eclipsed in bruising and blood. They were outside the speakeasy at the back of the laundry. It was strange. She could tell she wasn't completely asleep yet she felt stuck in the scene.

"What do you want to tell me?" she asked, trying to keep her words as steady as possible in light of the gory remnants of his face.

Eddie leaned closer, his putrid breath making her cringe. "What makes you think I need anything from you?"

"I'm a dreamist. I can help you."

"Ha! Don't need any help. Having too much fun scaring you." Festering lips peeled away from his yellowed teeth in a macabre grin.

"Obviously, you do need my help or you wouldn't be here." Proud of her strength, Sarah stood a bit taller. Until Eddie grabbed her throat and squeezed.

"No need to move on from putting women in their place. You all been too uppity for your own good. You need a lesson or two."

Despite being a dead man, his grip was strong, blocking air from entering her lungs. Sarah remembered a move from a self-defense class and brought her arms up, forcing Eddie to release his hold. Pleased with her ability to think so clearly, Sarah ran toward Hayden Place.

Bolting through the front door, Sarah gasped. This wasn't the house, at least not the one she knew. The walls were a drab gray like a stormy sky just before the first lightning strike. A heaviness blanketed the air. All of a sudden, the floor creaked behind her. She turned around but nothing was there.

Terror bumped across her skin when the sound of rushing water echoed through the space. Puddles formed at her feet, the frigid wetness soaking her sneakers. A thunderous sound rattled the walls and made the floors quake. The far wall collapsed, releasing a swell of water into the space. It lifted her like a feather on the wind carrying her through the front door, down the street, towards downtown.

Sarah did her best to swim but the current was too strong. The harder she tried the weaker she became. Panic took hold. Something bumped against her leg, making her gasp and letting the brackish water in. Her throat burned as she struggled to find something solid to latch onto. But the undercurrent was powerful and nothing was within reach.

You can't die she told herself in an effort to calm her panic. Without warning, the water receded, leaving Sarah standing amongst a garden of marble slabs at Colonial Park Cemetery. Relieved to be free from the torrent, she took in a deep breath.

"Amelia?" Sarah called. She had to be here. Eddie wasn't affiliated with this place which gave Sarah a slight sense of relief. Of course, he was a ghost so he could come and go as he pleased. She was safe for the moment, or so she hoped.

"Amelia?" she called again.

A warm breeze whispered through the tree branches overhead. That's when she appeared. Amelia stood before Sarah dressed in her flapper attire, a rosy hue to her porcelain skin.

"You're restored," Sarah said, tensing at the idea Amelia might revert to a bloated, decaying corpse at any moment. Except she didn't. "We know who killed you. Why are you lingering?"

"Not here," she said, pointing across the street.

"I don't understand."

Amelia's image began to waver like a TV screen losing power.

"Don't go!" Sarah hollered. "I know Eddie Porter murdered you. What else do you need?"

Amelia's image dissolved as the words "not here" floated on the breeze.

Sarah turned around and looked across the street. A three-story office building occupied the space. Then Sarah remembered something Willow had said during the cemetery tour about the original graveyard covering a broader area. The road cut through the sacred plot of land and buildings were constructed without removing the graves. Willow also said many of the graves were unmarked due to tombstones being destroyed or misplaced from the civil war and subsequent storms.

She followed the brick walkway as it wound through headstones and crypts to the street that divided it from the structure across the road. The office building towered before her but nothing happened. No chills, no whispers, no spirits. This wasn't where Amelia was leading her. Then Sarah recalled something else. Willow had also mentioned a pauper's cemetery during her tour. Where was it located? She never said.

You're close, brushed Sarah's cheek.

Sarah jolted up in the bed, sweat trickling down her spine. Rubbing her palms against her eyes, she groaned. Now, Amelia was saying new phrases that only complicated the situation.

She was tired of waiting for answers and trying to corral information. She didn't want to wait for the truth. Sliding from bed, she tiptoed from the room and down the stairs. The house was deathly silent as everyone slumbered.

Garrett's laptop sat on the island. Maybe she could find some information about the pauper's cemetery. Sarah slid onto the stool and squinted when the screen glowed brightly cutting through night's dark veil. Her fingers raced across the keys as she typed 'pauper's cemetery, Savannah, Georgia.' Her heart seized when a photo of an office building popped onto the screen. A history of the property from being a burial ground for the poor a century and a half before to the current office space tumbled across the page.

Sarah shivered. This was it. She could feel it. She'd share her discovery with the group in the morning. If she was correct, they'd find the answers the ghosts were trying to reveal with a visit to the office building that sat upon the graves of the poor.

"Sarah?"

Gasping, Sarah turned. Garrett stood in the kitchen doorway in his flannel pajama bottoms with a long sleeve shirt clinging to his upper body. His burnished hair was crumpled from sleep.

"What are you doing down here?" he asked.

"Chasing ghosts," she replied, a mischievous smile curling her lips. She was proud of herself for finding information that might actually solve this haunting.

"What happened?" Garrett said.

"Shhh...you'll wake everyone."

"Maybe they need to get up," he replied.

"Let them sleep. It's been a long few days and they need to rest if they're going to help me figure this out."

Sarah motioned him over to sit next to her. The stove clock alerted her to the 4:00 a.m. hour.

"How'd you get into my computer?" he asked, rubbing his eyes.

"Seriously?" she chortled. "Your password is Dallas. It didn't take long to figure that one out. You're not upset, are you?"

"No, just rethinking my password."

"Anyway, I had another vision but couldn't get back to sleep so I decided to check things out on my own," she said.

"Did you find anything?" he asked, his voice scratchy.

"Not sure. Amelia showed me the Colonial Park Cemetery and said 'not here.' That's when I remembered what Willow told us about the pauper's graveyard. I think Amelia wants me to know something about that plot of land."

"What would she want you to discover about that place?" Garrett queried.

Sarah shrugged. "I don't know but something tells me the answers to this mystery are there."

"Is it still a graveyard?"

"According to what I found online, there's an office building there now."

"Why do you keep saying vision?"

"I'm not sure I can explain it, but tonight I've been able to access the ghosts without actually falling asleep. It was more like being in a state of suspension."

Garrett ran his hand through his hair. "That's a new one for me. Don't remember Grams ever mentioning anything like that."

"It's on my list of things to investigate after we help Amelia and Eddie move on."

Nodding, Garrett smiled. "I'm wide awake now. Might as well get the coffee brewing."

Sarah yawned. "All of a sudden, I'm tired."

Garrett leaned in and kissed her. Her heart thudded against her chest. It felt like things were better and she was glad. She loved him and needed him to help her through this crazy haunted existence. Once this whole thing was wrapped up, she'd apologize properly for her moodiness.

"Why don't you try to get some sleep. I'll do some more

research. Maybe I can find more about what you discovered tonight."

"Thanks, I could use a little shut-eye," she said. "See you in a little while."

He kissed her once more and smiled. Sarah ran her hand along his cheek and returned the smile before plodding up the stairs to her room. Danni was still out as she slipped into bed and pulled the covers over her shoulders. This time sleep found her and escorted her to dreamland.

Sweat dripped down Theo's spine as he plummeted the shovel into the sandy soil. He straightened for a moment, brushing the back of his hand across his brow. A racoon scurried from the bushes nearby making him jump. He glanced around the darkened area to make sure nobody was watching before resuming his task.

Half an hour later, Theo rolled Eddie's lifeless body into the earth's cold embrace. Staring at what was left of his head, Theo sneered. "Stupid hick," he grumbled, spitting on the corpse. Theo covered the body and tamped down the fresh mound of dirt. "Guess this is goodbye, Eddie. You ruined my chances for a prosperous life when you killed Amelia. And now I shall leave you with the reputation you spent a lifetime creating."

Did me wrong!

Sarah spun around to find Eddie glaring at her, bits of dirt and debris clinging to his decomposing frame.

"I know he killed you," she said. "Why won't you go away?"

Eddie's blackened lips curled revealing blood-soaked teeth. "He's guilty."

"I know that!" Sarah hollered, tired of this carousel of accusations. "Why are you still here?"

Eddie's sinewy fingers wrapped around Sarah's throat and squeezed. "Revenge."

Sarah grabbed at his forearm, his skin sloughing off as she tried to break his grip. Increasing the pressure, Eddie laughed. "You'll do in his place!"

Sarah gasped for air, the disgusting odor of Eddie's rotting flesh coating her tongue. Then she remembered the necklace and Ola's words. Her other hand latched onto the thistle charm. Instantaneously, Sarah found herself standing in front of the Edwards' laundry building where police swarmed about the property. Across the street she spotted Theo chatting with one of the cops.

Meandering through the crowd of onlookers, Sarah made her way toward Theodore Warren. A triumphant smile creased his eyes as he patted the Sergeant on the back.

"Hope you get the credit for this one, Tommy."

"Thanks for the tip, Theo," the cop responded. "Any idea where Eddie Porter ran off to?"

Theo shook his head. "All I know is he offered to let me in on his liquor trade. I played along so I could get all the information you'd need to make the bust."

"And I appreciate it," Tommy responded. "The captain said there'll be a promotion in it for me."

"Glad I could help." Theo grinned.

"If there's anything I can do to return the favor, just let me know."

"Trust me, I won't hesitate to ask," Theo replied. "By the way, any news on the Edwards' family?"

"Not a trace of 'em. Maybe they're with Eddie."

Theo shrugged. "Perhaps."

Tommy strode across the street and joined the other police officers gathered at the cinder block building.

Sarah watched Theo walk down the street, a swagger to his

stride. He killed Eddie, disposed of his body, and then ratted him out to the cops about his running illegal liquor. No wonder Eddie was angry. Theo betrayed him in every way possible.

Sarah cried out as a hand grabbed her from behind, knife-like fingernails slicing into her skin.

Bolting upright in bed, Sarah sucked in a breath. Sleepiness sloshed around her brain as she took in her surroundings. Danni was standing near the bed, a worried expression knitting her brow. Sarah glanced at the night table clock. Seven in the morning.

"Why are you up this early?" Sarah muttered, surprised to see her friend already dressed for the day.

"Early?" Danni snorted. "Normally, you've already run a mini marathon, showered, and saved a ghost or two by this hour."

"There's nothing normal about me," Sarah groaned, massaging the back of her neck.

"That's beside the point," Danni replied. "You look pale. Something happen in your dreams?"

"Let me get dressed first and process all of it before I tell you about it."

"Hurry up. I found something too."

"What did you find?" Sarah asked.

"I'll tell you when we share everything with the team," Danni replied, lifting her chin.

"Extortion of information. Low blow," Sarah mumbled as she stepped into the bathroom and closed the door.

After a quick shower, Sarah dressed and made her way to the kitchen where the team was chatting over coffee and computer screens. A steaming cup of tea waited on the counter. Closing her eyes, Sarah lifted the mug to her lips, taking in the delicate scent of Earl Gray. Her body released the tension holding it captive as the hot liquid soothed the rawness of her throat. Apparently, screaming in dreamland was a strain on the vocal cords.

"What did you guys find?" Sarah asked.

"Not us, Danni," Harry replied.

"Turns out the link was off by one digit so the article didn't open the last time I was on this site," Danni said. "Apparently, I mistyped the URL this time, and voila, it showed up."

Danni turned the laptop so Sarah could see. A newspaper article from 1921 glowed on the screen. Stepping closer, Sarah began reading.

Police Investigate Illegal Liquor Trade in Hayden Street Neighborhood

An anonymous tip led police to a speakeasy set up in the back of a laundry establishment in the Hayden Street area of town. The Edwards' family business was a front for the illegal establishment. However, it appears they did not act alone. Eddie Porter, known for his unlawful activities, appears to have been the mastermind behind the business. According to a reliable source, Eddie owned several stills and transported liquor to various places across state lines. Attempts to locate him have been unsuccessful. A reward is being offered for any information leading to his or the Edwards' family whereabouts.

"Oh my gosh," Sarah exclaimed. "This is what I dreamt about!"

"Seriously?" Danni said, her brows arching.

All eyes were trained on Sarah as she shared the previous night's escapades.

"I saw Theo speaking with a police officer. Seems he's the one who tipped off the cops. He told them Eddie was the one behind the liquor trade at the speakeasy on Prince Street. This was after I saw him burying Eddie's body."

"Where did Theo bury Eddie?" Ralph queried, his eyes wide.

"Couldn't tell," Sarah replied, her shoulders slumping. "I suspect the reason Eddie can't rest is because no one ever knew he was dead, not to mention, he was blamed for the speakeasy and wasn't able to defend himself. He's pretty intent on revenge and seems determined to use me as his target."

Garrett reached over and took Sarah's hand in his. Sarah met his gaze and smiled. Things definitely seemed better between them. Now if she could just figure out how to get Eddie to move on.

"Don't know about you guys, but I'm hungry," Danni announced.

"Saw a bagel shop a few blocks from here when we were out exploring the other day," Ralph said.

"I could go for a bagel," Harry replied.

"I'll pick up breakfast while you guys work on figuring out how to get rid of Eddie," Danni offered.

An hour later, everyone was gathered around the kitchen island sipping hot drinks and munching on bagels. Danni's phone dinged.

"It's my friend, Dave, from the records office. He says Edward Porter had no family and disappeared just before the raid on the Edwards' laundry slash speakeasy."

The hairs on Sarah's neck and arms bristled with electricity. "Except Eddie didn't disappear per se. He was murdered by Theo who never paid for his crime. That's got to be the reason he's still haunting me."

"What about Amelia?" Garrett asked.

"She's not been as active but she's lingering. It may be because she's still attached to Eddie's spirit."

Pop! Pop! Pop!

Each of the bulbs in the pendant lights over the kitchen island blew out sending shards of glass raining down on the marble counter. Garrett and Harry ducked while Sarah, Danni, and Ralph scurried across the room. Dallas ran to the front parlor at the same time, barking and snarling.

"You guys alright?" Garrett asked.

Everyone nodded as they stared at the small bits of glass scattered across the countertop.

"Better get this stuff off the laptops," Ralph said, taking his computer to the trash can to clean it.

"Which spirit was that?" Harry queried.

"Not sure," Sarah replied with a shudder. "But I suspect Dallas knows." She headed to the front parlor with Garrett on her heels. Turning, she rested her hand on his forearm. "Let me do this. You might scare off whoever is waiting."

With a nod, Garrett stayed in the kitchen.

Sarah found Dallas in the front parlor still growling. "Hey little fella," she said softly. "Is someone here?"

The chandelier overhead, the one draped in plastic to protect it from plaster dust, flashed on and off. Chills skittered across Sarah's skin. There weren't any bulbs in the light fixture.

"Who are you and what do you want?"

Instead of charging like he normally did, Dallas lay on the floor and rested his snout on his paws with a whimper. It had to be Amelia.

"Amelia?" Sarah called. "Why are you still here?"

A misty figure wavered in the far corner. "Make him leave."

"Are you talking about Eddie Porter?"

"Too close."

Sarah cocked her head. The faint outline of a woman in a knee length dress formed letting her know it was Amelia's spirit. "Is he still connected to you?"

"Find me!" the ghost screeched swirling through the room. Dust formed a cyclone as the plastic on the chandelier came loose floating down in a phantasmic form. Dallas leapt to his feet sniffing the air as the plastic sheathing rested on the floor like a deflated balloon.

Rubbing her temples, Sarah exhaled. She thought she was close to solving this mystery yet it seemed the ghosts had taken a different trajectory.

"What happened?" Harry asked, standing in the doorway. Ralph and Garrett stood behind him. No doubt, Danni wasn't going to risk coming anywhere near the ghost and had chosen to stay in the kitchen.

"Amelia was here except this time she used new phrases."

Garett walked over to Sarah and grasped her hand. "What did she say?"

"She said *too close* and *find me*. It doesn't make any sense. I feel like we're starting all over again."

"Not when you have friends in good places," Danni announced, a Cheshire cat grin on her face.

"What do you mean?" Sarah asked.

"Remember the large office building that was built on the pauper's cemetery you found online earlier?"

"Yeah."

"Since it used to be the graveyard for the poor, there weren't any burial records. No one knows how many people were interred there or their identities."

"How does that help with this situation?" Ralph asked.

Danni's eyes formed slits. "Maybe Eddie's body was buried there."

"That's a pretty wild assumption based on a random fact," Ralph shot back, crossing his arms over his chest.

"Except the office building is empty," Danni replied, stepping closer to Ralph who uncrossed his arms. "The place has so many reports of unusual occurrences they can't get people to rent it. It's been empty for years because of the haunted activity."

"Still doesn't prove anything," Harry said, sheepishly.

"If that's the case, why did my computer screen flash on and off when I was typing the address?" Danni said with a shudder. "There has to be a connection."

"Can't hurt to check it out," Sarah said. "At this point I'm willing to try anything."

"Looks like we're going to visit the office building," Garrett replied. "Whether the bodies were removed or built upon, chances are the spirits are lingering there."

"If Eddie is among them, I'll know," Sarah said.

Danni groaned. "I'll stay here and do some more research."

"Nope," Sarah said, pursing her lips. "You're coming with us."

"Why?" Danni whined.

"You found the information and need to follow through."

"I'm the research department, not a ghost hunter. Why do I have to go?"

Sarah narrowed her eyes. "Because you're my best friend and I need you."

"That's a low blow," Danni retorted. "Pulling the best friend card is not cool."

Ralph snickered at the exchange, resulting in a glare from Danni.

Everyone piled into Garrett's truck and they drove across town to the building's address. Parking in front of a non-distinct structure, they got out and looked around.

"Not much to see," Ralph said.

Sarah's chest tightened. "There may not be anything visible but the feel of multiple spirits is oppressive." This was going to be more complicated than she'd realized. She hadn't considered being inundated by all the unknown spirits left to linger.

"Everything okay?" Garrett asked, squeezing her shoulder.

"Not sure," Sarah replied. "There's a lot of pressure here. I get the feeling the land was bulldozed and built upon without relocating the bodies."

Something moved near the bushes at the side of the structure, catching Sarah's attention. Whether it was a critter or something otherworldly remained to be seen. Something told her it was the latter.

"What is it?" Garrett asked.

Sarah waved him off and walked toward the back corner of the property where a small maple was surrounded by a cluster of azalea bushes. As she approached, the shadows shifted, stopping her. Closing her eyes, she tried to remember what she'd seen when she dreamed about Eddie's burial. Sarah touched the key fob charm to trigger her memory and saw the dreamscape clearly. There weren't any trees, only an expanse of land. But she still couldn't determine if it was the same location or not.

When she opened her eyes, Eddie appeared; his face restored to its living appearance. He was a rough looking character. It seemed they'd found his resting place. Hesitating, Sarah waited to see what he would do.

"Sarah?" Garrett whispered.

"This is it," she replied in a hushed tone. "He's right in front of me."

"Ugh," Danni moaned, taking a step back. "This is too weird."

"It may be weird but it also means you'll likely win the wager with Walter. Even better, Eddie appears to be in a restored state," Sarah added. "Which means he should be able to move on now. We've solved the mystery behind his death and where he was buried."

"So, we're done," Harry said.

All of a sudden, Amelia appeared behind Eddie, a grim expression clouding her visage.

"Not quite," Sarah whispered. "Amelia's still here."

"Why?" Ralph asked.

"Don't know," Sarah replied. "I assumed the connection between Eddie and Amelia was the fact he killed her." Out of the corner of her eye, Sarah noticed movement at the other side of the property as the words, *not far*, brushed against her ear.

"Stay here," Sarah called over her shoulder as she moved behind the building toward something shimmering near a clump of overgrown shrubs at the far end. Weeds slithered through the woody branches of the unkempt boxwood hedge. Amelia flickered in and out as Sarah approached.

"I don't understand," Sarah muttered. "What are you trying to say?"

Find me, floated through the air as Amelia dissipated.

Frustration filtered through Sarah's body and her chin dropped to her chest. Without thinking, she fidgeted with the necklace. At that moment, a skeletal hand burst from the weeds and latched onto Sarah's ankle. She sucked in a breath as the hand retreated back into the dirt. Kneeling down, Sarah rested her palm on the ground. Amelia's image flashed through her head as clear as a photo. She could make out every detail of the spirit's face with her hazel eyes and coffee brown hair.

No wonder neither ghost could move on. They were both dumped in the pauper's graveyard without ceremony or identification of where they were. The irony of being buried so close to each other wasn't lost on Sarah. Perhaps that's what had linked them in the afterlife.

"Guys!" Sarah hollered. "Come over here."

"What did you find?" Garrett asked as Dallas scurried to Sarah's side and started digging.

"No, Dallas!" she scolded, holding the little dog back. "Amelia's buried here."

"How do you know?" Ralph asked.

"It's one of my skills. I can touch something and get visions of the ghost's life. When I touched the ground, Amelia appeared as she did in her living years."

"That is so cool!" Ralph declared.

"And seriously disturbing," Danni moaned.

"This must be why she didn't go away once I discovered how she died. Think about it. The phrases *find me* and *too close* could mean that Amelia has been lost all this time and that her murderer was nearby. Supposedly, her father had her interred somewhere in Atlanta, but it seems he was angry enough to do something as underhanded as burying his only daughter in the pauper's cemetery."

"That is despicable," Harry said. "No wonder she couldn't rest."

"Now what?" Danni asked.

"We go back to the house and see if either ghost shows up," Sarah replied.

"We can't just leave them here," Ralph said. "We have to let the authorities know where they are."

Sarah stood. "How do we explain locating the bodies? We can't tell anyone about my dreamist abilities. Besides, no one would believe us."

"If we don't have the bodies moved, they could continue haunting," Harry suggested.

"Maybe knowing where they are will be enough. I won't know for sure until we go back to the house," Sarah said.

Chapter Sixteen

Garrett pulled the truck down the driveway and parked. Everyone got out and started for the house when a cold breeze ruffled Sarah's pony tail. Something was nearby.

"You guys, go inside," Sarah said quietly. "I need to do something."

No one questioned her. Without a word they all climbed the back stairs and went into the kitchen. Sarah could feel them watching her through the window over the sink.

"Amelia?" she called.

The breeze picked up whispering through the leaves of a towering live oak at the edge of the property. Amelia appeared.

"I'm sorry you were buried near your killer and that you haven't been able to rest in an unmarked grave," Sarah muttered. "There's not much I can do except apologize."

With a nod, Amelia gave a slight smile before dissipating on the breeze like dandelion seeds.

Tears trickled down Sarah's cheeks. Amelia's family had

been a wealthy, prominent force in the area and in the big city of Atlanta but she'd been dumped with others in an unmarked grave only to be bulldozed and built upon as if she'd never existed. Even worse, her murderer's body was buried nearby. No wonder she'd not been able to rest.

Wiping the tears from her cheeks, Sarah joined the group inside.

"Well?" Garrett said.

"She's finally at peace," Sarah replied.

"How do you know?" Ralph asked.

"I can't explain it," Sarah said. "I could tell she was content with the truth being known by someone. And she was alone. Eddie was nowhere around."

"How will you know if Amelia and Eddie have really moved on?" Ralph queried.

"We won't know for sure until I go to sleep tonight," Sarah responded.

Everyone gathered at the kitchen island with steaming mugs of coffee except for Sarah who sipped hot tea. Dallas was curled at her feet. The guys went back to reviewing the previous night's footage. Walter was still running it through his programs and was confident something notable would show up. Danni went upstairs to wrap up in a blanket while she searched for more information about the building site where the pauper's cemetery had been.

Thirty minutes later, Danni bolted into the kitchen with her laptop. "You won't believe what I found."

All eyes turned toward her. Even Dallas watched her.

"Apparently, there was a scandal regarding the sale of the pauper's cemetery land to developers. Most people knew it was an old burial ground but the plans for the building were approved and construction began. A court order halted it temporarily so they could determine if an archeological dig was needed."

"I thought that was standard practice," Ralph said.

"It is unless a wealthy developer thwarts it," Danni replied. "The archeological search never happened and the building was constructed."

"That's awful," Sarah said.

"It gets worse," Danni replied with a scowl. "The developer was Teddy Warren the fourth."

"As in a descendant of Theodore Warren?" Sarah asked.

"Yup. Looks like sleazy is imbedded in the family DNA."

Woof!

Sarah reached down and scratched Dallas's head. "Pretty bad when the dog knows it too."

Ralph's phone rang. "Hey, Walter...yeah...no way! Send it! Thanks!" Ralph hung up and rushed to his laptop. He cued up the video and pressed play. Everyone gathered round and watched as the misty form of a woman materialized near the pantry before vanishing. "That is the clearest image we've ever captured," he said, excitement in his voice.

"Unbelievable," Harry declared.

"Disturbing!" Danni hollered, taking a step back.

"It's definitely Amelia," Sarah added.

"We can't see enough for an identification but it's a woman's spirit which should garner a lot of attention on YouTube," Garrett said with a broad grin.

"Let's film again tonight in case the spirits make one last visit," Harry suggested.

"Sounds good to me," Garrett answered.

Over the next hour, the team arranged cameras in the areas where most of the activity had been captured. After a quick bite from a nearby fast-food place, everyone went to their places. Garrett was in the front parlor, Harry was on the third floor, and Ralph manned the monitors in the kitchen. Sarah and Dallas stayed with Danni on the second floor. Weariness weighted Sarah's eyelids making it difficult to stay awake. Curling beneath the blankets, Sarah closed her eyes.

"I'm going to sleep," she announced.

"Goodnight," Danni said, typing away on her laptop. "Keep the spirits in your head please."

"I'll do my best," Sarah giggled, getting a nudge from her friend.

"You better or I'm outta here."

Dallas snuggled beside Sarah, adding warmth. Knowing this would be the last night in the house was a relief. Hopefully, the haunting was over and she could sleep without interruption. Her breathing steadied as she drifted off.

Sarah walked down the street along a row of businesses, reading signs affixed to each building. Johnson's Mercantile, Nelson Smith Druggist, Knapp Five and Dime, and First Colorado Bank. Except this wasn't the Lowcountry. There were no live oaks, no Spanish moss, no marshes. Mountains capped in white bloomed from behind the row of storefronts with pines and maples dappling the landscape. Where was she and why was she here? Had another haunting already begun?

At the end of the dusty street was a small sign that read *Harrison Laundry & Alterations*. The wooden structure was welcoming with its tin roofed porch and two large picture windows on either side of a glass paneled door. Despite its quaint appearance, it was indistinct almost as if the building was trying to cower in the shadow of the other edifices.

Sarah traipsed over and peered inside one of the picture

windows. A dark-skinned woman, her hair contained beneath a kerchief, sat behind a wooden counter stitching a pair of trousers. She recognized that face. It was Mrs. Edwards. But it couldn't be. Or could it?

"Help them," resonated in Sarah's head.

Whipping around, Sarah gazed at Amelia in her silk flapper dress and cloche hat. "Is this who you wanted me to help?"

Amelia nodded.

"I don't understand. How did Mrs. Edwards get here? Where's the rest of the family? What about Jackson?" The words fell from Sarah's lips in a jumbled rush.

Amelia cocked her head. "Wrong conclusion. Help them."

Sarah sucked in air as Dallas licked her cheek. Morning light filtered through the curtains, tiptoeing across the floor. Sitting up, Sarah looked around the room. She was at Hayden Place in Savannah.

Sarah glanced at the clock. It was six in the morning. She'd slept through the night yet the dream was brief. As she ruminated on the scene, she tried to make sense of everything Amelia had shown her. It would have taken a great deal of energy for Amelia to accomplish what she'd done so why not just tell Sarah what she was trying to convey? Then again, Sarah knew the spirit world wasn't always logical. Dallas jumped to the floor, rushed to the door, and whimpered.

"Need to go outside, little fella?"

Bark!

Climbing from bed, Sarah opened the bedroom door and followed Dallas down the staircase. Everyone was still asleep. Must've been a late night of filming for them. Sunlight glimmered across the sandy expanse as she opened the back door and watched the little dog frolic along the foundation of the house. He turned the corner and Sarah saw dirt flying in the air.

"Dallas, no!" Sarah commanded. She ran to his side and nudged him. "Stop digging. Do your business so we can get back inside. It's cold out here."

Like a disappointed child, he did as he was told while Sarah bobbed up and down on her toes and rubbed her upper arms. She should've grabbed her jacket on the way out.

Once he finished, they hurried back into the kitchen, Sarah exhaling as she stepped into the warm space. Ralph was preparing coffee, his blondish hair darting in all directions.

"Mornin'," he croaked.

"You're up early," Sarah said.

"Couldn't sleep," he replied as the coffee pot sputtered. "We're missing something and it's bothering me."

"What exactly?"

"The video from last night showed high activity in the pantry area again," he said. "It doesn't make sense."

Sarah chewed her lower lip as Ralph poured a cup of coffee and settled at the island in front of his laptop. Seemed the more they discovered, the more complex it became. The strange dream about Mrs. Edwards bounced around in Sarah's head. Amelia had inferred the Edwards were the ones who needed help. But they weren't haunting Sarah. She'd share it with the team once everyone was up.

At that moment, a scratching noise emanated from the pantry, startling Sarah and Ralph. They exchanged glances before heading that direction. Dallas was scrabbling at the wood floor.

"Dallas! Stop that!" Sarah hollered, scooping up the dog before he damaged the wood planks. "What has gotten into you this morning?"

"He did this earlier?" Ralph asked.

"Not in here. He tried digging near the corner of the foundation out back."

"The area behind this room?"

"Yeah," she replied, goosebumps prickling her skin. Sarah's gaze met Ralph's. "In the same location I found the old skeleton key a few days ago. Something must be there."

"Good morning," Harry said, appearing in the doorway. "What're you guys doing in the pantry?"

"Trying to figure out what Dallas is telling us," Sarah responded. "Is Garrett up yet?"

Harry nodded. "He was getting in the shower when I came down."

"I have a theory but let's wait until Garrett joins us," Sarah said with a clever grin.

"What about Danni?" Ralph asked.

"She's still asleep." Sarah responded.

Twenty minutes later, the team gathered around the island, steaming drinks in their hands.

"What's going on?" Garrett asked.

"Amelia showed me Mrs. Edwards in my dreams last night. They were the ones she was speaking of when she kept saying 'help them.'"

"That's weird," Ralph said.

"Exactly what I thought. Except this time, she added, 'wrong conclusion.'"

"What does that mean?" Harry asked.

"Nothing at the time," Sarah continued. "Dallas woke me up. I thought he needed to go outside but now I believe he's trying to show us something. He tried digging near the foundation where I found the key. Shortly after I brought him inside, he started scraping at the floor of the butler's pantry."

"Something's got to be there," Garrett said boldly.

Sarah waggled her brows. "That's what I'm thinking."

"Considering all the activity we caught on film in that area, I'd say we've definitely found something," Ralph added.

"How do we gain access to the underside of the house?" Harry queried. "Whatever entry was originally in the floorboards is long gone."

"Don't know why I didn't think of it before," Garrett said. "The plumbing and ductwork are down there which means there has to be an entry point. I just have to find it and crawl to the area in question."

"I should be the one to go," Sarah offered. "If something is down there, the ghosts will be able to guide me."

"Guess the haunting isn't over after all," Garrett said.

"In a sense it is," Sarah replied. "Amelia appeared as her old self and Eddie never popped up. I think Amelia is trying to reveal something about the Edwards' family in an effort to help them."

"Should we wake Danni?" Ralph asked.

"I'll get her up. I need to change into something warmer anyway."

Sarah rushed up the stairs and found Danni sleeping soundly. She hated waking her and decided to let her sleep instead.

Sarah slipped on a pair of jeans, a sweatshirt, and a jacket and met the group downstairs. They went outside, the brusque winter air like a slap in the face. Garrett located the entry point for the crawl space underneath the back stairs. Sarah scooted through the small opening with Dallas behind her. Once in the crawl space, she was surprised at how easy it was to move about. She couldn't stand up but she was able to crawl on all fours instead of having to scoot along on her stomach like many of the homes in the area.

Dallas bolted to the wall where they'd found the key and started pawing at the ground with a whimper.

"Give me a minute to get there," Sarah called out, making her way to him. By the time she reached him, he'd made a decent hole in the ground near the wall. Sarah looked up and smiled. It appeared she was below the spot in the butler's pantry where the images had flashed on the tape. She pulled out the trowel Garrett had given her and started shifting the sandy soil into a pile. Sarah gasped when the trowel clinked against something solid. After digging around the hard surface, she pulled a black metal lockbox from its tomb.

An image of Bessie Miller flashed through Sarah's mind. Excitement radiated through her limbs as she held the box to her chest with her right hand. This could be what they needed to finally settle Amelia's ghost. Crawling toward the entry point, Sarah called to Dallas, "Come on buddy!" The little dog scurried past her and waited as she lumbered across the sandy ground.

Squinting in the sunlight, Sarah emerged from the darkened space. Garrett's eyes widened when she handed him the box and got to her feet. Years beneath the sandy soil had corroded the metal casing of the small container. Hopefully, whatever was inside was still intact.

The team hurried into the kitchen with their treasure and watched as Garrett grabbed the small key they'd found by the foundation.

"Let's see if this fits," Garrett said, wiggling the old key in the padlock until it popped open.

Holding her breath, Sarah watched as he tugged at the lid until it broke free from the grime sealing it shut. Everyone gasped.

Inside was a ledger, its leather cover cracked and missing in places. Underneath were several letters addressed to Mrs. Bessie Miller. The return address was the same on all of them. The Harrisons, Boulder Colorado.

Sarah removed the ledger and set it on the marble counter-top. A musty smell wafted from within as she opened the cover. Running her finger down the rows of entries, she was puzzled by the cryptic notations.

"Is it the inventory for the speakeasy?" Harry queried, looking over her shoulder.

Sarah shook her head. "It appears to be payments made to the First Colorado Bank."

"Did the Miller's own property there?" Garrett asked.

A chill slinked down Sarah's spine as she fingered the key charm on the necklace. The previous night's dream came flooding back like a trailer for a movie. In all of the excitement, she'd forgotten about it. "The Edwards were there. Mrs. Edwards was working in Harrison's Laundry and Alterations."

"Do you think the Miller's owned the business?" Ralph asked.

"Doesn't make sense," Sarah replied, puzzled by the new visions and references to Colorado. Amelia's phrase of, *wrong conclusion*, echoed in Sarah's mind. Reaching into the box, Sarah removed one of the letters. The hair on the back of her neck bristled as she carefully unfolded the parchment and started reading aloud.

Dear Bessie,

Colorado was the perfect place for our escape. The city is large enough that we blend in but not so big we feel lost. We miss the warm breezes of the Lowcountry but are settling in to our new home. I must admit, it took some time getting used to our new last name! I can't tell you how often I almost intro-duced myself as Mrs. Edwards. All the same, we are thankful for your efforts in helping us to relocate. Jackson was depressed at first but has finally opened his garage. Business is booming for him with all the new automobiles arriving in town. He met a young lady at church and I believe there might be a spark in his eye for her. We'll have to wait and see. The rest of the children are doing well with their schooling.

We miss you terribly and continue to grieve Amelia's death. I don't believe Jackson will ever be free from his sorrow. But being here helps a bit. May the Lord keep you all safe and fill your days with joy.

Sincerely,

Mrs. D. E. Harrison

Everyone stood in silence as they absorbed the contents of the letter.

"The Millers helped the Edwards' family leave town and reestablish themselves in Colorado," Sarah muttered. "And yet, the locals continued to believe they'd been solely responsible for the speakeasy. That must be what Amelia meant when she kept saying *help them*."

"Except, the Edwards' family didn't need help. They escaped without incident," Harry said.

"But their reputation didn't escape scrutiny and scandal." Sarah pursed her lips. "We need to correct this."

"How?" Ralph questioned.

"We go through these papers and make a timeline of events. We can research the Edwards living as the Harrisons in Colorado and show they were good folks who were forced to flee. As much as the Millers were nice people, they put the Edwards in a precarious situation when they decided to house the speakeasy in the back of the laundry."

"Not a bad idea," Garrett replied.

"The museum across the street showcases the neighborhood with little about the Edwards' family except that the house belonged to them and they ran the laundry. Maybe this is what Amelia meant when she kept repeating *help them*," Sarah said. "Perhaps Amelia wants them to be recognized as a contributing family to the neighborhood without the stigma that was placed on them."

Danni trudged into the kitchen, went straight to the coffee pot, and poured a cup. Turning, she stared at everyone, her eyes drooping with sleep. "Anything important happen last night?"

"You could say that," Sarah said. "Hurry up. We have some investigating to do."

Danni trudged up the stairs behind Sarah, grumbling the entire way.

"You realize this is only my first cup of coffee. I'm useless until the second one."

"Don't wanna hear it," Sarah replied playfully. "You're always claiming to be the research department so let's get started."

"I really need to find a friend who doesn't do mornings as energetically as you," she groaned as they sat on the bed. Danni took a long sip of java, set the mug on the night table, and grabbed her laptop. "What are we looking for?"

"Anything about the Harrison family in Boulder, Colorado around 1921."

Danni gave her a sideways glance. "You seriously think I'm going to find something with a name as common as Harrison?"

"I could always ask Walter to look," Sarah retorted.

"You're so mean," Danni groused. "Is there anything that might narrow my search?"

"As a matter of fact, yes. Look for Harrison Laundry and Alterations."

"You could've started with that." Danni sighed and started typing.

Sarah watched as Danni scrolled through record after record.

"You gonna share what happened last night so I can have some context as to what I'm searching for?"

"I dreamt about the Edwards family only they'd changed their name to Harrison and were living in Boulder. Then Dallas and I discovered a metal box buried under the house. It had bank records and letters between the Millers and the Edwards."

Danni's hands hovered over the keyboard as she stared at her friend. "Your life is so strange," she said in a deadpan voice. "But definitely interesting." She shook her head as she resumed her search. Moments later, Danni shouted, "Got it!"

Sarah leaned in to see the document on the screen. The typewritten form was faded but the names were clear enough. The Harrisons had purchased the building in Boulder along with a small cottage about two miles from there. The dates corresponded with the time of their disappearance showing they'd taken possession of the property shortly after the raid on the speakeasy.

"Amazing," Sarah muttered. "See if you can find anything on Jackson Harrison."

Moments later a broad smile spread across Danni's face as she turned the screen toward her friend. "Ask and you shall receive."

"Only because the caffeine is starting to kick in," Sarah chuckled, nudging Danni's shoulder.

The documents on the screen showed Jackson had purchased a garage where he ran a successful repair business. He'd married and had two children, a daughter and son. The name on the business was Harrison and Son. By all accounts, the Harrisons had done well for themselves after leaving Savannah.

"It's a shame they had to go that far and change their identities," Danni said. "Looks like they prospered though."

"There's no way they could have stayed here after that raid.

As a black family the law would have been harder on them and not accepted any defense."

"Looks like I'm gonna win the bet this time." Danni grinned, her eyes glinting.

"Better tell the guys before Walter beats you to it. You know Ralph probably texted him about all this."

Danni and Sarah took the laptop downstairs and shared the new information with them. The men showed the footage from the night before with the bursts of light near the pantry.

"I feel certain this was what Amelia needed to convey," Sarah replied.

"We'll keep going through the tapes. So far, we have enough for a great YouTube segment," Harry said, excitement in his voice. "I think this is the break we've been hoping for."

Garrett smiled at Sarah making her stomach flip. This would also make up for the trouble she'd inadvertently caused when they were at the Borden House in Fall River. Even though she wasn't technically to blame, being Garrett's girl-friend had poisoned the network floozy against the team.

"I'm going to take a shower," Sarah said.

Trudging up the stairs, Sarah went over everything they'd learned. Amelia's father sent her away because she refused to marry Theodore Warren, the man he'd chosen for her. Theodore in turn tried to convince her to marry him and when that didn't work engaged the help of a low-life criminal, Eddie Porter. Eddie was only supposed to frighten Amelia but instead lost his temper and drowned her in the Savannah River. Theo killed Eddie to cover up everything related to Amelia's unfortunate demise. All of this mess led to a raid of the speakeasy in the back of the Edwards' laundry. The Millers funded the Edwards' relocation to Colorado and the raid went unsolved with no one to arrest.

Sarah exhaled. So many people had been impacted by the

greed of one man vying for power in congress. George Danburty had inadvertently set a series of tragic events in motion through his selfish ambitions. Hopefully, this new knowledge would give the spirits the peace they so eagerly sought.

Chapter Seventeen

S tepping out of the shower, Sarah towel dried her hair and plunked onto the bed. The mystery behind the spirits' deaths seemed to be solved which meant the haunting was likely coming to an end. She leaned against the headboard, closed her eyes, took in a deep breath, and exhaled. It seemed as if everything was done. Cheryl would be able to resume the restoration on the house without ghosts interfering.

A slow smile crept across Sarah's face. It felt good to have helped Amelia move on and rid Cheryl of her haunted dilemma. She was even pleased that Eddie could finally rest if for no other reason than keeping him from terrorizing someone else.

All of a sudden, Sarah saw Bessie Miller standing in line, a straw hat perched on her coiffed hair. This must be another vision, Sarah thought. She knew she wasn't asleep but in a state of relaxation. With a few more deep breaths, Sarah let the scene unfold. The haunting was over but apparently there were still things that needed to be revealed.

A smile creased Bessie's eyes as she entered a building with a handmade sign on its brick exterior that read "Vote Here."

"She did it," a voice echoed from behind Sarah.

Wheeling around, Sarah watched as Amelia approached.

"You're ready to move on now," Sarah said.

"I am. Thank you."

"Your aunt was finally able to vote."

"She fought hard for it," Amelia said. "Spent years in secret meetings helping ensure that women got that right. When the rest of the country ratified the 19th Amendment in 1920, she and her friends had to continue their battle. Georgia women wouldn't vote until 1921."

"Amazing," Sarah replied. Not being able to vote was something she'd never experienced, and she was thankful for the efforts of those before her who'd made it possible.

"I'm sorry Eddie slipped into your dreams along with me," Amelia continued.

"I'm sorry you were connected to him," Sarah responded. "Sadly, I don't have a choice in which ghosts I help."

"I understand," Amelia stated. "Couldn't stand being around him. Made it more difficult for me to communicate with you."

"It's strange. This is the most I've ever spoken with a spirit before."

"It's the necklace." Ola said, materializing next to Amelia. "The charms together allow for the ability to speak clearly with the ghost."

"Why didn't it work before now?" Sara queried.

"It only works once the spirit is at ease with the situation. Amelia's secret has been resolved. Now she can share things more fluidly."

"Thanks again for your help," Ameila whispered and vanished.

Sarah smiled. "That was incredible."

"Enjoy these moments. There will still be difficult entities and gruesome scenes but it gets easier as you adjust to being a dreamist. You're doing well," Ola said.

"Can you tell me more about this necklace?"

"The only thing you need to know for now is that the emerald-cut peridot gives you clarity, the key unlocks memories of previous dreams, and the thistle charm can repel troublesome spirits. And as you've just discovered, it can also allow you to speak openly with them once they're released from their turmoil."

"Amazing," Sarah muttered, fidgeting with the charms.

"Indeed, it is. However, if not handled properly, it can also weaken you leaving you open for..."

Ola's image began to fade.

"Open for what?" Sarah exclaimed.

"Another time...just don't..."

Ola disappeared. Sarah's heart pounded against her chest. What was she supposed to avoid doing? And why hadn't Ola been able to maintain her presence?

Gasping, Sarah jolted upright. She fingered the key charm and Ola's words came back to her. The necklace was there to help her but could also be dangerous if she did something. Except Ola disappeared before she could say what that was.

Sarah slid from bed. She needed to share what she'd just witnessed with the team. Maybe Garrett knew what Ola was trying to warn her about.

Everyone was gathered in the kitchen, Walter's voice booming from Ralph's cell phone.

"Well done, Miss Cook," Walter said. "While I appreciate your detecting work, your proximity definitely had an impact. If I'd had access to the information recovered from beneath the house, I may have won."

"You were informed of the documents," Danni replied.

"True, but it's not quite the same. I suppose I'll be coming to Beaufort next weekend to take you to dinner," Walter said.

"Actually, I was thinking I'd like something in your area," Danni responded.

Walter hesitated. "We can go to the place I would have chosen, if you'd like."

"Sounds good to me."

"We'll work out the details later," Walter said, a hint of excitement in his voice. "Congratulations."

"Thank you," Danni replied, the smile on her face broadening.

Sarah gave Danni a thumbs up. Her friend had a big heart. Offering to go to Walter's choice of dining establishments was Danni's way of being a gracious winner. Where she dined was irrelevant. The fact she won was enough.

"You guys are tied now," Ralph said.

"Huh?" Danni replied.

"You've each won one. Wonder who will win the next challenge."

Danni pursed her lips. "I will, of course. He just got lucky the first time."

An hour later, Cheryl arrived to hear the outcome of the team's investigation. The men explained everything in a way that excluded Sarah's abilities since there was a strong possibility Cheryl would share the information with Sarah's mom. No sense stirring up that drama, especially when Sarah was so close to discovering her mother's true views on the spirit world. They also shared a few clips with Cheryl on Ralph's iPad.

"There hasn't been any more activity since we made these

discoveries," Garrett explained as Cheryl sat at the kitchen island wide-eyed.

"This is incredible," she replied. "I can't believe you were able to capture all of this on video."

"Thanks for allowing us to film here," Ralph said. "Hopefully, we'll get a lot of views on YouTube."

"Glad I could help," she answered. "Have you spoken with your mother about this?" she asked, looking at Sarah.

"Not yet. I thought it would be better coming from you."

Cocking her head, Cheryl furrowed her brow. "Why would you think that?"

Sarah glanced down and fidgeted with the edge of her shirt. "She's never been open to the subject of ghosts."

"She believes," Cheryl grunted. "I'll talk to her about it."

If Cheryl could get Sarah's mother to admit to believing in ghosts it would make her life much easier. After a lifetime of hearing her mother say that ghosts were nothing more than an overactive imagination, it would be nice to share the true nature of Sarah's haunted past with her parents. Until then, her secret about being a dreamist would remain with the team and her best friend. Maybe someday, Sarah thought, she'd be able to explain to her mom that she hadn't been crazy or attention seeking as a child. She had a special skillset and her visions were real.

More than anything, Sarah was relieved to finally be going home. She rode with Danni so the guys could go straight to Edgefield. Garrett was going to come to Beaufort the following weekend and Sarah was looking forward to it. There was so much she wanted to discuss with him from explaining her moodiness at Hayden Place to what Ola had almost revealed about dangers associated with the necklace. But she needed to be alone with him without all the distractions of ghosts and guys.

Chapter Eighteen

An hour later, Danni pulled out of Sarah's driveway after dropping her off. Sarah grabbed her bag and started for the back door when she spotted a crow, its ebony wings shimmering in shades of deep blue and green.

Caw!

"You again," she muttered. "Unless you're a different one."

Caw!

The bird hopped toward her. Something was in its beak. Astounding, she thought. The bird can talk with its mouth full. It dropped the item and flew off, cawing all the way.

Sarah leaned over and lifted it from the gravel drive, a tingle racing up her arm. A tiny key with delicate scrolls embedded in the bow. With a chuckle, she shoved it in her pocket. "Looks like I have an admirer," she mumbled to herself.

After unpacking her things, Sarah fixed a cup of tea, grabbed her *Dreamist* book, and curled up in the leather chair in the front parlor. She paged to the quote she'd found while at Hayden Place and reread it several times. There was no doubt about it. Her family had a talisman. It appeared all dreamists did. Since her biological mother, Edie, was deceased Sarah had no idea what the family talisman might be.

Then it hit her. Both sides of her biological family had dreamists which meant there was more than one talisman. Sarah groaned. She had no access to the paternal side of the family and she didn't want it. The Deverauxs nauseated her, except for her great-grandmother who visited her in her dreams last Christmas. She seemed like one of the few decent members of the clan.

Exhaling, Sarah leaned her head back, closed her eyes, and sulked. As she shifted in the chair, something poked her thigh. She reached into her pocket and pulled out the key, her fingertips prickling.

Great, she thought, the ghost attached to this is probably trying to communicate with me. I can't get a break.

Caw!

Sarah jumped up from the chair, the key clattering to the floor. The crow was perched at the window staring at her with glimmering eyes.

Caw!

And it flew off.

What was happening? Was she being haunted by crows now? She picked up the key and turned it over in her hand, bits of electricity stinging her skin as she held it. This was something important except she had no idea where to begin looking. A random crow brings her a random item and somehow, she's supposed to know what to do with it? As if her life wasn't complicated enough, now she was expected to add ornithology to the list. Closing her eyes, she exhaled. An image flashed through her head. All of a sudden, she knew what she had to do.

· · ·

The next morning, Sarah showered, had a cup of tea, and headed across town. She pulled onto the oyster shell driveway of Deveraux Real Estate Agency and parked. The Beast's engine sputtered and coughed as she turned the key and stared at the building. Her heart thudded against her chest which felt like an overtightened drum. She fiddled with the small key, the tingling sensation giving her the courage to go inside.

She'd only known about being adopted for two years. The shock of discovering Devereaux was her biological father had been revolting to her. His son William, her half-brother, had spent most of their high school years trying to hook up with her. The entire family was a disgrace and it irked Sarah that she shared DNA with these people. Of course, Mr. Devereaux wanted nothing to do with her which made this visit tense.

She entered the building and found it to be the typical high-end real estate office with local art on the walls, plush chairs, and a Keurig machine on a Bombay Company side table. A receptionist sat behind a cherry desk, her blond hair pulled neatly into a pony tail. A name plate on the desk read Carly Jones.

"Good morning," Carly chirped. "Welcome to Devereaux and Son. How can I help you today?"

Son? Sarah thought. Looks like William was moving up in the world. He'd made partner in their father's real estate business.

"I need to speak with Mr. Devereaux, Senior please," Sarah said, a slight quiver pulsing through her limbs.

"Do you have an appointment?"

"Um, no."

"Mr. Devereaux's son is available. I'm sure he can find a property you'll love." The receptionist lifted the receiver and started to press a button on the phone.

"No!" Sarah declared, stepping closer. "I need to speak

with Mr. Devereaux, not his son."

"I'm afraid I can't do that unless you have an appointment. He's a very busy man."

Sarah exhaled. This wasn't going as she'd hoped.

"Please tell Mr. Devereaux that Miss Holden is here to see him. I assure you; he'll be willing to make an exception for me."

Carly's face paled as she lifted the phone to her ear and pressed a few numbers. "Mr. Devereaux, there's a Miss Holden here to see you." She replaced the receiver and gave a half smile. "He'll meet with you. It's the first office on the left."

"Thank you," she said.

Sarah walked into her biological father's office and took in the grandeur of the space. So, this is what cheating people gets you, she thought. A large window spanned the wall behind his desk with a panoramic view of the marsh. Sunlight glistened across the choppy tides coming in for the day. A tide clock hung to the right of the window along with a print of shrimp boats moored at the docks.

Mr. Devereaux sat behind his desk with a scowl on his face. Dad, she thought to herself and cringed. But now wasn't the time to think about her revulsion. She had a mission and it needed to be completed if she ever hoped to understand and improve her dreamist skills.

"What do you want?" he growled.

Something inside Sarah bubbled, an anger and determination she didn't recognize. Fidgeting with the necklace, she felt a strength rising inside her.

"I'm your daughter. Is it so offensive that I've come for a visit?"

A sneer wrinkled his upper lip. "Humph. You've finally come to bleed me dry. I knew it was only a matter of time. How much do you want in order to walk out that door and never come back?"

Sarah sat in the chair across from his desk. A bookcase to his left housed several framed photos of family, no doubt, to make him look like a good man to his clients. Sarah knew better. Scoundrel. One photo showed him and William standing on a boat in the river. Father and son enjoying their wealth. Others showed college graduations, birthdays, and vacations. His family history perched on a shelf. Well, the ones he acknowledged.

"I don't want your money," Sarah responded, shocked at the calm in her voice. "I'm here about something that belonged to my great-grandmother. Specifically, a piece of jewelry."

Mr. Devereaux's face turned a deep shade of crimson. "How dare you? You'll not get one thing that belonged to my grandmother," he said between gritted teeth. "I'll not have the likes of you touching any of her things. She was a fine lady."

"The likes of me? You mean your daughter? I have a right to her things as much as your other children." Sarah's hands began to shake. How could he dismiss her as nothing more than trash? Her adoptive father's face flashed in her head. Thank goodness he was her dad. Being raised by this man would have been horrible.

"You were nothing more than a one-night stand. Biggest mistake of my life. Edie Monroe was a temptress and I was..."

"Drunk. Yes, I've heard your tale of victimhood," Sarah retorted. She may not have known Edie Monroe personally but she felt a responsibility to her. After all, she was her biological mother and did what she had to do for Sarah's sake. "I'm not asking for all the family jewels. I only want one thing, something from my family line."

"And I said you'll not get your grubby paws on anything that belonged to my grandmother," he thundered, his fist slamming against the desktop as he stood.

Sarah's heart pounded at the violent nature of his response.

She could feel the key in her pocket, burning as if it had been held over a fire.

Standing, Sarah forced a smile. "I'm trying to be reasonable. But I can always show up at your house. I've never met your wife before. I've heard she's a hospitable woman. I feel certain she'd welcome me into your home for a chat."

Mr. Devereaux's eyes widened as the flush drained from his cheeks. Grinding his jaw, he sat back down, his fingers curling into fists. "Come back tomorrow. I'll bring the jewelry box with me. But you can't have it all. Only one thing."

"Thank you," Sarah said, turning to leave. She stopped in the doorway and looked back at her biological father. He looked so defeated and it filled her with satisfaction. "And don't take anything out of it. Trust me, I'll know if you do."

She left his office before he could respond feeling stronger and lighter than she had in weeks.

The following day, Sarah drove to Devereaux's office and met with her biological father. A deep red velvet box sat on his desktop. Silver swirls decorated the lid with her great-grandmother's initials in a center oval.

"I don't know how you know about this box, probably that idiot son of mine, but here it is. Don't have the key so you'll have to find a way to open it without doing any damage," he said with a wicked smirk.

"Not a problem," she replied, pulling the key from her pocket and holding it up. "I deal in antiques and figured there might be a lock so I brought a key with me just in case."

His eyes grew wider as the smirk faded from his face. Sarah slipped the key into the ornate lock that matched the scrolling silver on top of the box. A satisfying click sounded as the key released the lid from its base. Sarah opened it and stared inside, her breath catching at the exquisite collection of baubles. She didn't know what she was looking for but knew it would reveal itself.

"Remember, only one thing," Devereaux barked.

Sarah ignored him. She'd met her great-grandmother in a dream and she had been so unlike the family Sarah knew now. A diamond and pearl brooch sparkled from within along with a coral beaded necklace, an emerald and ruby bracelet, and a pair of garnet earrings. Then she saw it. Nestled beneath the other pieces was a small pocket watch, its golden surface shimmering from the back corner of the jewelry box.

As if calling to her, she reached for it, her fingertips warming as she lifted it from its velvet tomb. This was it. The family heirloom for the dreamists on her paternal side. She recalled her great-grandmother saying something about the ability skipping several generations until Sarah which explained why the talisman was still in the jewelry box.

Devereaux grunted. "What's so special about that? These jewels are worth a small fortune, and you choose a trinket. Makes me think there's some hidden value in that little bauble. You being an antique *expert* and all," he taunted.

"I told you I didn't want much. Just something from my family line. Whether we like it or not, we are biologically connected."

"Humph," he grunted.

Sarah dropped the watch into her pocket and stood. "Thank you."

"Don't thank me for something you extorted. I don't ever want to see you here again."

"Rest assured, I won't be back."

As Sarah passed through the front office, Carly gave a weak smile. "Thank you for doing business with Devereaux and Son."

"It was a pleasure," Sarah retorted with a smirk.

Pleased with her fortitude and her find, Sarah marched out of the office feeling stronger than she ever had. For the first time in her life, she'd taken control of a situation and it felt good. Would she ever feel this way as a dreamist? She hoped so. With a renewed sense of self-confidence, Sarah cranked the Beast and drove home to Monroe Manse.

Sarah parked and started for the back door when the crow landed in front of her.

Caw, caw!

"I don't know how you know all of this but thank you for bringing me the key. It opened the jewelry box, but I suspect you already knew that."

The crow cocked his head from side to side, its onyx eyes fixed on her.

"Too bad you can't get my great-grandmother's *Dreamist* book. That I could really use," Sarah sighed.

The crow took flight, squawking as he flew away.

Once inside the house, Sarah pulled the watch from her pocket and examined it. It appeared to be real gold with roses engraved on the case. She pressed the crown and the cover popped open, revealing a porcelain face with tiny pink roses circling the dial. Strange, she thought, it was ticking. Then she remembered a horologist telling her you could gently shake a pocket watch to get it running. She must've shaken it up a bit when she shoved it in her pocket.

The next morning, Sarah took her cup of tea to the back gardens. As she approached the bistro table, she noticed something sitting on top of it. Chills bumped along her skin as she neared, her eyes growing wider. She set the cup of tea down and lifted the small brown leather tome with *Dreamist* in gilded letters across the cover.

Caw, caw! skittered across the air.

Sarah looked up. The crow was perched in a branch of the massive live oak.

"Thank you," she muttered, astounded by this bird and its apparent understanding of what she needed. Was it a real bird or a ghost? At this point, she didn't care. Somehow this crow had brought her the key to unlock her great-grandmother's jewelry box and retrieved her *Dreamist* book. Since the bird was becoming a regular visitor, Sarah decided to name him. "How about Corsallus?" she said to the ebony bird.

Caw!

Sarah jumped when her phone rang.

"Hey, Garrett."

"Are you alright? You sound funny," he said.

"Got some strange stuff going on. I'll fill you in when you get here this weekend."

"Sounds good. I wanted to let you know that Cheryl called me. The house has been ghost-free since we left. Hopefully, Ralph and Harry will finish editing everything so we can post it on YouTube by the end of the month."

"That's great," Sarah said. "Can't wait to see you."

"Same here. Gotta another call coming in. Talk to you soon."

Sarah shoved the phone in her pocket and took a sip of tea. "What other skills am I going to discover?" she mumbled to herself, paging through the *Dreamist* book as Corsallus looked on.

* * *

Garrett sat across from Sarah at the old pine harvest table in her kitchen. Reaching across the table, he took her hand in his. Dallas was sprawled on the floor catching rays of sunlight filtering through the back door.

"I need to say something, but I want you to hear me out before you respond." He looked up, his deep green stare locking onto hers. "I know things have been a bit rocky between us the past week or so."

Her chest constricted. Was he breaking up with her? They'd argued a lot at Hayden Place but things seemed to be okay when they left. That was one of the things she'd planned to discuss with him this weekend, alone. Perhaps she'd waited too long. Bile rose in her throat as her stomach churned. She could feel tears brimming.

"I've been talking with the new owners of Rose Hall, an 1858 mansion in Bluffton over the past few weeks. It's one of the few remaining examples of Gothic Revival architecture in the area. They want to do a complete renovation of the place and have negotiated a contract with me. I start next week."

Sarah released the breath she'd been holding. It's a job, one that would have him closer to her than Edgefield. So, why all the drama? Sarah bit her lip to prevent the questions from springing forth. He'd asked her to wait until he finished, and she was determined to do so.

"It's going to take several months so I'll be staying at a cottage on the property. I was wondering, and you can say no if you want, but I was thinking that maybe...would you stay with me?"

"On the weekends?" she asked.

"Everyday."

Sarah inhaled sharply. This was huge and she didn't want to blow it. "Are you asking me to move in with you for a few months?"

"I am," he replied, his thumb caressing her fingers.

"Will Dallas be there?" she asked coyly.

Rolling his eyes, Garrett sighed. "Yes."

"Then count me in," Sarah giggled.

"My dog wins again," he chuckled.

"Is the cottage as old as the house?"

"It was built as a guest cottage in the 40s when the Sturgeons owned the property."

Sarah swallowed. "Is it haunted?"

A sly grin lifted the right side of Garrett's mouth. "I suppose you and my dog will figure that out."

Mulling it over a moment more, Sarah contemplated the entire scenario. She and Garrett would be living together for an undisclosed period of time in a potentially haunted cottage. Granted, the cottage was mid-twentieth century and had only housed guests which meant its haunted aspects were probably negligible if there were any spirits there at all.

"Sounds good to me. I doubt there's anything significant lingering there."

Garrett brought her hand to his lips and kissed it. "Thanks for agreeing to this. I've been a little worried about us and wasn't sure where we stood."

Sarah sighed. "I'm so sorry. Everything got to me with three ghost hunts in a row, the mystery behind Ola's necklace, and having to deal with two spirits at once. I didn't mean to take it out on you."

"I wasn't sure what to think. I knew you were going through some stuff and I wanted to help but didn't know how."

"It can't be easy dating a haunted woman," Sarah huffed. "I wanted to tell you what I was going through and yet I wasn't sure I understood it myself. Thanks for sticking by me."

"I love you."

"Love you," she replied, her stomach fluttering with excitement. Or was it dread? Stop it, she scolded herself. All that mattered was she and Garrett would have a chance to take their relationship to the next level. What could a ghost do to disrupt that?

Epilogue

Smoke snaked through Sarah's chest squeezing the air from her lungs. Her eyes burned as she crawled along the floor, stopping every so often to bring her shirt over her nose. If only she could get a tiny breath. Her mind began wandering unable to focus. She needed to get out of there before the smoke consumed her. Behind her, she could hear the sounds of wood crumbling and flames crackling.

Then another sound. This one more frightening than the rest.

Cannot go on like this. No hope.

Chills swept across Sarah's skin despite the rising heat around her. Where was she? More importantly, was someone here with her? Perhaps somebody was trapped deeper in the building where the fire was more intense and needed her help. Except she didn't know where they were or how to find them. She couldn't even see in front of her to know how to escape herself. Something behind her collapsed sending sparks like fireworks falling around her. The building was collapsing. She had to get out of there.

Buzz, buzz, buzz.

Sarah jolted awake, gasping for air.

Buzz, buzz, buzz.

Grabbing her phone, Sarah answered, her voice still scratchy from the smoke in her dreamscape. "Hello."

"Sarah?"

"Mom? Is everything okay? You sound panicked."

"Have you seen the news?"

"No, I was asleep," she replied, sitting up and brushing her hair from her face. "What's going on?"

"It's Virginia Intermont. It's on fire."

Wakefulness took hold as her mother's words flooded her consciousness. "What?"

"It's all over the news," her mother sobbed. "My beautiful campus is up in flames."

Sarah swallowed the lump forming in her throat. "Mom, let me get online and check this out. I'll call you back."

"No rush," she replied, a whimper in her voice. "I only wanted you to know since you and the team were just there."

"I'll talk to you later. Love you, mom."

"Love you, darling."

Sarah tapped Virginia Intermont College into her phone and was inundated with report after report of the school in flames. The inferno could be seen for miles and several fire departments were on the scene battling the blaze. Tears spilled from Sarah's eyes as she watched the 1891 structure devoured by flames. She thought back to all the spirits who'd appeared to her, pleading for someone to save the school that last day she and the team were on campus. Even the building had said it didn't want to die.

She recalled the deteriorating state of the college buildings. Ceilings caving in, rotted floors, mold climbing the papered walls, graffiti from vagrants. After one hundred thirty years of educating students, the college had become nothing more than a decaying corpse of what she once was.

Had to go on my terms.

Sarah shuddered at the words. Was it possible? Her gut churned as she watched the horrific scenes on her phone. She realized she'd been dreaming about the school when her mother called. It was the building communicating with her. Old buildings were alive and this one was taking her own life.

A slight sense of satisfaction coursed through Sarah's mind. The old girl went out in a blaze of glory, on her own terms instead of rotting to the ground or being taken down by a wrecking ball. Nevertheless, Sarah's chest ached. She was heartbroken it had come to this. If only she'd had the means, she'd have gladly brought the buildings back to their former glory. As it was, she was honored to have walked through her halls and heard her final words.

Sarah wiped her tears as a slow smile crept across her face. How fitting, she thought, for a building who had seen so many through the good and the hard times to leave in her own dramatic way.

"Everything alright?" Garrett asked, towel drying his auburn locks as he stepped from the bathroom.

Sarah blew out a long breath. She handed her phone to Garrett with the scene of the college in flames. "It's been on fire for a couple of hours now."

"This is awful," he muttered, sitting on the edge of the bed. "We were just there."

"We might have some of the last footage of the school."

"Since there was no electricity to start the fire, I'm guessing it was one of the vagrants trying to stay warm."

"Don't think so," Sarah replied.

"They already know how it started?"

"No, but I do."

Garrett furrowed his brows. "What are you talking about?"

"I was dreaming that I was in a burning building. I was trying to escape when my phone rang. It was Mom telling me about the fire. Then I heard, *couldn't go on* and *had to do it on my terms*. It was the building communicating with me like it did when we were on campus."

"You're telling me that a building told you it was going to destroy itself?"

Sarah hesitated. She'd never seen Garrett surprised by anything she shared and it scared her. "Yes, that's what I'm telling you."

He rubbed his chin. "Better tell the guys. We probably need to delay the YouTube release until things settle down."

"No," Sarah said. "I think you should release it. The college and the alumni deserve recognition, especially now that the buildings are gone."

Garrett nodded. "I'll let them know."

He left the room leaving Sarah feeling queasy. Pulling her legs to her chest, she rested her chin on her knees and contemplated how crazy her statement had been. Yes, they knew she could pick up on memories stored within the walls of old structures which made more sense than buildings actually communicating with her. Yet she knew what she'd dreamt and it was definitely the old dorm telling her what it had done.

Sarah slid from bed and changed. By the time she made it to the kitchen, Garrett was sipping coffee, his eyes glued to the computer screen as the inferno raged on the old Virginia Intermont campus. She fixed a cup of tea, sat next to him, and watched in silence. Even Dallas seemed forlorn.

"I can't watch anymore," Garrett said, going to refill his cup.

"It's devastating," Sarah said, trying to tear her attention from the conflagration. Her phone rang, breaking the spell.

"Hey, Mom," she said. "Are you okay?"

"Not really," she replied. "I've been on the phone with my college friends for the last hour. We're all in shock."

"I can only imagine."

"When are the men going to release the videos they took of the campus?"

"Garrett talked with them and they decided to post it in the next few days," Sarah replied.

"Thank goodness," her mom said. "The girls and I feel now is the best time for the world to see our haunted campus as she was in her final days."

Sarah gasped. Did she hear what she thought she had? "Mom, what are you saying?"

"I'm ready to tell you about my time at Virginia Intermont, ghosts and all."

Author Notes

.

The Haunting of Hayden Place was a fun story to write. Much of the history is true although I took artistic liberties with certain aspects. The house in which the story is set was actually built by a local grocer in the 1880s. There are several tiny cottages and a cinder block cottage behind the structure on the street perpendicular to the house. The cinder block building was a laundry at the turn of the century. The Vaults and tunnels also exist although none of them run beneath the house or the old laundry building.

The prohibition history in the book is accurate including the part about income tax being enacted to make up for the lost taxes from liquor sales. Prohibition was a rocky time in our history with stories of fast cars, illegal stills, and gangsters. My research for this part of the story took place at the Prohibition Museum in Savannah. I highly recommend a visit to the museum. It's informative and entertaining.

An underlying facet of the story addresses the 19th Amendment granting women the right to vote. Although the 19th Amendment was ratified in 1920, Georgia did not allow women to vote until 1921. Furthermore, they didn't ratify the amendment until 1970. Ladies, please embrace the privilege of being able to vote as many women were beaten and jailed so you could have that right.

The entire setting for this book was serendipitous. While visiting my husband's friend and fellow clock collector, Ron Horton, at his clock shop in Savannah, we met his wife, Cheryl. Like most Savannah natives, she was proud of her city. When I told her I was looking for a location for my next book in the Dreamist series, she suggested I set it at a Second Empire house they were renovating in the heart of Savannah. As soon as I saw a picture of the home, I knew it was the right place. Ron and Cheryl were gracious enough to give me a tour of the home and share the history they'd garnered about the place and the surrounding structures. It was only fitting to name the home owner in the book after Cheryl who provided the idea for the setting.

Sara Ann Knight was kind enough to share her storytelling talents and knowledge of the Colonial Park Cemetery. Most of the graveyard stories are based upon factual events.

The Edwards family, Amelia, and the Millers are all fictional characters.

Acknowledgments

To my husband, Darryl, thank you for your love, support, patience, and for helping me with my books! I love you!

To my mom, Karen Oates, thanks for reading, editing, and cheering me on! Love you!

To my writing coach, Charlotte Rains-Dixon, thank you for always helping and encouraging me to be a better writer. You are the best!

To my 'other mother', Millie Boyce, thanks for always being there and encouraging me! Love you!

To Sara Ann Knight, haunted tour guide extraordinaire, thanks for sharing your enthusiasm and knowledge of Colonial Park Cemetery!

To Ron and Cheryl Horton for sharing their beautiful house and inspiring the setting for this book. Thank you!

To the businesses who carry my books, Nevermore Books, Beaufort Bookstore, McIntosh Book Shoppe, Sassafras, Emry's Bookshop, and Grayco, thank you for your support!

To my friends and family who cheer me on, Joan Jones, Aimee Tidwell, Darlene Stokes, Lynn Bristow, Diane Morrison, Mary Beth Klinar, Kay Keeler, Richard Norris, Jo and Ralph Beaver, Teresa Partin, Chris Crooke, Charlie Frost, Peggy Callahan, Janell McClure, Sarah Hetzler, Kelly Taylor, Bernie Ladd, Jonathon Haupt, Karen Neumeister, and Janet McCauley -thank you for your ongoing support! Love you all!

To all my readers- I appreciate each and every one of you!

Thank you for reading my books! Your kind words and continued support mean everything!

Most importantly, thanks be to God! With Him all things are possible!

In Memorium:

Thanks to all those who supported me over the years but have gone on to Heaven. Harvey and Catherine Oates, Michael Wiegel, David Clark, Sam Poovey, Rachell Poovey Navratil, Tom Boyce, John Keith, Phyllis Sooy, Cathy Benson, and Becky Baldwin. Love you always!

About the Author

Kim Poovey is a storyteller and best-selling author of gothic horror and historical fiction. She has traveled the Southeast for more than 20 years presenting on 19th century fashion, mourning practices, and other Victorian era topics. In 2011 she portrayed Mrs. Stanton, wife of Secretary of War Stanton (Kevin Kline), in the Robert Redford film, *The Conspirator*. In addition, Kim has written for several magazines to include Beaufort Lifestyles, Bluffton Breeze, Citizen's Companion, and the Civil War Times. Kim lives in a haunted 1890s Victorian cottage in the SC Lowcountry with her husband, Darryl, and their furry children.

Also by Kim Poovey

Also by Kim Poovey

<u>Dreamist Series</u>

The Haunting of Monroe Manse

The Haunting of Edgefield Manor

The Haunting of Borden House

The Haunting of Intermont Hall, A Novella

The Haunting of Hayden Place

The Haunting of Christmas Present (short story)

<u>Shadows Trilogy</u>

Shadows of the Moss

Shadows of the War

<u>Other Titles</u>

Truer Words

Recipe for Writing

Through Button Eyes; Memoirs of an Edwardian Teddy Bear (out of print)

Dickens Mice; The Tails Behind the Tale (out of print)